"I want to leave you with two things to think about, Reggie."

He held up one finger. "For your own safety, put whatever you know or think you know about me or the Paladins or the Regents right out of that pretty little head. Destroy the hard copies and never access that site again."

She glared up at him. "What makes you think I made hard copies?"

He smiled down into those angry, long-lashed eyes. "Because, Reggie, that's what I would've done. Clear out the copy you made on a flash drive, too. Better yet, destroy the damn thing. Don't keep anything that can be used against you."

For the first time she looked worried. "Seriously, D.J., you're not trying to tell me all that crap was real?"

He wished he could, but that wasn't happening. "No, I'm trying to tell you to keep that cute nose out of my business for your own good."

She wasn't buying it, not for an instant, which was why he'd be sticking around for a while. ⟨...⟩ what he'd told her about ⟨...⟩ ⟨...⟩uld figure out some ⟨...⟩ ⟨...⟩he'd keep an eye on he⟨...⟩ ⟨...⟩ny-one was coming af⟨...⟩

"Okay, so that ⟨...⟩e?"

He shouldn't d⟨...⟩ really, really shouldn't. But then he'd never had much luck with impulse control.

"Think about this, Reggie."

And he kissed her.

Turn the page for red-hot reviews of
Alexis Morgan's seductive novels. . . .

"The sparks fly off the page. . . . Fantastic."

—Fallen Angel Reviews

"Thank you, Ms. Morgan, for another great read!"

—Night Owl Reviews

"Good stuff!"

—*Romantic Times*

DARKNESS UNKNOWN

"A fabulous read. . . . Passionate, hot, and very sexy."

—Fallen Angel Reviews

"Fresh and exciting with the same depth of character and emotional punch we've come to expect from Ms. Morgan."

—Fresh Fiction

REDEEMED IN DARKNESS

"Captivating, compelling, and totally hot!"

—Alyssa Day, *USA Today* best-selling author of
Atlantis Unmasked

IN DARKNESS REBORN

"Utterly compelling. . . . Really terrific and totally unique."

—Katherine Stone, *New York Times* best-selling author of
Caroline's Journal

These titles are also available as eBooks.

The DARKNESS Beyond

A *Paladin* Novel

ALEXIS MORGAN

Pocket Star Books

New York   London   Toronto   Sydney

Pocket Star Books
A Division of Simon & Schuster, Inc.
1230 Avenue of the Americas
New York, NY 10020

First Pocket Star Books paperback edition June 2011

POCKET STAR BOOKS and colophon are registered trademarks of Simon & Schuster, Inc.

For information about special discounts for bulk purchases, please contact Simon & Schuster Special Sales at 1-866-506-1949 or business@simonandschuster.com.

The Simon & Schuster Speakers Bureau can bring authors to your live event. For more information or to book an event contact the Simon & Schuster Speakers Bureau at 1-866-248-3049 or visit our website at www.simonspeakers.com.

Cover design by Lisa Litwack. Illustration by Craig White.

Manufactured in the United States of America

10 9 8 7 6 5 4 3 2 1

ISBN 978-1-4391-7605-4
ISBN 978-1-4391-7608-5 (ebook)

I dedicate this book to all of the women and men who serve our country—past, present, and in the future— and to their family and friends, as well. We owe you a debt we can never repay. Thank you.

Acknowledgments

To Micki Nuding, my brilliant editor; and to Michelle Grajkowski, my incredible agent: a special salute to both of you from me and the Paladins for your support and friendship. Every book is a team effort, and this one was no exception.

Chapter 1

$\mathcal{A}$ ball of wadded-up paper flew past Reggie's head to hit a bank shot into the trash can. She ignored both it and the argument that had been going on for the past ten minutes.

"I'm telling you, no matter what Big Ed thinks, it's our very own Regina Morrison who is going to bring down the Knightwalker!"

Cody, her cubicle partner, was a college student who worked part-time for the firm, his hours arranged around his class schedule. The kid had more energy than any other three coworkers combined, and she liked his enthusiasm. Well, at least when he wasn't trying to make a killing in the office pool by betting on her skills in tracking down hackers.

He threw another "ball" toward the garbage. This time it missed and landed on her desk. She picked it up and tossed it back over her shoulder, her aim spot-on after months of practice.

"Thanks, Reggie."

Cody snagged the paper out of the air without missing a beat. "Seriously, I'm betting Reggie nails the target to the wall by Friday, next week at the latest. The Knightwalker's ass will be toast," he continued.

"Drop it, Cody," she told him.

He paid about as much attention this time as he had to her past dozen attempts to stop him. As he wadded up another piece of paper, he went right on talking her up.

"You know her skills are smokin' hot. If we pool our resources, we can make a killing."

The sound of heavy footsteps put a sudden end to the conversation. Reggie immediately cleared her screen and brought up another case just as a shadow fell across her desk and a meaty hand landed on her shoulder. She gritted her teeth and set her keyboard back on the desk so she could move quickly if need be. Ignoring her unwanted company, she kept right on typing.

"Hey there, Cyberqueen. Your little buddy Cody here might be backing your play in this particular game, but don't let it go to your head. You and I both know that I'm the big dog around here when it comes to catching a hacker like the Knightwalker."

"Get your hand off me, Ed."

She'd give him two seconds to comply before demonstrating why she was the star pupil in her self-defense classes. Most men never saw past her dark blond hair and baby blues, sorely underestimating her strength and speed. The guys in her dojo only made that mistake once.

Ed would learn differently, too, if he kept pushing her. The mental image of Big Ed curled up on the floor, holding his personal package and squealing like a pig, held a great deal of appeal. Luckily for him, he stepped away before she gave in to the impulse.

She went back to ignoring him. Ed's sense of self-importance had taken a beating lately because Reggie had led the office in closing cases for five of the past six months. Prior to her joining the team, he'd been the undisputed leader of the pack. Never one to accept second place at the best of times, losing out to a newcomer—and especially a woman—was more than Ed's poor ego could handle.

She winced as Cody picked up right where he'd left off. "Ed, I still think our girl here is going to find the Knightwalker before you do."

Cody was one of her favorite people, but she really wished he'd shut up. His ringing endorsement of her abilities was only making a bad situation worse. Sure enough, Ed's voice took on a new threatening tone. She braced herself for the inevitable; somebody was going to get hurt, and it wouldn't be her.

"Like hell she will, kid, but go ahead and put your money on her. I'll enjoy eating a steak dinner at your expense."

Ed leaned down over Reggie's shoulder to study her computer screen, his smoker's breath tickling her skin. Disgusting. Did he really think she was stupid enough to be working the case where he could watch? Idiot.

Then he whispered right next to her ear, "Play your

cards right, Reggie, and maybe you and I will be ordering that steak dinner as room service."

Then his hand started to slide down over the front of her blouse. Okay, that did it. Abruptly, she shoved her chair back from her desk, running over his foot and in the process making sure she elbowed him right where it hurt. Ed stumbled back, banging into the wall of the cubicle and almost knocking it over.

His face was red, his eyes furious as he waited for the pain to pass. She rose to her feet, ready to meet his next challenge head-on. Her next stop would be the boss's office, but to leave now would only convince Ed that she was afraid of him.

"You bitch! You did that deliberately," Ed wheezed.

She balanced on the balls of her feet, ready for action, her adrenaline levels skyrocketing. "Damn straight I did. I've warned you before about keeping your hands to yourself."

Ed straightened up. "The boss will fire your ass when I tell him what you did."

Reggie really hoped Mr. DeLuca wouldn't do any such thing. She needed the paycheck too much. Fortunately for her, Cody had already called for the cavalry because the boss was standing right behind them. There was no mistaking the fury in his expression when he looked at Ed.

"No, I won't be firing Reggie, Ed. I heard what you said to her and saw what you did. Now you will apologize to her and then hobble your way to my office so we can continue this discussion in private."

Then he got right up in the other man's face. "I will make this much clear right now: if I find you back in here hassling Reggie again, you'll be the one looking for a job and with no references from me. Got that?"

Ed's jaw dropped in shock. "But—"

"A simple yes will do, Ed. Now go, before I rethink my decision to let you stay."

The big man shot Reggie a look that promised trouble in the future, but at least he started to leave. Mr. DeLuca stepped back to let Ed pass, waiting until he was out of sight before speaking again.

"Sorry about that, Reggie. I never thought he'd take things that far."

"I probably overreacted."

Her boss shook his head. "No, you didn't, and I meant what I said. If he bothers you at all, I want to know. He's good at his job, but you're better. The trouble is, he knows it."

Then he shot a look in Cody's direction. "And by the way, Cody, that betting pool you've started isn't helping things. You know what Ed's like when it comes to Reggie's record. Why rub his nose in it?"

Cody hung his head. "Sorry, boss. I'll put a stop to it."

"See that you do."

Reggie sat back down, hoping the two men didn't notice how badly her hands were shaking. Cody was usually oblivious to such things, but nothing much ever got by the boss. At least he changed the subject.

"So, any progress on the new case?"

She shook her head. "I've only just started. The client's firewalls haven't been breached again, but we know hackers of the Knightwalker's caliber are rarely able to resist coming out to play for long. I'll be waiting for him."

"Good. Keep me posted." He rubbed his hands together with a wolfish smile. "I've been hoping for a chance to go after this guy. God knows, enough people have tried to track him down. If we pull this off, it will solidify the company's reputation. It won't be easy, though—this guy knows how to cover his tracks."

"I'll do my best, sir."

"I know you will." Her boss backed out of the cubicle. "Well, I'll leave you to it. Cody, I'll want those reports by closing today."

"You'll get them."

As soon as he was gone, Cody stopped all pretense of working. "Look, Reg, I'm sorry if the betting caused you problems with Big Ed."

She waved it off. "It's his problem, not ours. If it hadn't been this case that set him off, it would've been another one."

Cody lowered his voice. "To tell the truth, part of me will be really sorry if you do manage to nail the Knightwalker. He's been a hero among the geek crowd for a long time."

She knew just how Cody felt. Rumors about the shadowy hacker had been circulating for years. Most people she knew spoke his name with a note of reverence in their voices. Reggie had been following the *über*hacker's career herself, but with one major differ-ence: she'd actually *found* the Knightwalker. She even knew his real name—D. J. Clayborne.

Now she just needed to decide what to do with that knowledge. Despite her determination to bring cyber-criminals to justice, the Knightwalker was different—and not just because he was the best. If she had to char-acterize his forays into hacking, she'd say he was playful rather than destructive. Most of the companies he went after had actually benefited in the long run because he always pointed out the weaknesses in their security pro-tocols.

Get in and get out. That's all he did. Illegal, yeah. Irritating, most certainly. But most of all, intriguing. What did that say about her? Unwilling to pursue that line of thought any further, she put on her headphones and cranked up her iPod. She couldn't afford to pick and choose which criminals she went after.

It was time to hunt.

Hi, there, Knightwalker. Want to come out and play? Meet me tonight and we'll talk. I hear the deejay there is special. R.

D.J. stared at the cryptic signature in the e-mail and cursed long and loud. He was getting sick and tired of this. He had the laptop in his hands, ready to heave the damn thing as far as he could throw it when the voice of reason intervened. Unfortunately, he wasn't the one speaking.

"Damn it, D.J., if you throw that laptop, the next thing that dents the drywall will be your head."

D.J. set the innocent machine back down on his desk and waited for Devlin to speak his piece. It shouldn't take long; the big man never minced words.

"I don't know what's gotten into you lately, but the next computer you pound into dust comes out of your paycheck or maybe your hide. Seriously, I don't care which."

"Fine." D.J. forced himself to relax. "Sorry, Dev."

His friend's face changed from its usual pissed-off expression to one of worry. "Okay, that rips it. What the hell is wrong with you?"

D.J. lurched to his feet and got right up in Devlin's grill. "Why does something have to be wrong?"

Dev held his ground but lowered his voice. "Because you just apologized without me having to kick your ass up and down the hall first. That never happens."

"Sure it does," D.J. lied. "I apologize all the time. I'm fine."

His friend snorted. "Yeah, right. Even if I was willing to believe that, I'm not the only one who's noticed something has been bothering you for weeks. If you don't want to tell me, tell Cullen or even Laurel."

Like that was going to happen. D.J. flopped into his chair and pinned his attention back on the computer screen. Anything was better than staring into Devlin's eyes, which always saw straight through any bullshit. D.J. tried to come up with some excuse for why he'd been off his stride lately because he knew Devlin wouldn't go away until he did. The man was relentless once he caught the scent of a problem.

"I've just pulled a few too many long shifts this week."

That much was true; it just wasn't all of the problem. He leaned back in his chair and plunked his feet on the scarred surface of his desk. To keep his hands busy, he picked up his favorite stress toy and started working it for all it was worth.

Devlin rolled his broad shoulders and sighed. "Yeah, we all have. I just checked with Lacey down in the geology lab a few minutes ago. She said the readings are all stable and look like maybe they'll stay that way. I was on my way to tell you and Lonzo to knock off early and take some downtime."

D.J. tried to look happy about it but wasn't sure how successful he was. The last thing he needed right now was more time to sit around at his apartment with nothing to do but wait for another e-mail.

His hand automatically reached for the mouse and clicked. Nothing. Good. He really preferred not to go ballistic again in front of Devlin. He sure as hell didn't want to explain that he'd been playing e-mail tag with another hacker, one good enough to breach the security measures he and Cullen had installed to protect the secret world of the Paladins.

"You heard me, didn't you?"

Devlin waved his hand in front of D.J.'s face to draw his attention away from the computer screen.

"What?"

"I said you should get out of here for a while. It wasn't just a suggestion."

D.J. swallowed hard and nodded. "Fine. I have a few things to finish and then I'll go."

As if arguing with Devlin ever worked. The head Paladin immediately crossed his arms over his chest and went into glare mode. "Now."

D.J. could be stubborn, too. "Damn it, Devlin, cut me some slack. I've spent so many hours at the barrier this week, the post office is delivering my mail there. I want to clear up a few things and then I'll go." He crossed his heart and then held up his hand. "I swear."

Devlin's hand shot out to sweep D.J.'s feet off the desk. "I'll give you ten minutes and then you'd better be gone. Don't make me bring Laurel in on this. I bet she'll bring one of those extra-large syringes with her if I ask nicely."

"Fine, but using your wife as a threat is really low, Devlin, and you know it. Now go bother someone else so I can get packed up."

He tossed his toy back on the desk and started keyboarding at his usual lightning-fast pace. His search brought up nothing. His elusive quarry had once again evaded D.J.'s attempts to track him. Well, D.J. could work just as well from home as he could from the office. At least at the apartment, he had a cold six-pack waiting for him and his favorite pizza parlor on speed dial.

He shoved the laptop into its case and grabbed his jacket. "I'm out of here."

Devlin looked up from where he'd been conferring with his fellow Paladin Trahern.

"Take tomorrow and the next day off, too," Devlin said. "If I need you, I'll call."

D.J. waved at his friends. "Sounds good."

Not really, but he wouldn't get anywhere by arguing. Besides, they both knew that there was no predicting how long the barrier would behave. At the first sign of instability, Devlin would be calling everyone in. That's how things were for them: hours of brutal warfare alternating with hours of boredom.

Outside, the cool air felt good as he headed toward the parking garage to get his truck. Some of the guys had talked about meeting up at the local watering hole for a few cold ones, but he wasn't in the mood. Crowds made him edgy at the best of times, and that was the last thing he needed right now. He punched the button on his key to unlock the truck and tossed his computer over onto the passenger seat.

Traffic was on the light side, so the trip to his apartment up on Capitol Hill went faster than usual. After parking the truck, he took the steps up to his apartment two at a time. Once inside, he cranked up the stereo. As soon as he punched the button, the sound of steel guitar and fiddles filled the air. Lately he'd been liking more twang in his music.

He found himself really relating to the lyrics about a lover who only existed in the singer's dreams. It had been a long while since he'd had more than a casual relationship with a woman. Most of the time, the best he could hope for was hooking up with someone who wanted a few nights of hot sex and no commitment. In his experience, women like that were rare enough to belong on the endangered species list.

He popped the top on a beer and ordered his pizza, tacking a second one on to the order more out of habit than need. It used to be that he could count on friends stopping by to watch whatever sport was in season. Lately, though, his closest buddies had good reasons for sticking closer to home. Devlin had married their Handler, Dr. Laurel Young. Trahern had hooked up with the daughter of one of the Regents, and Cullen had an instant family he'd brought back from his foray into another world.

Even the two Kalith warriors who'd become part of the inner circle of the Paladins were now paired off with human women. Hell, Larem was even going to be a father soon. No one had seen that coming.

After hanging up the phone, D.J. wandered toward his media room. The glow of computer screens and the soft hum of hard drives always soothed him. Or at least they used to when he was still king of the cyberworld. He briefly hesitated in the doorway. If his stalker wanted to meet in a cyberbar, fine. Determined to prove his supremacy in the world of hackers, he headed for his favorite computer and prepared for battle.

Chapter 2

*R*eggie's pulse stuttered a bit. She'd been waiting for hours for the Knightwalker to make his presence known. The second he'd entered the room, she'd felt the familiar sizzle of high-octane energy that came from the hunt.

Her fingers hovered over the keyboard. Bracing herself for a lively encounter, she watched as her newest avatar strolled up to the bar to order a drink. This model had fiery red hair, bright blue eyes, and an athletic build. She'd chosen the redhead because she was everything Reggie wasn't—tall, voluptuous, and a guy magnet.

Her avatar deliberately ignored the man at the other end of the counter. Granted, she couldn't be sure it was really D.J. because the avatar wasn't the Knightwalker's usual one. The previous model had the overdone muscles of a bodybuilder. This one was tall, with broad shoulders, looking more realistic than his norm.

He made no move to approach her, leaving Reggie no choice but to wander back to the table she'd staked out in the corner. That didn't mean the Knightwalker was ignoring her though. Maybe she was imagining things, but as soon as he looked at her, she could swear the temperature in the cyberroom rose ten degrees.

Every incarnation the Knightwalker used was hotter than the last. This one had dark brown hair that brushed his collar and dark chocolate eyes that secretly followed her every move. The two avatars had yet to actually engage; instead, they circled each other, watching for any sign of weakness. So far, those had been few and far between.

Finally the teasing dance ended as the handsome avatar picked up his drink and headed straight toward her table, against the back wall. After setting his drink down, he straddled the chair next to hers.

The Knightwalker's smile sent a sweet chill of awareness through her. It was as if this encounter was taking place in real time, in a real place, instead of online.

"It's about time we introduced ourselves, don't you think?"

She manipulated her cyberself carefully to look at him more directly, aiming for cool and detached. "Any particular reason?"

He arched a brow. "Because you're the one who's been yanking my chain. I thought it would be nice to put a name to the talent."

"I already know who you are." She smiled and added, "Knightwalker."

He actually looked disappointed. Had he really expected her to admit to knowing his real name? "Okay, lady, so what should I call you?"

"Ruby will do for tonight."

He shook his head and downed the rest of his drink before standing up. "'Bye, Ruby."

She didn't like watching him walk away. She tried one more time. "Why are you in such a hurry to leave?"

"Because I don't have much use for cowards, *Reggie*."

She swallowed hard. "I said to call me Ruby."

The avatar shook his head. "You've been taunting me for weeks with your cryptic little e-mails. Now that I've found out your real name, you still want to hide behind your avatar. That hardly seems fair."

He started walking away again, but then stopped to look back one last time. "When you're ready to really play, you know where to find me."

Then his avatar blinked out of existence, leaving both Reggie and Ruby alone and confused.

D.J. shut off his monitor, feeling better than he had in ages. Nothing like confronting the enemy directly to raise the stakes in the game. He'd suspected for a while that the hacker who'd been chasing him was one of the avatars he'd encountered in the gaming rooms. Even now, he knew little more about the hacker than the name Reggie.

This time the avatar was female, but that didn't mean much. More than once he'd used either demon or female designs to hide his own identity. Reggie could've chosen the gorgeous redhead just to attract his attention. But now that he had a name to work with, it would be only a matter of time before he located Reggie in the real world. Of course, the name could be another fake, but his instincts told him differently. Now the real games could begin.

He reached for one last piece of pizza, not caring that it was cold and a bit past its prime. After a couple of bites, he tossed the rest back in the box. It was definitely time for some shut-eye. Maybe if Lacey was right about the barrier remaining stable, he might even get to sleep in tomorrow.

No sooner had that thought crossed his mind than his cell phone started vibrating and dancing across the desk. He picked it up without bothering to check the caller ID. Devlin was the only one who would be calling at this time of night. Grabbing his weapons bag, D.J. headed for the front door.

"I'm on my way."

Ten hours later, D.J. fell back against the wall to catch his breath, grateful for the support of the cool stone. His legs burned with exhaustion, and his arms ached from swinging his ax for hours.

The barrier that separated the tunnels under Seattle from the alien world of Kalithia had decided to prove Lacey's predictions wrong in a big way. The damn thing had been flickering in and out like an effing strobe light at a seventies disco club.

D.J. used a handkerchief to wipe the blood off his ax and hung his throwing hammer back on his belt. Now all he could do was wait to see if the barrier would finally make up its mind to behave or if he was going to have to wade through another river of blood before he could find a corner and grab some much needed sleep.

Trahern staggered over to join him. The man sported a makeshift bandage around his sword arm, but otherwise looked sound. Besides, like all Paladins, he would recover from any wound far faster than a normal human would.

Hell, even death only slowed them down for a short time.

Trahern didn't so much sit down as collapse. "Devlin said the guards would be around soon with food and water. I hope they get here before we have to dance again."

D.J. nodded, too tired to talk. At the sound of footsteps, he straightened up and braced himself to fight if it was another straggler being herded back toward the barrier. As soon as he spotted one of the older guards heading in his direction, he relaxed a bit but not entirely.

Technically the Paladins and the guards fought on the same side, but lately there'd been a lot of tension between the two groups. It had been only a few weeks ago that a new transfer had shot Lonzo and tried to kill one of the Regents who oversaw the entire organization.

They all knew that most of the guards were on the up-and-up. The trouble was that it was impossible to separate the good from the bad. Until Devlin and the Regents got to the bottom of the conspiracy that infected every level of the organization, they were all being careful about who they trusted.

The guard was cautious in his approach, holding out two paper bags with grease stains. "Here you go. I'll stand watch while you two eat. Coffee and bottled water are on the way."

"Thanks, Jack." Trahern accepted both bags and tossed one to D.J.

Then, in a show of good faith, the guard turned his back to them as he watched the flickering light of the barrier. D.J. sank down on the floor next to his friend, both of them careful to keep their weapons within easy reach. The way things had been going, they'd be lucky to finish half their makeshift meal before the barrier failed again.

The hamburgers and fries were barely warm, but considering how many hours had passed since he'd eaten that last piece of pizza, they tasted pretty damn good. Trahern wolfed his down and was already reaching for a second burger before D.J. was halfway through his first. Just as promised, another guard came into sight with a sack of bottled water and a thermos of coffee.

As soon as he spotted them, he veered in their direction. Holding out the sack, he said, "Take a couple of bottles each. No telling how long before I can make rounds again."

Then he filled two oversize cups with coffee. "Sorry, they forgot the cream and sugar. Maybe next time."

D.J. mustered up a smile. "No sweat. Thanks for this much."

The guard wandered on down the tunnel to the next cluster of worn-out warriors. Meanwhile, Trahern nibbled on his fries while watching D.J. out of the corner of his eye. Clearly the man had something on his mind. D.J. wished he'd just spit it out, whatever it was.

Finally Trahern did just that. "Dev's worried about you."

A flash of frustration gave D.J. a brief surge of energy. "God, not you, too. I swear, everyone has turned into a bunch of nosy old women. I already told Devlin that I'm all right."

Sort of, anyway.

His friend's pale eyes flashed hot. "That's bullshit, and you know it. You've been moping around here for weeks. Devlin's not the only one to notice. He's just the first to speak up."

At least Trahern was the kind who normally kept his observations to himself. Anything D.J. told him would remain confidential unless the big man thought it endangered the other Paladins. Unfortunately, D.J. had no idea if Reggie's incursions were a threat to anything other than his own ego.

By rights, he should've reported the security breach weeks ago, but he'd been convinced he could handle the situation himself. Once he realized he'd come up against someone who was every bit as good as he was, he'd been intrigued. Now he was just worried.

If he didn't find some way to block Reggie for good, he'd have to admit his failure and hope that he hadn't allowed the hacker to do irreparable damage to the Regents' security. That wasn't the half of it though. He had no doubt that Reggie was some idiot kid who was in over his head without knowing it. The minute the Regents got involved, the kid wouldn't know what hit him.

"I've been having trouble with some computer programs I've been working on, and it keeps me up nights. Between the barrier being unstable and my mind revving a million miles an hour, I'm not getting enough sleep."

True enough. Now if Trahern would accept his explanation D.J. would be all right for the time being. His friend picked up a few more fries, but he was frowning big time as he ate them. He looked as if he was about to say something else when a flash of light had both warriors scrambling back to their feet and grabbing their weapons.

It was a hell of a thing to be grateful for the barrier failing, but as D.J. charged forward, his ax at the ready, that's exactly how he felt.

Reggie stretched her arms over her head and sighed as she worked out the stiffness that came from sitting at her computer for too long. The sun was rapidly disappearing over the horizon, and the evening air was definitely chillier than it had been only an hour before. Time to head back inside.

After setting her laptop on the desk, she went into the kitchen to zap some leftover pizza in the microwave. While it did its thing, she poured herself a glass of wine and considered her options. She'd worked four tens that week, so tonight was the start of her weekend. She was definitely entitled to kick back and relax a bit. Maybe watch a movie or read a book.

Her eyes strayed back to where she'd left her computer. No use in lying to herself. Once she refueled, she'd be right back at the keyboard. Call it an obsession but she couldn't remember the last time she'd enjoyed tracking an adversary this much.

Yeah, come Monday she'd be back on company time where she'd have to report any progress she'd made to her boss. But now, at home and on her own dime, she could enjoy the challenge the Knightwalker presented while ignoring any guilt about having to bring his career to an abrupt halt.

She finished off the last of her dinner and cleaned up the kitchen before sitting down at her desk. Maybe her efforts would be more productive this time. She'd been checking out the Knightwalker's usual haunts for hours but with no luck.

Where did D. J. Clayborne go when he disappeared for days at a time? Did he have another online persona she'd yet to uncover? Somehow she didn't think so. He was too confident in his abilities to go into hiding now.

While she'd been hunting earlier, she had discovered an interesting link though. Maybe she'd do some more exploring to see if she could find a way to break through some pretty powerful firewalls. She had no doubt they were some of D.J.'s handiwork.

Following the same links she'd tracked before, she soon cracked the code and stumbled across a report written by someone named Brenna Nichols. She snagged her favorite stress reliever ball and worked it with her left hand as she scanned the introduction.

Why was that name so familiar? She tossed the ball back on the desk and started typing.

A quick search brought up several popular nonfiction books written by a woman of that name, the last one released three years before. This particular Brenna Nichols was a historian who specialized in making history come alive for the general public.

If this was her next book, why was it hidden in a bunch of corporate files? And who were these Regents the document referred to? For sure they didn't appear to be connected to any university. There was only one way to find out.

Before logging off, Reggie saved the report to her flash drive and made a hard copy. When the printer quit running, it had spewed out more than a hundred pages of information. She curled up on the couch and started reading.

Two hours and a pot of tea later, Reggie set the stack of paper on the coffee table. She stared up at the ceiling as she tried to make sense of the report. It read like nonfiction, complete with footnotes, even though the subject matter clearly belonged on the urban-fantasy shelf at the bookstore. The premise was ridiculous. Whoever heard of modern-day Paladins who guarded the world against invasion, armed with nothing more than swords?

Besides, if aliens ever did show up on Earth's doorstep, wouldn't they arrive in spaceships and sport more sophisticated weapons than blades? Ray guns or some kind of lasers at least. She'd taken only one physics course in college and knew even less about geology, but she was pretty darn sure that if an energy barrier was all that separated this world from one filled with crazies called Others, it would've been all over the evening news.

She ran her hands up and down her arms trying to smooth away the goose bumps that rippled across her skin. Had she locked the doors? As soon as the thought crossed her mind, she was up and heading to make sure. She threw the dead bolt on the front door and then the latch on the slider that led out to the balcony. After a quick check of the window locks in the bedrooms, her pulse slowed to a more normal pace.

Being scared was silly—no doubt her overactive imagination running out of control. She'd be far better off focusing on something real, like checking to see if D. J. Clayborne was around yet.

A few minutes later, her avatar was back at her favorite table, watching the crowd for any sign of the Knightwalker. Reggie sipped her tea, dividing her attention between the cyberworld displayed on her laptop and the latest installment in her favorite romance series. At the moment, the book was definitely the stronger draw as she lost herself in the growing tension between the hero and the heroine.

When she finally looked up again, she jumped. How

long had the Knightwalker been standing there staring at Ruby? Reggie dropped the book on the desk and started typing.

"Knightwalker, how nice of you to drop by."

As soon as she hit Enter, the handsome avatar pulled out a chair and sat down. "I'd said hello three times. I was beginning to wonder if either you or Ruby here had fallen asleep at the keyboard."

"Sorry," she typed. "By the way, earlier I was reading a fairy tale that you might find interesting."

"Really? What makes you think that?"

She hesitated, but there was only one way she was going to find out the truth about the files she'd stumbled across. Taking a deep breath, she started typing.

"It's written by an author named Brenna Nichols."

No response.

She tried again. "Since you call yourself the Knightwalker, I figured you'd find a story about Paladins fascinating. Maybe I was wrong. Perhaps you'd prefer some *Other* story."

This time there was definitely going to be a response. The Knightwalker's avatar leaned in close to Ruby, his expression one of shock and then fury. When he finally spoke, it scared her far more than anything her own imagination had come up with.

"Listen, kid, I hope you erased your tracks. Whatever you do, don't go there again. Chasing me is one thing, but trust me on this, Reggie. Going after the Regents will land you in a world of trouble."

Then the Knightwalker blinked out of existence.

• • •

Son of a bitch! D.J. stared at the blank screen, his hands clenched in tight fists. What the hell was he going to do now? He should make a beeline for Devlin's office and tell him that the organization's firewalls had been well and truly breached. The minute that happened, the Regents would start a witch hunt to track down Reggie. God knows what they'd do to the kid.

That it had gone this far was solely D.J.'s fault. If he'd reported the first incident, maybe he and Cullen or even Jake could've found a way to stop Reggie's forays into Paladin territory. Instead, his ego had taken control, refusing to admit that some punk could best him at his own game.

D.J. would give himself until Monday to handle the problem on his own. If that didn't work, he'd talk to Devlin and hope he survived the conversation.

Chapter 3

Todd Bedford walked into a coffee shop twenty miles from his office and spotted his coworker Ray sitting at a table in the back corner. Rather than head straight there though, Todd stopped at the counter to place his order, giving Ray a chance to watch for anyone who might be a little too interested in Todd's activity. If he saw anything suspicious, Ray would walk out without acknowledging Todd's presence.

This far from the Regents' headquarters, it was highly unlikely that would happen, but neither of them had gotten where they were by being careless. So far, no one had connected either of them with the activities of the infamous Colonel Kincade. Sure, the Regents suspected that the man's tentacles had extended far beyond his home turf in the Pacific Northwest. But suspecting and knowing were two different things.

The colonel was now under house arrest while the Regents went through the man's affairs with a fine-tooth comb. It was a sure bet that anyone implicated in Kincade's systematic theft of money from the organization would join the man in a prison cell. The thought gave Todd nightmares.

When his coffee and scone were ready, Todd did one last visual sweep of the room before making his way to Ray's table. While keeping a pleasant smile on his face, he injected enough temper into his voice to make the other man twitch.

"So, Ray, by all rights I should be on my way home for dinner. What was worth me driving all the way out here for a damn cup of coffee?"

Ray set his own drink down with more force than necessary. "As I recall, you said you wanted to be notified off the record if anyone ever breached our security. Excuse me for assuming that meant you wouldn't want me barging into your office to deliver the message."

Okay, so maybe the trip had been necessary. Todd pulled out a chair and sat down. "What happened?"

"I'm still working on it, but it appears that a hacker made it at least as far as the archives."

Todd almost spewed his coffee on the table. "What did they get?"

"As far as I can tell, all the guy downloaded was a copy of Brenna Nichols's ongoing history of the Paladins."

As if that wasn't bad enough. Todd closed his eyes and gritted his teeth. He'd tried to tell the board that having a historian poke around in those confidential files was nothing short of stupid. The woman was too high profile even if she'd kept her word about maintaining the secrecy of the organization. Hard-copy files of the Paladin history could be protected. But anytime there was a computer file, there was a hacker waiting to find it.

"Was anything else compromised?"

"Not that I could tell." Ray smoothed down the wisps of hair that failed to hide his shiny scalp, a clear sign he was nervous. "Whoever this guy is, he's good. Damn good, in fact. It was only by sheer dumb luck that I found any trace of his incursion."

Todd set his coffee aside. He was revved up enough without adding caffeine to the mix. He considered his options.

First thing, he needed to soothe some ruffled feathers. "You did the right thing by calling me. I should've known you wouldn't have requested an unscheduled meeting without good reason."

Ray nodded, looking marginally happier. "I didn't want to risk anyone at the office finding out about this before I had a chance to run it by you. I *should've* reported the incident to the Regents first, not to mention my boss in Security."

The man was right, of course, but following protocol was out of the question now. If Ray were to go ahead and report the breach, how could he explain the delay? With everything going on connected to Kincade, Security took a very dim view of anyone who didn't follow the rules inside or outside the organization. Filing a report now was clearly out of the question and they both knew it.

Whoever the hacker was, it took some serious mojo to circumvent all the security protocols maintained throughout the Paladin organization. One had to tread carefully to avoid being caught, thanks in large part to the two premier hackers within the Paladins themselves.

In fact, Todd's first thought was to wonder if D. J. Clayborne and Cullen Finley were up to their old tricks. Those two Paladins loved nothing more than sneaking around in the organization's files for no other reason than to prove the systems were vulnerable.

The problem was that neither of them had any reason to download a history of the Paladins, not when they were living it. Besides, they were friends with Trahern, Brenna Nichols's Paladin lover. If they'd wanted a copy of her work, they probably only had to ask.

That left an unknown hacker. Todd hid his rising excitement. If they could catch the guy without raising the alarm, maybe they could put him to work. Rumor had it that Kincade had left money squirreled away in hidden accounts. As the former Regents' representative in the Seattle area, he'd had his fingers in all kinds of pies. Some of that money had been promised to Todd and Ray for their help in covering the man's tracks.

So far, those who were interrogating the bastard hadn't gotten very far in recovering the Regents' losses. In Todd's mind, all of that money was now fair game. Finders keepers and all that. He'd considered having Ray hunt for it, but neither of them could risk discovery.

No, it'd be far better to outsource the job. And once the hacker did his job, well, accidents happened. There were ways of dealing with loose ends, ones that wouldn't lead straight back to Todd's door. Shove a human across the barrier at the right time, and he wouldn't last long enough to realize that he was bleeding out on alien soil. Todd smiled at his companion.

"Find this guy."

Ray's eyes narrowed and he frowned. "Are you sure? If he's as slippery as I think, he'll be hard to control."

"You let me worry about that. Once you've located him, call me and I'll get you some backup."

Ray nodded although clearly still not happy with Todd's decision. Too bad. Todd checked the time. "I've got to get back. The wife's family is coming for dinner tonight."

Todd smiled again. "See that this happens, Ray, and I'll make it worth your while. I'm sure your bookie will appreciate getting paid for once."

Then he walked away without looking back.

"Gotcha, you little jerk!"

D.J. grinned at the information on the screen, basking in his hard-fought victory. He'd found Reggie. This R. Morrison he'd tracked down had to be the guy. If so, his nemesis lived right down the I-5 corridor, just outside of Portland. He printed out the address and a map so he could find the place when he got there.

Next up was telling Devlin that he'd be out of town for the weekend. Timing was everything. Rather than risk having his friend ask too many questions or even order him to stick around, he'd text him at the last possible minute. Better yet, he'd send the man an e-mail.

With luck, it would get lost in the dozens of messages Devlin got every day. Heck, maybe Devlin wouldn't even see it until Monday morning. To be on the safe side, D.J. waited until he was packed and ready to leave before hitting the Send button. Unfortunately, as he merged onto the southbound lanes of the interstate, his cell phone rang. He checked the caller ID.

Damn it, just as he'd feared.

Luckily, Washington state law made it illegal to drive and talk on a handheld phone. As a law-abiding citizen, D.J. couldn't possibly take the call. He powered off the phone and kept driving. Once he confronted Reggie and showed the kid the error of his ways, he'd head back to Seattle and face Devlin's wrath.

Hell, he was on Dev's shit list so often, one more time wouldn't matter. Right? Now if only the growing knot in his stomach would buy into that idea. Unfortunately, there were only two things D.J. took pride in. One was his skill with computers. The other was his loyalty to the men he fought beside.

If Devlin needed him, he'd turn around and head right back to headquarters. He pulled off at the next exit and stopped in a convenience store parking lot. Holding his breath, he dialed Devlin's number and waited. When it went to voice mail, he didn't know what to think.

Was the barrier down? He closed his eyes and reached out with his senses, searching for the familiar buzz of high energy. Paladins were all attuned to the frequency of their stretch of the barrier. Once he located that frequency, he followed it back toward the tunnels under Seattle. Good, it felt normal, healthy. That could change any second, but for now it seemed stable. Rather than stew about it, he punched in another number.

Cullen answered on the first ring. "Hey, D.J., what's up?"

His friend sounded calm. Good, that probably meant the barrier was all right for now.

"Devlin was looking for me, but he's not answering his phone. I just wanted to make sure nothing was going on."

"Not that I know of. Did you check his office? Maybe he's on the other line."

Okay, truth or lie? D.J. hedged his bets. "Uh, I'm not exactly at headquarters or even in Seattle. I have a few things to take care of, so I'll be out of touch for a couple of days."

Several seconds of silence passed before Cullen spoke again. "Buddy, I hope you know what you're doing. I'll try to avoid Devlin, so maybe that will buy you some time. But if he finds me, I'll have to tell him if he asks."

The offer made D.J. smile. It wouldn't be the first time the two of them had combined efforts to deflect Devlin's attention. This time, though, was far more serious.

"Thanks, Cullen, but don't do anything to get him pissed off at you, too. No use in both of us being on his shit list."

He could almost see Cullen shrug. "I've been there before and survived the experience. In the meantime, is there anything I can help you with? Like those mysterious e-mails you've been getting?"

Son of a bitch, how did he know about those? Stupid question. The two of them were pretty much on a par when it came to computers.

"Maybe. I'll let you know how it turns out when I get back home."

"Okay, but don't hesitate to call for backup if you need me. I'm always up for a little cyberwar."

D.J. could hear voices in the background, most likely the two kids Cullen had unofficially adopted. It was time to get off the line and back on the road.

"Talk to you soon, Cullen. Tell Lusahn and Bavi hi for me, and give Shiri a hug."

"Will do."

When the line went dead, D.J. shut the phone off, telling himself he didn't want the distraction as he drove. That wasn't the real reason though. If Devlin called again, D.J. couldn't risk telling him the truth, but neither would he willingly lie to his friend. And if that wasn't a helluva position to be in.

Rather than dwell on it, he gunned the engine and tore off down the highway. The sooner D.J. found Reggie, the sooner he could go back to his life.

Reggie had spent far too many hours pacing back and forth in front of the computer, watching her avatar sit alone at the cyberbar. She'd been hit on by a number of others but none of them was the Knightwalker. Even if he'd changed avatars again, she would've known him. She was sure of it.

Obviously she'd struck a chord when she'd mentioned the Paladins and the Others. Were those code names for some kind of secret government project? That didn't feel quite right, but it was the best explanation she'd been able to come up with.

The walls were closing in on her. She'd been shut inside all week at work, and it was past time to burn off some energy. Should she go for a run or settle for working out inside? She'd let the weather decide.

A quick peek outside had her shoving her feet into her running shoes. After putting a bottle of water into her fanny pack and grabbing her keys, she trotted down the steps and cranked up some red-dirt rock on her iPod. Outside, she stretched before setting off at a slow jog, giving her muscles a chance to finish warming up.

At the corner, she kicked it into high gear and circled the block. Unfortunately, the sidewalks proved to be crowded, no doubt thanks to the beautiful weather. Rather than deal with the frustration of weaving in and out of the mob, she headed down to the track at the local high school.

Once she fell into the familiar rhythm of the run, her thoughts turned back to the Knightwalker. What was he up to? What did D. J. Clayborne, the man behind the avatar, do besides create havoc in other people's computer files?

She'd tried every internet search technique she could think of and failed to turn up anything. Maybe if she had some idea of where to look for him. As far as she knew, he could live on the other side of the world.

Obviously D.J., if that was even his real name, knew how to hide in plain sight. Well, when she was back in the office on Monday, she'd try again. As much as she'd enjoyed the game of tag they'd been playing, it was time to get serious and track him down. If she could pinpoint his location, she'd turn the information over to her boss and let him take it from there.

Her decision was made, and she'd live with the consequences. D.J. was like any number of other hackers she'd brought down over the years. Yeah, and if she kept telling herself that, she might just believe it.

Time to head home. At the next turn, she peeled off the track and cut across the grass to the driveway that emptied out on a busy arterial. She ran full out the rest of the way, stopping only to do her cool-down stretches in the parking lot.

As she straightened up, someone tapped her shoulder. She shrieked as she spun around, ready to go on the attack until she recognized Cody. She smacked the nitwit on the arm hard enough to sting but not bruise.

"Darn it, Cody, how many times have I told you not to sneak up on me like that?"

He rubbed his arm and glared right back at her. Then he reached out to yank her earphones off her head and dangled them in front of her face.

"I didn't sneak. I called your name twice. It's not my fault you didn't hear me. You're the one with your iPod cranked up so loud the whole city can hear it."

Only slightly mollified, Reggie pushed past him to head inside. "Did you want something or were you just hanging around hoping to scare a couple of years off my life?"

Cody trailed along behind her, clomping up the steps to her apartment. "I thought you should know that Ed has been messing in your files and maybe working on your case."

She stopped at the landing. "Which case?"

Although she knew. That jerk! After the incident the other day, Mr. DeLuca had specifically told Ed to back off and leave the Knightwalker to her.

"Did you actually catch him in the act?"

The kid shrugged as she unlocked the door. "Not exactly."

Inside her apartment, she handed Cody a bottle of water and twisted the top off one for herself. "Okay, start at the beginning and tell me what you did see."

Cody flopped down on the couch. "I left my calculus textbook at the office and stopped by to pick it up. On my way in, I saw Ed's car pulling out of the parking lot. I didn't think much of it. Lots of us work weekends."

He stopped to take another drink. "But inside, our cubicle reeked of cigarette smoke, and your chair wasn't pushed in all the way. You never leave it like that. Besides, nobody else would have the balls to smoke in the office. Even if it weren't illegal, we both know Mr. DeLuca wouldn't put up with it."

That was true. Their boss was a serious health nut and encouraged his employees to be the same way. Ed had been hired by the previous owner and had stayed on after Mr. DeLuca bought the company. The relationship between the two men was an uneasy one. She suspected that if Ed hadn't been so good at his job, he'd have been fired long ago.

She closed her eyes and sighed. "Darn it anyway. I had a feeling Ed wouldn't drop the investigation even after the boss told him to. Well, he wouldn't have found much. I've been doing most of my work on my laptop here at home for just that reason."

There wasn't anything she could do without hard evidence. She looked at Cody and caught him eyeing the basket of fruit she had sitting on the kitchen counter. He never complained, but between his tuition and rent, she knew money was tight. Too tight for him to always have enough left over at the end of the month to eat much more than cold cereal.

She would have to play this carefully because the kid had his pride. If he thought she was offering him a handout, he'd take off out of sheer stubbornness even if it meant going hungry for the night.

"I was going to order some takeout for dinner, but I don't have the energy to go pick it up."

She sagged back against the wall to give credence to the lie. "If I buy, will you go get it?"

He eyed her suspiciously but then nodded. "If you're sure."

She tossed him the menu. "I'll take broccoli beef and spring rolls. In fact, order me cashew chicken and a double order of fried rice and get whatever you want. If there are any leftovers, I can take them for lunch next week."

"Sounds good."

As he reached for the phone, she dug her spare key out of her junk drawer. "Here, take this so you can lock the door on your way out. I'm going to grab a quick shower while you're gone."

He caught the key and nodded while he rattled off their order. She was glad to hear he'd taken her seriously about ordering extra. Knowing Cody's appetite, she doubted there'd be more than a few grains of rice left after he was done eating. That was okay. She didn't have that many friends; she couldn't afford to let one starve to death.

Chapter 4

$\mathcal{D}$.J. hung back and watched the door to the apartment building. By his calculations, R. Morrison lived on the second floor, in the end apartment. He'd been unable to determine if the initial stood for Reggie for certain, but his gut told him he was on the right track.

He spotted a kid who looked to be about twenty cutting across the parking lot. The guy headed right for the apartment building with a bag of what looked like takeout. He twirled a key ring on his finger. This was definitely promising.

For one thing, he looked like the quintessential computer jockey. He was too skinny for his height, vibrated with overloaded energy, and wore glasses. His complexion was on the pasty side, as if he spent far too many hours at a computer and not nearly enough outside.

D.J. smiled. He liked the kid already, even if the punk had been leading him on a merry chase for the past couple of months. He planned on getting right up in his face about pissing in the wrong person's pool, hoping to put an end to Reggie's forays into Paladin territory. He had his doubts though. The forbidden fruit was always more tempting to a dedicated hacker.

He should know.

D.J. remained in the shadows long enough to give the kid time to get inside and feel safe before making his move. Five minutes later, he headed for the door. Time to go introduce himself to one Reggie Morrison. This should be fun.

Inside the building, he took the steps two at a time. A hunter by nature, he automatically avoided making any noise right up until he was ready to announce his presence. No use in giving his target any advance warning.

D.J. stopped to listen before knocking. Crap! Reggie wasn't alone. He should've guessed that was the case considering how big the bag was that the kid had been carrying. There was definitely a woman inside the apartment. The door muffled the conversation too much to make out what they were saying, but it didn't really matter.

D.J. hadn't driven four hours and risked his friendship with Devlin to give up now. He needed to get this mess settled so he could head back home and get with the program. He rapped on the door and then stepped back to wait.

Reggie handed Cody a couple of plates and dug out some serving spoons. The rich scents of ginger and garlic made her stomach growl. Judging by the speed with which Cody was opening all of the cartons, she wasn't the only one hungry.

She was about to ask him what he'd like to drink when someone knocked on the door. Who could that be? No one other than Cody was in the habit of dropping by uninvited. She took two steps toward the door and then froze, oddly reluctant to open it. She didn't want to be bothered.

Cody looked up from reading the slip of paper he'd pulled out of a fortune cookie with a grin. "Want me to get it? This says that 'The winds of change will come knocking and the daring will profit.' I'm not sure how wind is supposed to knock, but I could sure use a little profit about now. My tuition is almost due."

She waved him back to his seat. Her home, her duty to answer the door. "No, I'll get it."

The peephole didn't tell her much other than that the unexpected guest was tall and male. She slipped the chain in place and opened the door far enough to peek out.

"May I help you?" she asked before she got a good look at the guy.

When he moved directly under the light in the hall, her stomach lurched as if the floor had just dropped out from under her feet. The Knightwalker's avatar had come to life and was standing right outside her door. She blinked twice to make sure.

The avatar was speaking, but the only thing she could hear was a loud roaring in her ears. Instinct had her slamming the door closed and throwing the lock, but that accomplished nothing. As soon as she did, a big fist pounded on the door and an irate male voice shouted her name. This time, from behind the dubious safety of her door, she made out every word.

"Reggie, let me in. We need to talk."

"What does he want? Should I call the police?" Cody was already reaching for the phone.

"No, that's okay. He's okay." She hoped. "I just wasn't expecting company."

"Are you going to let him in?"

She'd have to. Damn, damn, double damn. What had she been thinking by toying with the Knightwalker? She should've handed everything she had over to her boss the minute the case landed on her desk.

The pounding started again. The last thing she needed was for one of the neighbors to get involved. Besides, she didn't want Cody to know who was standing out on the landing. As much as she liked the kid, he couldn't keep his mouth shut on a bet. If he had any inkling he was about to meet the Knightwalker in person, he'd be blabbing it to the world.

Reggie wiped her sweaty hands on her jeans and braced herself. As soon as she touched the chain, there was blessed silence. She slid it free and yanked the door open.

"What a surprise, D.J.! I had no idea that you were in town." That much was true. "Come on in. I'm sorry, but my friend Cody and I were about to sit down to dinner, so—"

At least now she wasn't the only one who looked

confused. D.J. glanced past her to where Cody was now standing and then back to her.

"You're Reggie?" he mouthed, his eyebrows arching high in surprise.

She nodded.

He let out a deep breath and then a slow grin spread across his handsome face. "Yeah, Reggie, I'd love to join you for dinner. Suddenly, I seem to have developed quite an appetite."

Short of slamming the door again, which would put her right back between a rock and a hard place, she had no choice. One way or the other, she was going to have to deal with the man. At this point, all she could hope for was that Cody would take off after they ate. Once he was out of the line of fire, she'd figure out what to do about D.J.

And didn't that thought bring a lot of interesting ideas to mind? The man would definitely be in the eye-candy aisle at the store. In an effort to clear her head, she performed the necessary introductions while she dug out one more plate and poured three glasses of iced tea.

"Cody, this is D.J., an online acquaintance of mine. D.J., this is Cody."

The two men shook hands, obviously sizing each other up, trying to figure out where each of them fit in the scheme of things. Poor Cody, he was seriously out-gunned and he knew it. Despite having seen D.J.'s most recent avatar, she would never have guessed that he'd based the character on his actual appearance.

If she thought the animated version was attractive, it had nothing on the man himself. D.J. was tall, broad shouldered, and had the kind of muscles that came from physical work, not a gym. His dark hair had a definite wave to it and was considerably longer than current fashion. Those dark brown eyes sparkled with a good bit of humor, all part and parcel of a complete rogue.

Her apartment was plenty big enough for one woman living alone, but it was amazing to see how much room the two men took up. She felt crowded—no, make that cornered. D.J. knew it, too, and clearly thought it was funny. Not that he made any threatening moves. Instead, he seemed completely at home in her tiny kitchen eating dinner with two total strangers.

He heaped his plate high, deliberately brushing his fingertips against hers as he passed the cartons. When she dropped a piece of chicken on the table, he quickly snapped it up with his chopsticks and held it up to her lips. She'd rather bite his hand but accepted the offering with barely disguised disgust.

The jerk actually winked at her before turning his attention to her coworker. "So, Cody, Reggie never mentioned you to me. How do you know her?"

Her friend shot her a hurt look before answering. "We work together. Come to think of it, she's never mentioned you either."

Okay, this could get ugly. "Cody, I only just met D.J. recently. If I'd known he was coming into town today, I would've mentioned it."

Not.

The conversation ended there. The two men at her table kept a wary eye on each other as they finished every last scrap of food Cody had ordered. Knowing her young friend had a sweet tooth, she offered him her secret stash of homemade chocolate chip cookies from the freezer. Those didn't last long either.

As she finished the final one, she considered her options. Cody probably had studying he should be doing, but it was obvious he wasn't going to leave until D.J. did. Somehow she doubted the Knightwalker had plans to go anywhere until he was good and ready.

Fine. She'd kick both of them out at the same time. To give them the hint, she stood up, preparing to clear the table. To her surprise, D.J. refused to surrender his plate.

"Let me. You bought. He fetched. The least I can do is clean up."

Not to be outdone, Cody gathered up the empty cartons and tossed them in the trash. Robbed of anything useful to do, Reggie sat back down. She wasn't quite sure how to react to having two guys banging around her kitchen while she watched. It was hard not to smile at the obvious rivalry between the two. Cody was doing his best to make sure that D.J. realized how at home he was in Reggie's place.

D.J. was obviously well aware of what the younger man was doing. She liked the fact that he even conceded the point by asking him where things were kept rather than rooting around in her cabinets. But in a straight one-on-one comparison, there was no way for Cody to win. Eventually his body would fill out to match his height, and he'd be a very good-looking man. But D.J. was definitely already in his prime.

He moved with a grace and confidence that Cody could only hope to achieve someday. She liked her friend, but she wasn't attracted to him. That didn't mean she was happy about the way her eyes kept wandering back to D.J., watching the play of his muscles as he worked and admiring the fit of those well-worn jeans.

The man was a criminal, at least by the strict definition of the law, even though he wasn't into hacking for profit as far as she could tell. Though she still wanted to know what he did with the rest of his time when he wasn't waging cyberwar.

Martial arts, for one, she guessed. She'd spent enough time in gyms to recognize the significance of the calluses on D.J.'s hands. That would also account for how well he moved and the confidence he wore with the same ease as he did those faded jeans.

Oops, he caught her staring. He grinned as he folded the dish towel and hung it on the stove handle to dry.

"Thanks for doing that."

"No problem."

Before he could sit back down, Reggie stood up. "I hate to rush both of you off, but it's been a long day."

She expected an argument. Instead, D.J. dutifully led the parade toward the door. He pegged Cody with a questioning look.

"I've got my truck outside. Need a ride?"

Cody looked relieved as he picked up his backpack. "Sure, if it's not out of your way. I don't live far."

This was going to be easier than she'd thought, but then he'd made his point just by showing up on her doorstep. There would be no hiding from him now. And if she turned him in, he would know who'd done it. She forced a smile, not wanting D.J. to know how aggravated she was.

D.J. followed Cody out the door, saying, "On the way, maybe you can recommend a good motel nearby. I've decided to stay in town for the weekend."

"'Bye, guys," she called after them, closing the door with exaggerated care.

If she gave in to the urge to slam it, it would only put one more point on D.J.'s side of the scoreboard. As they clomped down her stairs, she ran to the balcony to watch them leave. She wrote down D.J.'s license plate number as the big truck roared to life, her first real lead in finding where the Knightwalker lived.

Oh, yeah, two could play this game.

D.J. let the silence in the truck drag on for several minutes after Cody gave him directions. He considered pumping the kid for information about Reggie but rejected the idea. Anything he said or asked would get back to her sooner rather than later.

"So you and Reggie work together."

Not exactly a question since the kid had already told him that much.

"Yeah, we've shared a cubicle for the past two years and hang out together on weekends and evenings when I'm not in class. She's taught me a lot."

The kid injected a little extra emphasis on that last statement, clearly still trying to prove that his relationship with Reggie was a special one. No doubt it was, but if Cody thought she was feeling anything for him other than friendship, he was sorely mistaken. She clearly treated him like a favored little brother.

No use in calling him on it though. "So what are you studying?"

"Computer engineering with a minor in business. I want to design and market my own games."

D.J. nodded in approval. "If you've got the talent for it, you could be set to make some major bucks when you graduate. I have a friend who does that. His newest game just hit the market."

He wondered what Jake would think about D.J. claiming him as a friend, especially considering the amount of time they spent just screwing with each other. Heck, if that wasn't friendship between hackers, what was?

For the first time, Cody dropped his attitude. "Really? Which game?"

"Clash of the Golden Dragons."

"No shit? You know the guy who designed that? The graphics are incredible!"

"I can put you in touch with him. You know, if you'd like to talk to him about the business."

"Think he'd mind?"

"No. Give me your e-mail address and I'll introduce you. He has another job that takes up a lot of his time, so don't think he's blowing you off if he doesn't respond right away."

"Sounds good." Cody was grinning as he pointed down the street. "That's my apartment building at the end of the block, on the left."

D.J. pulled into the parking lot and waited while Cody dug out a business card. "Thanks, D.J. I appreciate this."

"Not a problem. Maybe I'll see you again before I leave town."

"Cool."

Cody waved one last time before he disappeared into the rundown building he called home. It was clear that money was tight for him. If the kid was anything like D.J. had been in college, he put all his disposable income into his computers. Come to think of it, Cody reminded D.J. of his own younger self.

Sort of. Cody might be strapped for funds, but at least he had one trusted friend. D.J. hadn't had anyone like that in his life until the Regents found him and brought him to the Paladins, offering him the first—no, make that the only—real home he'd ever known. D.J. just hoped that he hadn't screwed that up big time by letting this mess get out of control.

He pulled back out into traffic and debated what to do next. A motel or back to Reggie's?

No contest. He circled the block in case Cody was watching to see which direction he went and then drove right back to Reggie's apartment. This was going to be fun.

When Reggie opened the door, he couldn't exactly say she looked surprised—or happy.

"Did you forget something?"

"Nope, but it's still early, and I've got a hankering for some ice cream. I spotted a place down the street and thought you might join me. I don't know anyone else in the area and hate to eat alone."

He stepped closer, deliberately crowding her. "Or I can go pick some up and bring it back here."

Her hesitation was only momentary. "Let me put on my shoes and grab my keys."

She left him cooling his heels on the wrong side of her door, but he didn't complain. He'd already pushed her enough by showing up unannounced and uninvited twice in one evening. He leaned against the wall and waited, listening to Reggie moving around inside her apartment. The thickness of the door did little to muffle the soft sounds, not with his Paladin hearing.

The padding of bare feet; the soft swish they made sliding into shoes; the jangle of her keys; her pulse picking up speed as she headed for the door. When it started to open, he stepped farther back to give her all the room she needed.

She ignored him as she locked the door and then shoved her keys into her pocket. "I'm ready if you are."

Without waiting to see if he followed, she started down the steps. Gutsy of her. Most women wouldn't trust a man they didn't know all that well at their backs. Even so, he followed at a respectful distance. When they were out on the sidewalk, she turned in the opposite direction from the place he'd had in mind.

As if sensing his curiosity, she glanced in his direction. "The ice cream is better at another place. It's only a little farther away."

"Sounds good." Distance translated as more time in her company.

They walked along in silence for a couple of blocks. Although the two of them had a lot to talk about, he was content to put the confrontation off as long as possible. After a bit, Reggie started playing tour guide, pointing out her favorite bookstore and several restaurants she thought he should try while he was in town. Finally, true to her promise, he spotted an ice cream shop at the end of the next block.

As they made their approach, he caught her attention. "So, Reggie, I've got a question for you."

She gave him a suspicious look. "Doesn't mean I have an answer, but ask away."

He pointed toward the shop. "Do you always order the same flavor or do you like to . . . experiment?"

Her fair skin flushed. Finally, she said, "Most of the time I keep things simple, boring even."

Somehow he doubted there was anything boring about her at all. He held the door open for her and then headed toward the counter to place their order. "Two waffle cones with double scoops of whatever the lady wants."

When she started to put some money down on the counter, he shook his head. "My treat. So, Reggie, what's it going to be? Let's see what you consider boring."

Reggie kept her attention focused strictly on the clerk behind the counter. "Double fudge mocha pecan."

D.J. grinned as he paid for their treats. He'd half-expected her to order plain old vanilla just to show him, but she'd been unable to resist the temptation of her favorite flavor. Good. He was having a difficult time resisting temptation himself. Rather than immediately head back out into the night, he took a seat at the one empty booth in the shop. It would be interesting to see whether Reggie sat across from him or if she was up to doing a little crowding herself.

She didn't even hesitate, sliding onto the opposite bench. Fine with him. All the better to keep an eye on her. He pretended not to notice when her legs brushed his as she scooted all the way to the far corner of the booth, but her eyes flared wide at the brief contact.

Good. He'd hate to be the only one who was almost painfully aware of their proximity. Hoping to cool off the direction his thoughts were headed, he tasted the ice cream. The rich combination of flavors exploded on his tongue. "Wow, no wonder you love this stuff."

She merely nodded, obviously more interested in her ice cream than she was in him. It was all he could do not to groan as her pink tongue darted out to catch a drip of ice cream running down the side of her cone. How sweet would her mocha-flavored kiss taste? Sadly, all things considered, he figured that wasn't on the menu for the night.

Odd how much that realization bothered him. After all, he was there to order a fellow hacker to back off before she got in over her head, relying on the same lies he'd been telling women for years. Somehow, he just couldn't bring himself to start spouting the usual load of crap.

So rather than say anything, he ate his ice cream and ignored the double scoop of regret that had settled in his chest.

When Reggie had polished off the last bite of her ice cream, she wiped her fingers with a napkin. "We should head back."

D.J. tossed the rest of his cone in the trash. "Sure."

Outside it had started misting, a common enough occurrence in both Portland and Seattle. Like most natives, the two of them ignored it as they walked along. But when he noticed Reggie shiver, D.J. peeled off his jacket and wrapped it around her shoulders.

She didn't quibble, instead laughing at the way it hung down almost to her knees. She had to really work to shove the sleeves up her arms far enough for her hands to show. She did a slow pirouette to show it off.

"Quite the fashion statement, don't you think? This thing is big enough to cover three of me."

Actually, he liked the way it looked on her, and he strongly suspected one Reggie was more than enough for him. Before he could bring himself to say so, they'd reached her building. She slipped off his jacket and held it out.

"Thanks for the ice cream."

He accepted the jacket, but not the implied goodbye. "We need to talk, and I'm guessing you'd rather we kept the discussion private."

She rolled her eyes and led the way up to her apartment. "Fine, but don't plan on staying long."

"Just as long as it takes."

Inside, she took the one easy chair, leaving D.J. the couch. He sprawled on it, automatically starting to put his feet up on the coffee table. Whoops. This wasn't his house. He froze in mid motion, lowering them back down to the floor.

Reggie shook her head. "Don't stop on my account. I do it myself all the time. That's what coffee tables are for."

D.J. nodded and plopped his size thirteens down on a haphazard stack of magazines. She curled up in the chair, her legs tucked to the side. From where he was sitting he could see one bare foot keeping time to a beat only she could hear. Seems they had more in common than just whacked-out computer skills.

She caught him staring and frowned. "So what do you think we need to discuss?"

"Like how you found me and how you managed to break into secure files. More important, what you plan to do with that information, not to mention why you were looking for me in the first place."

He alleviated the grim tone of his voice with a quick grin. "Although, now that I've seen you in person I can't say I'm sorry that I had to track you down."

"What does seeing me have to do with it?"

He gave her a deliberate look, from head to toe. "To be honest, I was envisioning you as looking a lot more like your buddy Cody. Believe me, it's been a pleasant surprise."

Her eyebrows shot up. "You thought I was a guy?"

"Most hackers are."

"But you'd met my avatar. If Ruby looked like a guy, maybe you need your eyes checked. Not that I'm anything like her."

There was an odd note in Reggie's voice when she said that last part. Clearly she thought he would've preferred her to be a tall, buxom redhead. That might have been true before he actually met her but not now. He suspected that underneath those baggy pants and oversize T-shirt there were some delectable curves.

She wore her dark blond hair pinned up on top of her head with a couple of chopsticks. Yeah, her expressive mouth was a little too wide, her nose a bit sharp, but it all fit together somehow. Besides, there was a great deal of intelligence shining brightly in those soft gray eyes, and smart was always a major turn-on for him.

He doubted she wanted to hear any of that from him. Not yet anyway. But, hot damn, he wanted to peel away all those layers of protective clothing to discover the secrets hidden underneath. He shifted his position on the couch, hoping she wouldn't notice what was going on south of his waistband.

"We both know things are not always as they seem in cyberspace. It doesn't pay to assume an avatar is ever an accurate representation of someone."

She played devil's advocate. "Yet your most recent one looked just like you. Seems like a risky thing to do. What if someone had recognized you?"

She was right. It had been stupid, but he'd grown tired of hiding who and what he was. Not just in the cyberworld either. For once, just once, he wished he had what his friends had: a woman who knew the truth of what it meant to be a Paladin and loved him anyway.

Definitely time to get to the point.

"I'm not here to talk about avatars, Reggie."

Her whole body went still. "So why are you here? Because I've got to tell you, having you hunt me down in person is veering pretty close to stalker territory."

"Yeah, right, Reggie." He sighed. "And leaving me cryptic messages for months doesn't fall into that category?"

A faint blush stained her cheeks. "Okay, so we're both guilty."

"I might sound like a five-year-old, but you started it. I think I have the right to know why. We both know I'm not the only hacker out there."

Her feet came down on the floor, propelling her up out of the chair. It was like watching a fast-paced tennis match as she paced from one end of the room to the other while he waited for her to answer.

Finally she stopped abruptly in front of the sliding door to her small balcony and stared out into the darkness. "You're a legend."

So that was it. Her interest was part of what he and Cullen called the "Fastest Gun in the West" syndrome. She was just another in a long line of computer jockeys out to earn her stripes by taking on someone higher up the food chain. That was pretty much what he'd figured. If it had been Cody instead of Reggie, he would've kicked the kid's ass for him and gone home.

But now having met Reggie, he wasn't sure of what

he was feeling. Disappointment for sure. Frustration of more than one kind. He doubted she'd want to do anything about any of it, which was a damn shame.

He stood and walked over to the counter, just to give himself something to do. What was there left to say? A couple of things.

"Well, congrats. You beat me, but don't expect a trophy."

Funny how that didn't make Reggie look any happier. She watched him much like a mouse watched a cat. A great big cat. At least she was smart enough to be wary of D.J.'s predatory nature. If she thought he was scary, she had no idea what she'd be messing with if the Regents caught wind of her escapade.

He stared at her, memorizing her pretty face. "This ends now, Reggie. Don't contact me again. Don't try to find me."

When her eyes immediately flicked in the direction of the kitchen counter, he picked up a scrap of paper and looked at it. His license plate number. No doubt she'd memorized it, but just in case, he wadded it up and stuffed it in his pocket.

He couldn't leave, not yet. He stalked toward her. That she stood her ground spoke to her courage, one more thing he liked about her. When they stood toe to toe, he leaned down close to her ear. The combined scents of soap and soft female skin filled his head. Damn, he was playing with fire.

"I want to leave you with two things to think about, Reggie."

He held up one finger. "For your own safety, put whatever you know or think you know about me or the Paladins or the Regents right out of that pretty little head. Destroy the hard copies and never access that site again."

She glared up at him. "What makes you think I made hard copies?"

He smiled down into those angry, long-lashed eyes. "Because, Reggie, that's what I would've done. Clear out the copy you made on a flash drive, too. Better yet, destroy the damn thing. Don't keep anything that can be used against you."

For the first time she looked worried. "Seriously, D.J., you're not trying to tell me all that crap was real?"

He wished he could, but that wasn't happening. "No, I'm trying to tell you to keep that cute nose out of my business for your own good."

She wasn't buying it, not for an instant, which was why he'd be sticking around for a while despite what he'd told her about leaving him alone. Maybe he could figure out some way to convince her. Meanwhile, he'd keep an eye on her until he knew for sure whether anyone was coming after her.

"Okay, so, that was one thing. What's the other one?"

He shouldn't do it. He really, really shouldn't. But then he'd never had much luck with impulse control.

"Think about this, Reggie."

And he kissed her.

Chapter 5

Was it possible to taste a smile? That's what she was sensing as D.J. captured her mouth with his. When she tried to protest, he only deepened the kiss, the velvet-soft glide of his tongue across hers melting away what little resistance she'd been able to muster up.

When was the last time a man had kissed her like it mattered? Maybe never, but right now she could barely process anything. Her brain had shut down, leaving only muddled thoughts of heat and need and want. Her hands dug into the muscles in D.J.'s shoulders and held on for dear life.

If he hadn't wrapped his arms around her, she wasn't sure she'd still be standing. Not when she was pouring every bit of energy she had into giving as good as she got. This was craziness, but sanity was an overrated commodity.

Incredible was the best description, but no ordinary words could come close to what she was feeling. The man was a definite tease. One second he brushed his lips against hers as if he'd never get back to the serious business at hand. Then he gifted her with a series of butterfly-soft kisses, scattering them across her cheeks and forehead, ending at the tip of her nose.

She put a stop to the play by grabbing his face with her hands and dragging his mouth back to hers. He seemed to like that, chuckling and murmuring his approval as he surrendered control to her. God, the man tasted like temptation, a flavor far too rich to possibly be good for her. But just like the ice cream he'd bought her, some things were worth the risk.

Tomorrow she'd run an extra lap to make up for the dessert. She wasn't sure what she'd be able to do to erase the effect D. J. Clayborne was having on her, though. When her feet left the floor as he pressed her back against the wall, her legs instinctively wrapped around his hips. His big hands cupped her bottom and settled her firmly against his body as he rocked against her.

Big mistake! The center of her hunger was in direct contact with the impressive evidence that she wasn't the only one veering out of control. She had to put a stop to this madness. Now, while she still had the strength to resist a complete surrender.

One last taste. She wanted that much, deserved that much. But each second she spent in D.J.'s arms made it that much harder to stop. Finally, she yanked her mouth free from his. "Put me down."

He slowly did as she'd asked. The sudden separation as he took a half step back hurt, but only on the inside where a shaft of disappointment stabbed right through her heart. D.J. allowed her some distance but kept her safe inside the loose circle of his arms.

His dark eyes stared into hers but gave her no clue as to what he was thinking. Was he feeling regret or triumph? She didn't want to know.

"You need to leave."

The words sounded breathy and far too indecisive to her own ears. He'd never take her seriously if she didn't sound more like she meant it. She tried again.

"D.J., you *need* to leave. Now."

He nodded, slowly, as if he was reluctant to believe her. Or maybe, like her, he wasn't processing things very well. She gave his chest a gentle shove, conveying the same thought with action.

His hands dropped to his sides, but the cocky grin was firmly back in place as he walked toward the door.

"Well, I guess that gave us both something to think about. Hope your dreams are good ones."

Before he left, he stopped and handed her a piece of paper. "Here's my cell phone number. If anything happens to worry you, call me. Don't hesitate, not for a second. Better a false alarm than to let the bastards get you."

He waited until she nodded and then said, "'Bye, Reggie. It's been a whole lot better than nice."

Then he was gone.

Okay, that was the stupidest trick he'd ever pulled. Sure, it wasn't the first time a plan had backfired on him, but right now he couldn't think of a single instance that had left him this badly shaken. Jumping in a tub of ice wouldn't be enough to quench this fire.

What the hell had he been thinking?

He had no idea. One taste of her lips and he'd frozen; in fact, one part of his anatomy had definitely been stiffer than the rest. Still was, in fact. If Reggie hadn't called a halt to the fiasco when she did, he would have for the sake of his own sanity.

Maybe he'd started off wanting to get a little of his own back by kissing her. He had to admit knowing she was capable of besting him at his own game smarted a bit. A lot, in fact, but that didn't give him the right to seduce the woman for a little bit of payback.

He was a better man than that. At least he liked to think so. For now, he'd get a room someplace close and crawl into bed. Alone—well, except for the memories of how she'd felt in his arms.

He'd been right about one thing, though. Reggie was hiding one hot little body under all that clothing. She definitely had curves in all the right places.

He almost spun around to head right back up those stairs to her apartment but managed to stop himself. Outside, he drew in a few deep breaths, trying to regain control by clearing his lungs of any lingering vestiges of Reggie's scent.

It didn't work.

He trudged across to where he'd left his truck. Maybe after a few hours' sleep, he'd be better able to decide what to do next. When he opened the door, he risked one last look up at Reggie's apartment. Just as he suspected, she stood outlined in the window, watching him from above. She might think the shadows prevented him from seeing her clearly. She would be wrong about that.

Paladins all had exceptional night vision. His allowed him to see the frown on that luscious mouth and the sadness in those pretty eyes. He could even see the slight tremble in her hand as she waved to him.

Rather than stare, he climbed into the truck and started the engine. When he pulled out of the parking spot, he rolled down his window and waved back. She nodded and stepped back out of sight, leaving him no choice but to drive away.

Alone, as usual.

D.J. seriously hated telephones. Especially ones rude enough to ring at . . . what time was it anyway? He groped on the bedside table looking for his cell phone and squinted at the screen. Okay, the sun was already up. That didn't mean he didn't hate the person on the other end of the line for disturbing his beauty sleep.

He punched the On button. "This better be damned important."

Devlin's voice was little better than a growl. "Care to explain to me why your worthless ass is parked down in Portland rather than here on duty?"

Oh, crap. He should've checked the number first. Obviously Devlin had finally opened his e-mail and then tracked him by the GPS chip in his cell phone. He sat up and considered his options. Would disconnecting the call be the smart thing to do or the coward's way out? Maybe a little of both. Eventually he'd have to face the music. Might as well hear the opening strains long distance.

"I had business down here. Personal business."

Silence. Long, heavy silence followed by more of the same. Okay, so Dev wasn't going to make it easy for him. He could try to wait him out, but they both knew who would break first.

"I should've told you I needed some downtime to take care of a problem, Devlin."

More silence, then a heavy sigh. "Does this particular problem have something to do with whatever has had you acting so twitchy lately?"

D.J. rubbed his forehead, anticipating the headache that was sure to follow this call. "Yeah, it does. I'm doing my best to fix it."

"Any chance it will blow up in your face?" Devlin didn't sound as angry as he did resigned.

No use lying at this point. "Maybe, but I can't be sure."

"When you get back, we'll have a long discussion about how you should've handled this, D.J. For now, if anyone asks, you're on personal leave."

"Thanks."

One of the knots in his gut eased up. That left only the worry about what the fallout would be for Reggie's brief foray into the Regents' server, not to mention why she'd been hunting for him. Despite her admission that she'd been out to best him at his own game, he sensed there was more to it than that.

"How long will you be gone?"

He'd already decided to stay in Portland for the weekend. Nothing had happened to change that plan, but he decided to build in some leeway for himself. "I should be back by the end of the week at the latest."

"Okay, but in case you're not?"

"Send the cavalry."

"Will do. And, D.J., one more thing."

"Yeah?"

"Whatever this is, I hope you can fix it permanently. We need you back at a hundred percent. The place isn't the same without you."

He had no idea how to react to the concern in his friend's voice. Normally Devlin yelled; he didn't coddle.

"I'm trying, Dev. I apologize for running out on you. I promise I'll explain everything."

"Okay, but watch your back. If you need to stay away longer, call. You know how Trahern gets when he's worried. It's embarrassing when he cries in front of all the guys, and the Others just laugh at him."

Another deep voice murmured something obscene in the background. D.J. grinned. It had to be Trahern. Damn, he missed the guys. He was so used to seeing them every day.

"See you soon, boss."

"Yeah, see that you do."

The phone went silent, but even that small connection with his friends had left him feeling energized and ready to face the day. The only question was, what would be the most productive use of his time?

Now that he had verified that R. Morrison was indeed Reggie, he could dig deeper into her personal business. She'd hate it, but turnabout was fair play. First things first. Shower. Get dressed. Eat breakfast. Then start shoveling.

His day planned, he grabbed his clean clothes and headed for the bathroom.

Saturday morning came way too soon. Reggie kicked her legs free of the twisted knot of blankets, the effort leaving her breathing hard and exhausted before she even got up. Not exactly the way she'd planned to start her day.

Sitting on the edge of the bed, she waited for her head to catch up with her body. Finally, she staggered toward the bathroom hoping a splash of cold water would clear some of the cobwebs. The rest would have to wait until she'd brewed her favorite dark roast.

Oh, yeah, that would work. Her mind journeyed back to the previous evening and memories of D. J. Clayborne. The trip was a short one because his image had filled her dreams almost from the second she'd crawled into bed to the moment she woke.

She had no idea where the man was at the moment, but she really hoped he was as thickheaded and grumpy as she was. Luckily she'd set up the coffeepot before turning in for the night. All she had to do was flip a switch and watch the magic elixir drip into the carafe.

While she waited, she booted up her laptop to check her e-mail. A couple of ads that she deleted. For the moment, she skipped the one from her boss probably asking for an update on her investigation. Finally, there was an odd one at the bottom of the list.

She filled her favorite oversize mug with coffee and then doctored it with three spoonfuls of sugar and a dollop of real cream. Yeah, another reason she'd have to add a couple of laps to her morning run.

As she took that first sip of caffeine, her conscience forced her to read Mr. DeLuca's e-mail. Just as she thought, he wanted to know if she'd made any progress, saying he didn't mean to pressure her. He was merely curious.

She could just imagine his reaction if she told him the truth, that she had both good and bad news. The good news was that the target had shared Chinese with herself and Cody last night, and his name was D. J. Clayborne. The bad news? She had no idea where he lived, where he was, or what she was going to do about the fact that she didn't want to turn him in. She hadn't wanted to from the beginning, but now . . .

Darn it anyway, she really liked her job. It would be a shame to lose it over a man she'd never see again. Rather than focus on that dismal possibility, she pulled up the next e-mail. She read it once and then read it again.

It was short and to the point: *If you want to know*

*the truth about the Paladins, meet me for coffee. You
pick the time and the place, and I'll be there.*

No signature. The e-mail originated from a free account, which meant the sender could be anyone, anywhere. Granted, if the sender really wanted to meet with
her, the person would have to be close by. She shivered.
Did the sender really know where she was? If so, how?
Not that it mattered. After all, D.J. had managed to find
her even though she'd covered her tracks. Or maybe this
e-mailer was waiting for her to pick a rendezvous spot
that would at least reveal the city she lived in.

She let the cursor hover over the Reply button, but
then chickened out. This was too big a decision to make
without some serious thought and maybe a bowl of cereal under her belt. When she sat down at the kitchen
counter, she spied the piece of paper D.J. had left with
his number on it.

He'd told her to call him if anything of concern happened. Was this what he was talking about? Obviously
her mystery sender knew something about the Paladins
or at least was pretending to. Her logical mind told her
that the whole idea was pure bunk. Secret warrior soci-
eties didn't exist.

Right?

But if that was true, why had D.J. gone out of his
way to warn her not to pursue the subject any further?
Maybe Brenna Nichols's paper was written in code, the
real facts hidden behind the fictional world she'd described. That still didn't feel right, but Reggie had read
the paper only once.

She shuffled through the pile of reports on her makeshift desk until she unearthed the printout. The stack of pages had her grinning, a reminder that she and D.J. definitely had a lot in common. No wonder he'd known that she'd not only made a hard copy of the report but had also saved it to her flash drive.

That wasn't the only thing they'd shared but she shoved that thought aside. It wasn't ever going to happen again because she was never going to *see* D.J. again. He'd disappeared from her life as quickly as he'd appeared. Her good mood faded away. Come Monday morning, she'd turn over what she'd found out about him to Mr. DeLuca and be done with it.

She just wished she felt better about a job well done.

Todd poked his head into Ray's office. "Has the hacker responded yet?"

Ray shot him a frustrated look. "No, but then it's the weekend. Some people actually take time off to be with their families or maybe play golf. Seriously, it's true. Just ask anybody."

God, Todd hated whiners. Yeah, it was Saturday morning, but hackers lived online, not out in the real world. Rather than antagonize Ray completely, he offered a compromise.

"Fine, I hear you. If you don't get a response in the next few minutes, go ahead and take off. You've earned it after all the work you put in tracking this guy down."

His coworker was clearly happier now. "I can always

check later, after I get home. If I do hear something, do you want me to call you or wait until I'm back in the office on Monday?"

"Sure, you can call, but only if you think the situation warrants it. I'll only be here at the office for a little while, so make sure you call on that special number I gave you."

Ray nodded, already packing up his stuff. "Fine. Once I know where the hacker lives, I'll send someone after him. We've got trusted contacts in most major cities, so we'll be able to snap him up without any problem."

Yeah, right. Like kidnappings always went smoothly. Once they had the hacker sequestered, they'd milk him for all he was worth. They just had to make it clear that the more useful he made himself, the longer he'd live.

"Talk to you soon, Ray. Enjoy your day."

"Thanks, I will."

Todd wandered back to his own office and studied the file he'd been compiling on Colonel Kincade's escapades. So far, he'd found information on three contacts the bastard had established on the other side of the barrier. One of them was now useless, thanks to the Seattle Paladins. When they'd caught Kincade with his hand in the till, they'd also found where he'd been trafficking with the Others.

Todd walked over to the window. The sun glinted off the St. Louis Arch, to the east. It had been built to represent the Gateway to the West, at one time a brand-new world for humans to exploit and explore. Little did those people swarming underneath the structure know that the real gateway to another new world already existed.

The Paladins saw the barrier as something to defend, a door they'd nail shut if they could. More forward-thinking men like Todd recognized it for the opportunity it really was: the route to a new land to exploit for profit. The entrepreneurs of an earlier era had funded the men who'd done the actual exploring.

Well, that and the dying.

Just like those pragmatic businessmen, Todd was willing to finance the rape of Kalithia. It might be possible to reestablish contact with the other two Kaliths on Kincade's roster. Considering how willing they were to sell out their own people in exchange for time spent in the light of this world, they'd no doubt deal with whoever could make that possible. Soon, he'd reestablish the flow of blue garnets across the barrier.

So far, the human scientists who'd been studying the blue stones hadn't had much luck replicating them or even generating the energy they were supposed to produce. The researchers insisted that eventually they'd be able to figure it out, but it was going to take more time and more money. Lots more money.

Which brought Todd back to the hacker Ray was tracking. Once they found the guy, they'd set him to work on finding the cash Kincade had squirreled away. In exchange, they wouldn't prosecute him for his illegal incursions into the Regents' server. Todd smiled. That was a bluff, of course. The Regents would never risk their existence becoming public record.

They normally found a way to leverage someone into keeping their mouth shut. Money bought an awful lot of silence. He, on the other hand, wouldn't bother with trying to finesse the situation. His Kalith business partners would take care of the problem for him in exchange for services rendered.

He stared out the window as he reviewed his mental checklist one last time. There was nothing more to be done until they found out if the hacker was going to take the bait. If not, they'd punt, but that didn't seem likely. As a breed, hackers were curious. It was part of what kept them parked at a computer for hours on end.

If they added a financial incentive, they'd reel him in. But enough of that. Ray had the right of it—it *was* beautiful outside. No use in wasting the whole day working.

A knock at the door startled Reggie into dropping the report, sending paper scattering all over the kitchen floor. She left them where they fell and hurried to the door. Her pulse picked up speed. Was D.J. back?

No, it was Cody. She ignored the brief surge of disappointment. What was he doing here? Only one way to find out. But first she needed to put on something besides her nightshirt.

She opened the door far enough to talk to him. "I'm not exactly dressed, Cody. Give me a minute and then come on in."

He frowned. "Am I early?"

Early? Oh, rats. No, of course he wasn't early. She was forgetful. But rather than risk hurting his feelings, she lied.

"I overslept, so I'm running late."

She wasn't sure he believed her, but there wasn't much she could do about that. After unhooking the chain, she took off down the hall.

She called back, "Okay, Cody. Give me twenty minutes and I'll be ready. Help yourself to anything in the fridge."

Reggie was already in the shower when she remembered the papers that had fallen on the floor. It was too much to hope that Cody would ignore them. She didn't care if he simply picked them up, but knowing him, he wouldn't be able to resist taking a quick peek. It was the last thing either of them needed.

She rinsed off and snagged a towel. After she yanked on her clothes, she twisted her hair up on top of her head. Back in her bedroom, she grabbed her shoes and hustled down the hall to the kitchen. She aimed for calm but doubted she could pull it off. Hopefully, Cody would just think she was frazzled from running late.

Just as she'd expected, the papers were piled on the counter in a neat stack. Too neat. Just great. He'd read them, all right, or at least he'd started to. The only saving grace was that she hadn't given him enough time to get far. With luck, he'd gotten bored and quit before it got interesting.

But he had an odd expression on his face.

"Is something wrong?"

"No, I was just curious. You didn't mention having any plans last night, but I tried calling you and got no answer."

She so didn't want to go there, but neither did she want to lie to her friend. "I went out for ice cream."

"Darn, you should've called. I would've kept you company."

She froze, caught between the need to get the Paladin report out of sight and keeping it low key while dealing with Cody's jealousy. Finally, she settled for first picking up the stack of papers and stashing them in a nearby drawer as if they were no big deal.

"Thanks for picking these up for me. I knocked them off the counter when I went to answer the door. Did you want some cereal before we leave or wait and get something at Saturday's Market? They're bound to have something good."

Her attempt to distract Cody failed miserably.

"D.J. came back last night, didn't he?" His eyes narrowed in suspicion as he stared down the hall, toward her bedroom. "Is he still here?"

Okay, the accusation in his voice had her feeling defensive. "Yes, D.J. did come back. Yes, we ate ice cream. No, he's not still here. But even if he was, none of this is your business, Cody."

Cody took a step back but then held his ground. "Aw, come on, Reggie, I know that. There's just something about that guy that seemed off, different somehow. What do you really know about him, anyway?"

She couldn't fault the kid's instincts. There was definitely something different about D.J.—particularly his effect on her. There was no way she was going to discuss that with Cody. He was already upset about D.J.'s return visit.

"As I told you, the two of us met online. D.J.'s plans changed unexpectedly, and he had to leave town today. Last night was our only chance to get together."

That much was true and seemed to satisfy Cody. It certainly didn't satisfy her, but at least one of them was happy about it. Cody's good mood would last right up until he learned he'd been in the presence of the Knightwalker without knowing it. He might not forgive her for that little omission.

Time to change the subject. She dug her canvas grocery bags out of the cabinet. "Let's get a move on. It's a beautiful day. I've got a class this afternoon, so I want to spend some time out in the sun while I've got the chance."

Cody looked marginally happier. "Okay. I'll skip the cereal and settle for a fruit smoothie and an elephant ear at the market then."

She gave him a mock frown as she thought about the delicious combination of fried dough, cinnamon, and sugar. "Only if you'll share it with me. I love those things."

He grinned. "Not a chance. You'll have to buy one of your own."

"Easy for you to say. You're not the one who's going to have trouble fitting into her jeans if she keeps eating all these sweets."

Cody snickered. "I'd say I like your jeans tight, but I've been afraid of you since you flattened Big Ed the other day. Anyone ever tell you that you've got one heck of a temper?"

"Yes, they have." She punched him lightly on the arm. "You'd best not forget it either. Now let's hit the farmers' market before all the good stuff is gone."

They raced down the stairs. She still hadn't decided what to do about the e-mail or about turning in D.J. when she saw her boss on Monday. For right now, though, she was going to enjoy her day off.

Chapter 6

$\mathcal{D}$.J. slouched down farther in his seat as Reggie and Cody came out of her building. Didn't she have anything better to do than hang around with that scrawny punk? Evidently not. At least if she was running around with Cody, that probably meant she didn't have a boyfriend in her life at the moment. Maybe other guys felt differently, but if D.J. had a woman like Reggie to call his own, he'd be the one hanging out with her.

But irritating as it was to see her take off with the kid, her absence offered him the perfect opportunity to do a little snooping. She'd never forgive him if she ever found out that he'd riffled through her personal belongings. Luckily, he had a light touch when it came to breaking and entering. She'd never know he'd been there. From what he knew of her, she'd have heavy-duty security protocols in place on her computer, but her apartment, not so much.

When she and Cody turned the corner, he waited another couple of minutes to make sure they weren't coming back before getting out of his truck. He crept up the steps, listening carefully to avoid being caught by her neighbors. He'd palmed the key that Cody had returned to Reggie last night, just in case.

What he was about to do was illegal as hell, but he wasn't worried about that. He was far more concerned about Reggie finding out. Reggie would kill him or at least give it her best shot.

The lock opened with a soft click, and D.J. eased through the door. At least she didn't have a dog to raise hell when a stranger came inside. He put the key back on the counter, tucking it under the edge of a plant where she should find it easily enough. Hopefully, she hadn't missed it already.

He looked around the small apartment. Where to start? The computer sat on a small desk in the corner of the living room. Most of the desktop was cluttered with toys ranging from cartoon characters to action figures, not to mention a nice selection of squeeze toys designed to relieve tension. He grinned. At least half matched the ones in his own collection.

He'd save her laptop for last because he could always hack into it from the outside. This might be his only chance to learn what he could from the nest Reggie had built for herself.

The kitchen revealed little that he didn't already know. Her taste in dishes was pragmatic, not fancy. She'd spent her money where it counted—good-quality cookware and high-end knives. Evidently a fondness for steel that would hold a sharp edge was something else they had in common.

The small living room was furnished with comfort in mind. The television wasn't as big as his, but her film collection was sizable, mostly science fiction and fantasy movies, but with a stash of chick flicks tucked away on the bottom shelf.

He moved down the hall, his steps slowing to a stop just short of the threshold to her bedroom. No, he wouldn't cross that line. She'd probably understand why he'd mess with her computer, especially considering that that was what she'd been doing to him. But there was no way she'd forgive him for venturing into her most private space.

If he was ever to spend time in Reggie's bedroom, it was going to be by invitation. So, okay, fat chance of that happening, but a man could always dream . . . and imagine. Yeah, he could just see the two of them picking up where they'd left off the night before, lips locked, legs entangled and burning up the sheets, her eyes huge as he took her for the first time. And the second.

Oh, hell, no. Was that a piece of black lace lying on the floor just inside the door? His unruly mind instantly pictured all too clearly what it would be like to peel lacy panties down Reggie's shapely legs with his teeth.

Mayday! Mayday! Sensory overload! He reluctantly retreated back toward the living room before his resolve weakened. It was bad enough that his imagination was running full throttle all on its own. There was no use in revving his engines with actual images from her bedroom.

It took him several more seconds to regain control of his motor functions. Once he managed to tear his attention away from that tempting scrap of fabric, he went back to study the living room again, looking for anything he might have missed, something to focus on that wouldn't send him into a complete meltdown. Nope, nothing stood out. He settled for checking out her computer.

Nothing like besting the woman at her own game. He grinned, happy to let his sneaky fingers dance across her keyboard. It didn't surprise him that she'd reinforced her firewalls and changed her passwords.

D.J. checked his watch. It was definitely time for him to be making himself scarce; any more exploring would have to wait.

As D.J. was about to log off, the phone rang, startling him. He stopped to listen, his curiosity getting the better of him. After three rings, the answering machine picked up. Her voice echoed in the small apartment.

"This is Reggie. Leave a message or don't. Your choice."

He grinned at her spunk. His smile faded when a male voice started speaking.

"Reg, I don't mean to be a pest, but our client is wanting a status report on the Knightwalker case. Can you give me an update on where we are? And don't take this to mean I want you to work all weekend . . . well, unless you want to. Let me know and I'll put you on the clock. Talk to you soon."

What the fuck?

D.J. reached out to hit the Replay button.

Big surprise, the message didn't change the second time around. She'd been chasing him because she was being paid to? He stared out the window, his fists clenched, the disappointment tasting bitter.

A game of hide-and-seek was one thing. That was half the fun of being a first-rate hacker. He liked the way her mind worked and the challenge she presented. It stung to find out that all he'd been was a means to a paycheck, maybe even some overtime. Damn, that kiss had felt like so much more than that.

No use beating himself up over the situation. She wasn't the first woman to lie to him and wouldn't be the last. He'd risk a quick search of her flash drive stash before making himself scarce.

Luck was with him. The second one he tried had the Paladin file on it. Stealing it wouldn't change a thing. She'd found her way in once; she could do it again. At least this way he'd know for sure what she'd seen and how badly the organization's security had been breached.

As he waited for the computer to shut down, he took one last look around to ensure that he hadn't left any signs of his visit. Yeah, she'd wonder when she discovered the missing flash drive, but that wasn't actual proof. Since she'd never let him out of her sight the night before, she couldn't exactly point a finger in his direction.

On the way out, closing the door felt so damn final. This wasn't the first time he'd walked out of her apartment, saying he'd never return. The difference was, this time he meant it.

• • •

One of Reggie's shopping bags slumped over on the counter, sending apples rolling all over the place. With a couple of quick moves, she managed to gather them up before they could fall off the edge. When she snagged the last one before it bumped into the African violet on the far end of the counter, she noticed a small gleam peeking out from under the plant.

Her spare key. How did that get there?

Oh, yeah, she'd loaned it to Cody when he left to pick up dinner the night before. Odd that he'd put it there. He knew where she normally kept it. Of course, nothing was exactly *normal* last night. Not with two men giving each other the evil eye over spring rolls and rice. She would've been flattered, but it was more of a pissing match between two males trying to stake out territory than anything to do with her. Poor Cody hadn't stood a chance against D. J. Clayborne.

Darn it, she did not need to be thinking about D.J., not now. It was bad enough that she kept smelling a lingering trace of his aftershave hanging in the air, no doubt thanks to her overactive, overheated imagination. Rather than think about it, she concentrated on putting away the rest of the produce she'd bought at Saturday's Market.

Looking at the clock, she had just enough time to eat a quick lunch and pack up her gear for her afternoon martial arts class. Nothing like pounding a few class-mates into the mats to relieve stress. Of course, sometimes she was the one to get tossed around like a rag doll, but that worked, too.

She waited for her homemade soup to reheat and checked her e-mail. While the computer booted up, she looked over at the answering machine. Odd. It showed one old message. She could've sworn she'd deleted the last one after listening to it. She punched the Replay button.

Her boss's voice filled the room. His message unraveled her nerves. As soon as he finished talking, she hit the Erase button and shoved the small frisson of fear down deep where it wouldn't interfere with her thought processes.

Think, Reggie, think.

Only three people had been in her apartment in the past twenty-four hours, and just two that morning—herself and Cody. She certainly hadn't heard the message before though. Besides, she'd been at the market when Mr. DeLuca had called if the time stamp was accurate. That meant Cody wasn't the culprit either. He'd been with her when the call had come in.

That left one obvious choice. She sniffed the air again, even more convinced that she could detect a certain hacker's aftershave. The pieces started falling into place, convincing her without a doubt that she was right. The key where it didn't belong. The aftershave. The message. She did a quick sweep through the rest of her apartment. If D.J. had rooted through her personal stuff, she'd kill him. The man would be on the floor, bruised and bleeding.

The air in the bathroom held just the barest suggestion of his scent. It was stronger in the hallway, as if he'd stood there longer, but the scent stopped just short of her bedroom door. There was no indication that the bastard had invaded her most private space. Smart of him. That little bit of restraint might have saved him some serious pain.

She hurried back to her computer desk. Her toy collection looked undisturbed, and nothing else appeared out of place. That just meant he'd been careful. It didn't take her long to determine that no one had breached her security measures, at least not yet. That didn't mean he hadn't tried though. What had he been looking for? After all, he'd already found her.

There was only one thing it could be. She yanked open the desk drawer and cursed. Just as she'd feared: the big jerk had taken the flash drive with the Paladin file on it. But being right didn't equal being relieved. Why bother stealing the file at all? He knew she could follow that trail again. Besides, she still had the hard copy. Didn't she?

A quick look in the kitchen drawer answered that. In fact, the report would make the perfect lunchtime entertainment. She poured her soup into a bowl, broke off a chunk of bread she'd brought home from the market, and settled in to read. When she was done, maybe it would be time to answer that mysterious e-mail offering to answer any questions she had about the Paladins.

• • •

Sunday morning dawned gray and drizzling. It suited D.J.'s mood. He'd spent the rest of Saturday on a pointless drive out to the Oregon Coast. No sooner had he gotten there than he'd given in to the compulsion to head right back to Portland.

He'd driven past Reggie's apartment, circling the block twice before returning to his hotel for what was left of the night. Now, after sleeping for only a handful of hours, he was pacing the floor. Maybe he should pack up the truck and go home. He'd be back in Seattle well before noon, giving Devlin plenty of time to work up a good head of steam once D.J. told him what he'd been up to.

Yeah, nothing like having a major butt kicking to look forward to. He sipped the coffee room service had delivered. It was the perfect jolt to get him moving. He did one last pass through the nondescript hotel room to make sure he wasn't leaving anything behind. He'd disappear from Reggie's life just as quickly as he had appeared.

Just in case, he'd do one more drive-by . . . although he had no idea what he expected to get out of it. Well, other than the possibility of one last glimpse of Reggie herself. He wanted to cement her image in his head— that kissable mouth, those sharp features, and that even sharper brain.

God, he was an idiot. The woman was little better than a bounty hunter, willing to work for anyone who could afford her services. She might tell herself she was on the side of justice, but that didn't make her any less a hacker at heart.

What really pissed him off most was the memory of how she'd tasted, and how perfect she'd felt in his arms. Was that part of her job description, too? Did she get bonus money for getting up close and personal when she encountered her victim in reality?

No. There'd been too much surprise and wonder in her kiss for that to be her regular process. Besides, she'd had no idea that he'd been coming for her.

He'd made his point, and she'd made hers. When he got back to Seattle, he'd enlist Cullen's help in finding out who'd sicced her on D.J. in the first place. Not that it mattered. He had no doubt they'd be able to fix that little problem, one way or the other.

That just left the Regents and Reggie's incursion into their server. If their IT guys found it, they'd be all over her. That wasn't going to happen, not if he could help it. If anyone was going to be all over her, it was going to be him.

Oh, yeah, he'd definitely be down with that.

Feeling better than he had all morning, he picked up his bags and walked out the door.

Reggie circled the block a second time, slowing to observe the people already seated under the awning at the small outdoor café. Despite the early hour and the intermittent rain, the place was already busy. She was supposed to recognize her mysterious date by the bright green cap he'd be wearing and the magazine he'd be reading. No sign of him yet.

She shoved her hands in her jacket pockets, taking comfort from the small stun gun she carried on one side and the pepper spray on the other. Meeting a total stranger for coffee might not be the dumbest thing she'd ever done, but she'd come prepared for the worst. She'd even taken the precaution of not driving herself, taking the Max instead. After the meeting was over, she'd hitch a ride on a different line of the light rail and then take a cab back to her apartment.

She'd also taken the precaution of sending Cody an e-mail on a time delay, one that she could cancel once she got home. In it, she'd told him what she was doing and that something must have gone wrong if he'd received her message. She'd debated long and hard about what specific instructions to give him next. Her first thought was to have him call their boss, but she'd learned over the years to trust her instincts. For some reason, she was convinced that D.J. was the better choice, so she'd sent Cody his cell phone number instead. He was to tell D.J. two words: Paladins and Regents. She was sure he'd know what to do from there.

God, maybe she should just give up and head back home right now. No harm, no foul. But tomorrow she'd have to face her boss, and she had just this one chance to learn more about this secret Regents organization before making her decision about the infamous Knightwalker. She could only hope that curiosity wouldn't kill the cat in this particular case.

How mad was D.J. now that he knew she was a gun for hire? Granted, he would've found out eventually. It went with the territory. She had no reason to feel guilty, but she did. There was more to the man than just a hacker out for fun. Hence the appointment she'd made for coffee and information.

She approached the open air café cautiously and took a seat near the exit. The place was gratifyingly crowded. Not much could go wrong in public. Crossing her fingers she was right about that, she placed her order and sat back to wait.

Thirty minutes later she gave up on her mysterious date and left the café. Obviously she wasn't the only one having second thoughts. She'd go home, cancel the e-mail to Cody, and settle in to watch a movie over a big bowl of buttery popcorn. Something sad so her tears had a better reason to fall than missing a man she'd only met twice.

Down the street, a panel truck abruptly pulled out of an alley, blocking the sidewalk as it waited to move out into traffic. Inconsiderate jerk! She circled behind it rather than step off the curb onto the edge of the busy street. But just as she stepped behind the truck, she realized her mistake.

Two men were waiting for her. Even with her extensive training, her reflexes were too slow. She'd barely gotten her hand on the grip of the stun gun when the man closest to her had her by the arm and was dragging her into the back of the truck. He slapped his meaty hand over her mouth with a noxious-smelling rag, which muted her attempts to scream and filled her lungs with a chemical that was making it hard to stay focused.

Inside the van, his accomplice slammed the doors closed and then quickly shoved a needle into her vein. It hurt like hell and scared her spitless. With her pulse outracing a jackrabbit, whatever had been in the syringe stole her strength first and her consciousness second. Fear mixed with darkness and her new, terrifying reality disappeared.

"What the hell?"

Cody read Reggie's e-mail again. Then he rubbed his eyes and tried once more. Nothing changed except the sick feeling in his stomach that intensified with each reading. If this was a joke, he wasn't laughing.

He hit Reply and sent her a succinct "*WTF*?" message. While he waited for her to respond, he punched her number on speed dial, first trying her cell phone and then her home number. No answer on either of them, so he left messages and hung up to see if he heard back from her.

While he waited, he paced the short distance from one side of his studio apartment to the other. With his long legs, it only took him five steps in each direction. Not nearly enough space to walk off his increasing fear for Reggie.

What was she up to that she'd felt it necessary to take such a precaution? As far as he knew, he was her closest friend. If there'd been any problems on the home front, he would've known, which meant this had to be something to do with work.

The only hot case she was currently working on was the Knightwalker. If she'd found him wouldn't she have said something? A victory of that magnitude would've been a major accomplishment for anyone in their business, giving her bragging rights for years to come. For sure, if he'd been the one to track the bastard down, he would've been shouting the news from the rooftops.

On the other hand, they did all their hunting by computer. There was no need to meet anyone in person. If there were special circumstances that required face-to-face contact with clients, Mr. DeLuca handled it. Another option eliminated. If this had to do with the Knightwalker, it was the man himself who was the real threat to Reggie.

Had she tripped some kind of alarm, alerting the guy to her interest in his affairs? Despite the hacker's near celebrity status, Reggie was smart enough not to meet with the guy. Not without backup. He popped the top on a cola and grabbed a handful of tortilla chips, fueling his body with junk food to keep his energy level high.

Was there someone who had it in for her? One answer jumped out at him. Big Ed had resented Reggie even before that latest incident. Cody was willing to bet that the jerk really hated her now that the boss had backed her play when she'd knocked Ed on his ass for getting handsy.

Would Ed have made a grab for her? Not openly.

The big slob was all bluster and no balls. He could've tricked her somehow though. But how and why? All of this was getting Cody nowhere. If Reggie really was in danger, the clock was ticking.

He checked his e-mail one more time. Nothing. The phone also remained ominously silent. What could be wrong enough for her to want him to contact D.J. for help but not the authorities? It made no sense. He reached for the phone. It was time to alert D.J. to the problem although Cody didn't want to.

After all, how long had Reggie known this guy? And how well? Okay, that last part was none of his business, but there'd definitely been a lot of hot energy humming between the two of them the other night. Reggie had never acted like that around anyone in all the time Cody had known her.

He'd had a big-time crush on Reggie himself from the moment they met. Looking back, he suspected she'd picked up on it, but she'd never treated him like anything other than a friend or maybe a kid brother. That was okay with him. Between work and school, he didn't have time to make a lot of friends, and he didn't have any family.

Neither did she, for that matter. So as the closest thing to a brother she had, it was up to him to raise the alarm. He'd notify D.J., but he fully intended to ask some questions of his own. Like what did Paladins and Regents mean? And why D.J.?

If he didn't like the answers he got, he'd be calling the police, Mr. DeLuca, and anyone else who might be able to help. He wasn't going to lose Reggie because she'd trusted the wrong guy.

"Can I get you anything else?" the middle-aged waitress asked with a dimpled smile.

D.J. studied the plate heaped high with bacon, eggs, and hash browns and shook his head. "This will do for starters."

She laughed. "I love a man with a healthy appetite. Let me know when you're ready for seconds . . . or dessert," she added with a wink.

He grinned back at her. "Don't worry. I will."

D.J. dug into his cholesterol-laden meal with relish and no regret. Thanks to his souped-up Paladin metabolism, he didn't have to worry about such things. After only a handful of bites, his cell phone rang. He yanked it out of his shirt pocket and glanced at the screen. It wasn't the number he had for Reggie, but it was from the Portland area code. Maybe she was calling from work.

Only one way to find out. He punched the button and barked, "You've got me. Speak."

A vaguely familiar voice stammered, "D.J.?"

Who the hell? Then it hit him. "Cody, how did you get my number?"

Sounding more confident this time, Cody said, "Reggie told me to call you if she disappeared."

D.J.'s fork clattered to the table as he tried to swallow the lump in his throat that had nothing to do with the eggs he'd just swallowed.

He had to grab his glass of water and take a big gulp before he could choke out any kind of response. "What the hell are you talking about? What do you mean she's disappeared?"

Cody's breath came in ragged tatters. "Reggie never told me what she had planned for today. She just sent me an e-mail saying that if I got it, she'd run into trouble. I was to call you and nobody else. She's not answering her phone or my e-mails."

Son of a bitch, what kind of trouble had the woman gotten herself into? "Was there anything else?"

"Oh, yeah, she said to tell you two words—Paladins and Regents. Is that some kind of code?"

For a second, D.J.'s world spun backward. "Yeah, it is."

"What's it mean?"

Like he was going to tell the kid that. "Look, Cody, I'm not in a place where I can talk. I'll call you back in a few minutes, but I'm on my way. I'm not in Portland now, so it will take me awhile to get back to you. In the meantime, stay away from Reggie's place. It's not safe."

He disconnected before the kid could ask any more questions and headed for the exit after dropping a pile of cash on the table. His waitress intercepted him, looking worried.

"Is everything all right? Was there something wrong with your meal?"

"No, ma'am, it was delicious, but I got an emergency call. I left money on the table."

The woman blocked his way. "You wait here. I'll be back in just a minute."

She was gone before he could protest. While he waited, he did his best to look calm when inside he was anything but. What kind of mess had Reggie gotten herself into? Hadn't he ordered her to stay out of Paladin business? Obviously she hadn't listened.

Good to her word, the waitress was on her way back with a bag in one hand and a tall coffee in the other. "Here, you take these. You'll need all your energy to take care of that emergency."

D.J. grinned and reached for his wallet again. She was already shaking her head. "No, just get going. I've held you up long enough."

He accepted the gifts and then leaned down to kiss her on the cheek. "Thanks, you're a lifesaver."

She blushed, but his gesture had clearly pleased her. "Stop in the next time you pass through."

"I will," he promised and then took off for the parking lot.

Outside, he set his coffee on the roof of the cab while he rooted around for his keys. Thank goodness he'd topped off the gas tank before stopping to eat. Now there was nothing between him and rushing to rescue Reggie except sixty-plus miles of highway. He couldn't risk wasting time by being pulled over by the cops. He'd have to keep his speed close proximity of the posted limits, despite the temptation to drive like a bat out of hell.

Once he was back on the interstate and cruising in the fast lane, he dialed Cody's number. He answered on the first ring.

"Tell me everything."

It didn't take long. All the kid really knew anything about was the e-mail Reggie had sent him. D.J. had him read it aloud, twice, but there was nothing in it that even hinted about what she'd been up to other than the two code words.

"Okay, Cody, you did the right thing by following her instructions. I'm about an hour north of Portland. I'll head for your place first so the two of us can check out Reggie's apartment together. We'll figure out where to go from there."

"Give me one good reason why I shouldn't call the police."

Okay, so Cody wasn't going to follow D.J. blindly. That made him respect the kid even more.

"For now, because Reggie told you not to. She had good reasons for that, ones I won't share with you over the phone. You can trust me to do what's best for her, but I also understand that you don't have any reason to believe that. But I'm not lying to you when I tell you that the police can't help you and might even make things worse for her."

"And who are the Paladins and these Regents she mentioned?"

"I'll tell you everything I can when I get there. Now let me hang up so I can drive."

"Okay, but get here as fast as you can. She's already been gone for hours. In fact, call me when you get into town and I'll meet you at her apartment. That'll save time."

D.J. gripped the steering wheel hard enough to

make his hands ache. Reggie would never forgive him for letting her young friend walk right into a trap. He injected as much authority into his voice as he could. "No, don't go anywhere near her place alone. They could be watching it."

He waited to let that much sink in and then added, "Got that?"

Cody didn't hesitate. "Yeah, but you'd better haul ass. I'll wait an hour and not a minute longer. If you're not parked outside my door by then, I'm calling the police. Got *that*?"

Ballsy kid. "Yeah, tough guy. I've got it."

Chapter 7

*R*eggie moaned and attempted to open her eyes. She immediately regretted the impulse when it set off a whole litany of complaints, from nausea to a throbbing pain behind her eyes. The good news was that she had to be alive. Death couldn't possibly hurt this much.

That one brief glimpse had been enough to show she was still inside the panel truck. Okay, the most positive spin was that she was no worse off than she had been. The interior of the truck wouldn't tell her much, so she kept her eyes closed and concentrated on what could be learned through her other senses.

The truck was still moving, accounting in part for her upset stomach. She'd never tolerated riding in the backseat of a car, much less lying down on the unpadded bed of a truck and feeling every bump in the road. She could hear the muffled sound of the radio coming from the cab of the truck, but other than teaching her that the driver liked vintage rock and roll, it wasn't much help.

Well, unless the deejay happened to mention the time. It would be nice to know how long she'd been unconscious. There was no way to know for sure, but hopefully Cody had received her e-mail by now. He'd hate contacting D.J., but she was pretty sure he'd follow her instructions. God, she hoped so. The cops might eventually find her, but probably not until her body was cold.

At least D.J. might know where to start looking. The man would be furious, but she had no doubt he'd come charging to the rescue.

God, she hated feeling helpless. How many hours had she spent training in self-defense only to end up trussed like a turkey, alone and hurting? A tear trickled down her cheek, the first of several. It would be nice to think her eyes were just watering, but that would be a lie. She was terrified of what might happen at the hands of her captors. If their intention was simply to kill her, surely she wouldn't still be breathing now.

What *did* they have planned for her? She refused to follow that train of thought. The possibilities were too numerous and ran the full gamut, from bad to horrific.

The truck abruptly made a sharp turn and then slowed to a stop, sending her rolling from one side of the truck to the other and banging her head. Despite the new wave of pain, she could hear the creak of metal on metal. As soon as the noise stopped, the truck lurched forward again. Through a gate, maybe? If so, it probably meant they were about to reach the end of the line.

Okay, that was ominous.

The drugs must have been clearing out of her system

because her mind felt as if it was finally hitting on all cylinders. She couldn't just lie there feeling sorry for herself. At the very least, she should be trying to free up her feet enough to kick the next bastard who put his hands on her.

Better yet, if she could get her hands loose, she might be able to find a makeshift weapon or even locate her jacket and retrieve her stun gun. This time, she forced her eyes open and blinked until her small bit of the world came into focus. Unfortunately, her hands were tightly secured with what felt like one of those plastic strips people used to tie wires.

Unless there was a handy sharp edge she could use to slice through the plastic, she was out of luck. Her feet weren't bound, though. If she could kick herself free of her captors, at least she could run. But where? There'd be no way to know if escape was even possible until she knew where they'd taken her. She could be ten blocks from home or a hundred miles.

Think, Reggie, think. Sitting up might help. Moving was awkward with her hands tied behind her, but not impossible. She managed on the second try, helped along when the truck lurched to one side, which sent her reeling in just the right direction.

If the driver and his buddy were aware of her moving around, they gave no sign of it. Maybe they couldn't hear her because of the wall separating the cab from the back of the van. There was a small window, but neither of them had even glanced through it to check on her.

She reassessed her situation now that she was upright and able to look around. Her jacket was tossed in the back corner. She inchwormed her way toward it, hoping against hope that they'd forgotten to check the pockets. She had to turn around and lean backward to pick it up. After several long seconds of fumbling, all she learned was that the pockets were empty. Her captors had taken everyting.

She dropped the jacket back down, trying not to let the disappointment paralyze her with fear. Okay, what else had she brought with her? Her cell phone! It had a GPS chip in it. Unless someone had disabled it, it wouldn't take D.J. long to track her whereabouts once he thought of that.

If he thought of that.

She shoved that bit of doubt right out of her head. This was no ordinary guy she was talking about. He was the Knightwalker, one of the world's premier hackers. There wasn't much he didn't know about the cyberworld and how to manipulate it. And Cody would be right there beside him to help.

The truck had slowed to a crawl, and it had been a couple of minutes since she'd last heard any traffic sounds. They'd definitely left the public roads behind. The suspension bounced hard a few times and then smoothed out again.

The silence was even more intense as the truck stopped moving altogether and the engine was shut off. The whole thing rocked a bit as the two men in the front climbed out. She held her breath, waiting to see if they were coming for her.

No, their footsteps quickly faded away. She didn't know whether to be relieved or terrified that they'd abandoned her for the moment. The continuing silence stretched her nerves to the breaking point. Would she die in this bucket of rust, alone and screaming for help that would never come?

Hysteria wouldn't solve anything. Rather than give in to it, she studied the back of the truck. Unless it was locked or chained shut from the outside, she might be able to kick it open and scream for help.

The only problem with that plan was that most likely anyone near enough to hear her was in cahoots with her captors. Why else would they walk away, leaving her unattended? Had they underestimated how long she'd be unconscious or did they know escape was impossible? Either way, she had to try.

Scooting to the center of the truck bed, she studied the doors. The handle would be easier to manipulate with her hands, but then she'd risk falling out backward if she lost her balance. Using the toe of her shoe she pushed the handle down and to the side. It wasn't locked! On the second try, she managed to unlatch it and used her foot to slowly push the door open enough to peek out.

She was in a warehouse, an abandoned one given its run-down appearance. Light filtered in through some filthy skylights overhead to illuminate the place enough so that she could see a doorway next to a much larger garage door. She eased her feet down to the ground, going slowly enough to make sure that she didn't take a header to the floor.

Once she was standing, she had to lean against the truck for support until the swirling dizziness eased. At least she didn't see any other people from where she was standing. Rather than take off blindly, she eased over to the edge of the truck and looked back in the direction she guessed her captors had gone. No one was in sight, but there was a staircase leading to an office at the top. The lights were on up there, highlighting the silhouettes of two men.

Time to get moving. She'd be in plain sight if they looked down. Rather than head straight for the door, she cut across to the far corner at a forty-five-degree angle to the truck, keeping it between her and the men upstairs.

She was breathing hard, mostly from nerves, when she reached the wall safely, but she kept moving. Staying low, she scuttled across the front of the warehouse, past the garage door to the exit. This time she had no choice but to turn around so that she could open it with her hands bound.

Damn it, it was locked.

She faced the door again and leaned down to study the lock. It shouldn't be a problem. Feeling her way with her fingertips, she found the latch easily enough and sighed with relief when it flipped. Grasping the doorknob she tilted her entire body in order to turn it. Again, success.

She pushed the door open far enough to see that it was still daylight outside. Unless the gods were really smiling on her this time, the sudden flash of bright light was bound to draw the attention of her captors.

It was now or never because they wouldn't stay holed up in that office forever. Reggie didn't hesitate, bolting through the narrow opening—and right into two long-haired men dressed in matching black costumes. There was no car in sight, so where had they come from? Not that it mattered. Ordinarily two such men wouldn't be her first choice of rescuers, but right now she couldn't afford to be picky.

"Please, you've got to help me! I've been kidnapped!"

The taller one looked at his companion with a freaky smile. "She must be the one they promised us."

She didn't need to hear another word, and took off running. They caught up within only a few steps. The second man latched on to Reggie by the hair and dragged her back the way they'd come. As they pulled her inside the warehouse, she could hear the men from upstairs pounding down the stairs. Worse and worse.

The two men in black waited for the others to join them. The taller one released her but stayed within grabbing distance. He studied her, his head cocked to one side.

"She's a bit on the small side, but I suppose we cannot complain. At least she's feisty. I like that in my women."

When his companion laughed, Reggie's last hope died.

Cody prowled the parking lot outside his apartment building. The seconds were ticking down. If that rat bastard D.J. didn't show up in the next five minutes, Cody was going to make good on his threat to call the police. He just wished he knew if that would further jeopardize Reggie's chances of survival.

What the fuck had she gotten herself into? D.J. better offer up some straight answers, and quickly. He stopped at the street corner and scanned in all four directions. No sign of that big mother truck yet. Where was he? If D.J. didn't remember where Cody lived, all he had to do was call for directions. The man had his number.

One more lap and that would be it. Cody started back around the lot, hoping against hope that this would be his last trip. He'd gone about halfway when his cell finally rang. When he saw the number, he cursed. It wasn't D.J., but Mr. DeLuca. What did the boss want on a Sunday? Cody wasn't scheduled to work until Tuesday afternoon.

He cleared his throat and answered. "What's up, boss?"

"Sorry to bother you on your day off, Cody, but I was wondering if you'd heard from Reggie. I left her a message yesterday, and it's not like her to not respond."

How worried was he? It was hard to judge. The temptation to confess all was almost overwhelming. Mr. DeLuca was a stand-up guy, and Cody had far more reasons to trust him than he did D.J. Before he could cave completely, though, he heard the rumble of a loud engine coming toward him. Seeing D.J. pulling into the parking lot bolstered Cody's determination to follow Reggie's instructions.

"No, sir, I haven't seen her since yesterday morning when the two of us went shopping together. Reggie didn't mention any specific plans for today, but she had a friend from out of town show up unexpectedly. Maybe they took off for the weekend."

He wasn't exactly lying, but he was sure skirting close to the far edge of the truth. At least Mr. DeLuca seemed to buy it. He definitely sounded relieved when he spoke again.

"Okay, good. That probably explains it. I just wanted to make sure she hadn't run into problems with the case she's been working on. Enjoy what's left of your weekend, Cody."

"I will, sir. You do the same."

He hung up, headed straight for D.J.'s truck, and climbed in. The man gave the cell phone a pointed look.

"I don't suppose there's any chance that was Reggie calling."

Cody shook his head as he fastened his seat belt. "I wish. It was our boss asking if I'd heard from her. Evidently he left her a message yesterday, but she didn't call him back."

D.J. was already pulling back out onto the street. "What did you tell him?"

God, Cody hoped he'd done the right thing. "I said she had a friend from out of town show up with no warning."

"Quick thinking. Sticking close to the truth is always best. We can't keep her disappearance quiet indefinitely, but you bought us some time."

As if sensing Cody's doubt, D.J. shot him a quick look when he pulled up to the stop sign down the block. "I know this is hard for you, Cody, and I promise to tell you everything I can. But if my suspicions are correct, believe me when I say that the regular authorities aren't equipped to do anything to help Reggie."

Okay, that sounded bad. "Are you thinking terrorists? Why would they go after someone like Reggie?"

D.J. didn't answer right away. When he did, he was obviously hedging his bets. "Not terrorists, at least not any you would've heard of. I'm thinking Reggie managed to stir up a hornets' nest when she poked that cute little nose of hers where it didn't belong. I tried to warn her, but I suspect she wrote the book on stubborn."

Cody had been slouched in the corner, but he jerked upright and slapped his forehead. "Why didn't I think of that? I know who this must be. That bastard. And here I was ready to blame Big Ed."

D.J. shot him a puzzled look. "What bastard? And who the hell is Big Ed?"

"Big Ed works with the two of us." Cody frowned. "Do you even know what Reggie does for a living?"

The jerk actually grinned. "Yeah, I know. She hunts down hackers. I assume you do, too."

"Yeah, well, Big Ed used to be the baddest of the bad when it came to hunting down the hackers our clients were having problems with. Reggie took over as top gun the minute she joined the company. There's only been one month since when she didn't top the list."

"I take it this Big Ed has a problem with that."

Cody nodded. "Yeah, he'd been giving her a hard time, but he eventually learned not to mess with Reggie." The memory still made him smile. "He harassed her one time too many."

D.J. clearly wasn't amused though. "What happened?"

"He said something under his breath and touched more than her shoulder, if you get my drift. Reggie rolled her chair over his foot and then elbowed him in his most prized possessions. Poor bastard was walking funny for hours.

"Not only that, but our boss saw the whole thing. He told Ed in front of everybody that he'd be looking for a new job if he tried anything like that again."

"He should've been kicked to the curb right then," D.J. snarled. His eyes were blazing when he asked, "Why don't you think he's the one behind this?"

"A couple of reasons. First of all, Ed's basically a coward. The man was humiliated in front of the office, but he backed down to our boss, who is half his size. More important, Reggie would never agree to meet the man outside work. She's smarter than that."

"We'll still check him out," D.J. said, nodding. "But who's the other guy you think might be involved?"

"Mr. DeLuca, our boss, gave Reggie a special project to work on a few days ago. She's supposed to be hunting down a hacker who's practically a legend. Reggie has been pretty secretive about the case, but I think she might have found him. She's sure been acting funny for the past few days."

Cody paused as they drove into Reggie's parking lot. He'd been hoping that her apartment lights would be on and that this would all have been one big misunderstanding. No such luck. Feeling a bit sick, he finished his story.

"She was hunting the Knightwalker . . . and I think the bastard took her."

Okay, it was hard not to laugh. The situation was so not funny, but the kid had lapsed into melodrama. At least D.J. could reassure Cody that Reggie wasn't in the clutches of the Knightwalker. He really wished she was.

He'd love to be the focus of all that intense energy she carried around with her, but now wasn't the time for that kind of thinking. He parked the truck and walked around to look Cody straight in the eye, hoping the kid would believe what he was about to tell him.

"It's good that you're thinking about possibilities, but I know for a fact that the Knightwalker doesn't have her."

Cody gave him a skeptical look. "And how could you possibly know something like that? If she didn't tell me anything about what she's found, she sure wouldn't tell you."

"I don't doubt that she trusts you more than she does me, but I have one thing going for me that you don't."

He clapped his hand down on Cody's shoulder. "She's actually been chasing the Knightwalker for months, not just the past few days, and I'm guessing she was doing so just for the hell of it. You're a hacker yourself. You know how much we love a challenge."

Cody nodded and frowned. "Yeah."

"So since she first found the Knightwalker, she's been sending him cryptic little e-mails just to be a pain in the ass. And being the kind of guy not to take that lying down, he turned the tables and showed up at her door."

"When? Why didn't she say something?"

D.J. offered Cody his best shark grin. "Because you were standing right there when he came knocking, or I should say, when *I* came knocking."

It didn't take the kid long to do the math. He went from puzzled to full-out pissed off between one second and the next.

"You bastard! Where is she?" Cody shrugged off D.J.'s hand and then took a swing straight at the man's jaw.

Rather than duck, D.J. let the blow connect and his head snapped back hard. Damn, Cody packed quite a punch, but the kid needed to burn off some of his anger and worry about his friend before he could start thinking straight again.

D.J. rubbed his jaw. "Feel better?"

Cody looked at him as if he was crazy, but then nodded as he gingerly flexed his hand. D.J. wasn't the only one hurting from the punch. That seemed only fair.

"Let's get inside where we can talk without drawing any more attention to ourselves."

Cody started across the parking lot, but then stopped. "We don't have a key."

"Trust me. That'll slow us down, but it won't stop us." D.J. patted the pack of tools he'd stuck in his shirt pocket.

"Really?"

"Really."

"Cool."

Ten minutes later they were inside Reggie's apartment. This time D.J. wouldn't hesitate to search her bedroom. In fact, he'd turn the whole damn place inside out if that's what it took. As much as he'd prefer to protect the woman's delicate sensibilities, this wasn't the time. They couldn't afford to leave any possible clue undiscovered, not with her life at stake.

"You start in the kitchen. I'll start in back. Look for anything out of place, any sign that she didn't leave of her own accord."

Cody stayed right where he was. D.J. figured he knew what was coming and waited for it.

"So, you're the Knightwalker."

"Yep, I am. Your friend Reggie is the only one who's ever managed to track me down. Like I said before, she's been getting through all my defenses and leaving me messages for a couple of months. Her avatar has been able to track mine even when I changed it."

He let his admiration for Reggie show. "I couldn't re-sist tracking her down. Hardest bit of hacking I've ever done. She's damn good."

The kid started going through the kitchen drawers.

"But if you're not responsible for Reggie disappearing, then we're back to Big Ed again."

Here came the part where D.J. had to do some dancing around the truth. "Not exactly. I work for an organization that values its privacy. She managed to get into some secret files that might have set off an alarm. If so, they may have come after her."

Cody pulled a stack of papers out of the kitchen drawer. "Could this have anything to do with it?"

Son of a bitch, he knew he should've taken the hard copy of Brenna's Paladin history. "Yeah, it could. I'll take those."

D.J. held out his hand for the papers, waiting patiently to see if Cody gave in and surrendered them.

"What's in them?" he asked, but his eyes shifted down and to the left.

Damn it, had the kid read the papers, too? That would be another clusterfuck in the making.

"Something you don't want to know about. Not unless you want the same thing to happen to you. Are you hearing me?"

Cody nodded as he finally offered them up. "There's nothing else in the kitchen that's out of place."

"Okay, you boot up her computer while I do a quick check of her bedroom and the bathroom. I'll be right back."

He stopped long enough to run the papers through the shredder in the corner just in case the kid hadn't already read through the report. It used up some valuable time, but D.J. couldn't risk Cody letting his curiosity get the better of him.

The bathroom looked the same as it had the day before, and her bedroom was pretty much what he'd expected. If he'd had to choose two words to describe her most private lair, he would pick "colorful" and "comfortable." The bed was made and all her clothes were either neatly put away or in the hamper.

The only bit of clutter was the haphazard stack of books on the bedside table. He paused long enough to check out her taste in reading material. Yep, just as he expected—she was a closet romantic. It went along with her wearing that scrap of black lace underneath her oversize T-shirts and jeans.

He studied the covers on the books. They all showed some heavily muscled guy carrying a sword or a gun. One model even had a double-bladed ax much like the one D.J. often fought with.

What did she think of the Paladins? He'd bet she found their history to be wildly exciting. Too bad the reality was anything but. It was hard to romanticize your own life, especially when it involved a heavy dose of killing on a regular basis.

Back to the problem at hand. There was nothing more to be learned from the apartment itself. He headed back to the living room to see if Cody had managed to get into Reggie's computer files.

"Any luck?"

The young hacker looked back over his shoulder with a frustrated frown. "Not so far. The passwords I wasn't supposed to know have all been changed."

No surprise there. If she was like D.J., once he'd

made direct contact, she would've gone through her entire system and changed all her settings.

"Let me try."

Cody stayed right where he was. "She won't like you rooting around in her files. She'd be mad at me, but in your case, she'd go ballistic. You might want to remember what she did to Big Ed. The woman's got a temper when she's provoked. Besides, if our boss finds out, she and I will both be looking for work."

"If your boss values the company's security more than he values his employees, he doesn't deserve either of you."

Cody grimaced. "Easy for you to say. I've got tuition due in a couple of weeks. I'm finally closing in on my degree and can't afford to blow it now."

D.J. understood exactly where the kid was coming from. He'd struggled to make it through college on his own, too. "Don't sweat it. I have contacts in the business. If this all goes to hell, I'll make sure you have any kind of job you want."

He would, too. In fact, the Regents could always use another resident hacker on the payroll.

"Now get out of my way."

Cody vacated the chair. "I'm going to watch over your shoulder."

"I wouldn't have it any other way. First things first though. I'm going to see if I can track her through the GPS chip in her cell phone."

No dice, but that didn't surprise him. If the bastards who'd taken her had a brain cell functioning, disabling her phone would've been one of the first things they'd done. Still, he'd continue to monitor the situation just in case.

Now on to her files.

After that, the only sound in the apartment was the pounding of computer keys and the ticking of the clock.

Chapter 8

*I*t took D.J. the better part of an hour to crack Reggie's firewalls. He leaned back in the chair and stared at the screen. Before going any further, he needed to think, which meant he needed to be up and moving. He instinctively grabbed one of Reggie's stress toys and started working it hard as he paced the floor.

Cody had given up staring over D.J.'s shoulder after the first half hour. Now he was sprawled on the sofa playing a computer game, losing himself in a cyberworld to avoid thinking about what might be happening to Reggie.

D.J. reached for his wallet and pulled out two twenties. "Cody, do me a favor. We're both running on empty here. Would you mind picking up something for us to eat?"

He dropped the money and his truck keys on the coffee table. "I'm not picky. Get whatever you like, but get double what you normally order."

The kid eyed the money. "I can buy my own food."

D.J. recognized pride when he saw it, so he lied. "Don't sweat it. It's a business expense for me."

He wasn't sure if Cody believed him, but at least he pocketed the cash. Not the keys though. "There's a great deli on the next block over. I'll get sandwiches and a couple salads. Dessert, too, if you want."

"Sounds good."

As soon as Cody was out the door, D.J. returned to the computer to study the files he'd uncovered. Just as he'd feared, Reggie had triggered an alarm at the Regents' headquarters. But as far as he could tell, they'd mounted no defense against the incursion. There were definite protocols in place for dealing with this kind of situation, but none of them had been activated.

True, they might be trying to hide their actions, but he'd left a back door or two into their security programs when he and Cullen designed them. After coming at the problem from every possible direction, he couldn't find any sign that they were officially hunting Reggie.

That left an unofficial, off-the-books response, a much scarier proposition. If he'd had any doubts that that was what was happening, they'd been dashed when he finally got into Reggie's personal e-mail. Sure enough, someone had dangled a promise of information about the Paladins and Regents in front of her, and she'd obviously taken the bait.

Were they using local talent? Most of the Regents and their lackeys were stationed in the Midwest. Who would they have used out here? Definitely not someone from among the Paladins themselves.

Could this get any more screwed up? God knew who had her or what their plans were. He began a more thorough search through the Regents' files to determine the most likely culprit.

It didn't take long. There were only a handful of people who had that kind of talent. He saved his findings to a flash drive to pass along to Cullen. Maybe he'd have better luck.

Too restless to stare at the screen any longer, D.J. stepped out onto Reggie's small balcony for some fresh air. He took a deep breath and looked out at the parking lot, where he spotted Cody. D.J. went back inside to wait for him, figuring it wasn't smart to spend too much time outside where Reggie's neighbors might spot him. There was no way of knowing if they were the kind of folks who kept track of her business. Better to err on the side of caution.

Cody slipped back through the door. "Hope you like your sandwiches loaded, because that's what I got."

"Perfect. After we eat, I'll show you what I've found."

As D.J. spread out the food, Cody got out plates and silverware. Before he took a bite, he paused, his expression worried.

"Think Reggie's okay?"

"Yeah, for now." D.J. concentrated on peeling back the wrapper from his sandwich, mainly to hide his own concern. "Don't worry, Cody. We'll find her."

"And then kick their asses?"

"Oh, yeah, we'll definitely do that, too. Now eat. You need to keep up your strength."

"Don't worry about me. I never get sick. I even have some kind of revved-up metabolism. I also heal faster than anyone I've ever met. It used to freak out my foster parents, I can tell you." Then he dug into his sandwich.

D.J. studied his companion for several seconds, using his enhanced Paladin senses. Oh, yeah, he picked up on a familiar vibe. Almost immediately Cody frowned and looked around, obviously detecting something odd but unsure of what it could be. D.J. recognized it for what it was: like calling to like. How the heck had he missed picking up on it sooner? The organization would be recruiting Cody, all right, but not for his hacking skills. At least not the computer ones.

Devlin and the other Paladins would be pleased to meet the kid. Finding one of the lost was always something to celebrate. D.J. should know. He'd been out of step with the whole world until the day a Paladin recognized him for what he was and brought him into the fold.

The storeroom was only slightly more comfortable than the back of the truck. At least they'd cut Reggie's hands free before shoving her inside and locking the door. They probably figured she wouldn't be able to get into much trouble in the cramped, dusty, dirty room.

She cautiously peered out of the small window in the door. Unfortunately, the room was located off a narrow hallway, so the view was too limited to be of much use. She'd already surveyed the place and had come up with nothing that would enable her to stage a daring escape.

She upended a cracked plastic bucket and used it to sit on. Studying her surroundings, it was hard not to give in to utter despair. How could she fight back when she had no idea who the enemy was or what they wanted with her? She'd been an absolute fool for answering that damn e-mail. Despite her precautions, she'd badly underestimated the danger.

She wondered what Cody and D.J. were doing. Probably ransacking her apartment looking for clues. Any other time she would've resented the intrusion, but right now they were welcome to root through anything that might help them find her.

If only she'd been able to keep at least her cell phone hidden on her person. That was probably the first thing they'd taken from her. As long as they kept it turned off, there was no way for D.J. to track her through it.

Rather than spin in circles over what couldn't be changed, she concentrated on her captors. She was pretty sure there'd been three in the alley near the café: one to drive, two to make the grab. But on the way to the warehouse, there'd only been two in the truck with her. So what had happened to their cohort?

Then there were the two men who'd caught her trying to sneak out of the building. They were definitely an odd pair, that was certain. Their clothing was almost identical, perhaps a uniform of some kind although she'd never seen anything like it before. Their hair was an uncommon color as well, sort of iron gray and black mixed in equal amounts. She hadn't been with them all that long, but if she'd had to guess their ages, she would've put them in their late twenties, early thirties at the most.

Who were they? And why did they think she'd been brought there for them? She rubbed her arms to fight off the chill that swept through her. She'd only heard a small part of what they'd said to the pair who kidnapped her. Their accents were thick and unusual. Where were they from?

So many frustrating questions.

From what she could tell, they were all waiting for yet another man to arrive. Maybe he was the one with the answers, but at the moment she wasn't sure she really wanted to know them.

The sound of footsteps approached. She cocked her head to the side and closed her eyes to listen. Most likely just one set but definitely coming her way. She stood up, not wanting to greet her captor from a position of weakness.

The door opened, revealing the guy who'd grabbed her in the alley. He held out a cardboard tray with a soft drink and a bag from a fast-food chain.

"Here. Eat."

She silently accepted the offering, only then realizing how hungry she was.

"Before I do, can I use the restroom? I'd like to wash my hands."

He rolled his eyes, but nodded. "Don't try anything or I'll tie your hands again and let you go hungry."

Then he stood back and let her pass. "It's over to the left."

She'd secretly been hoping there'd be a window in the cramped bathroom that she could crawl out of, but no such luck. It was on an inside wall with no exit other than the door she'd entered through. Like everything else in the warehouse, it was also filthy. She took care of business and then washed her hands in the grungy sink. No paper towels either. She settled for wiping her hands on her pants.

On the way out, she deliberately tripped, falling against her escort. He cursed at her clumsiness, but grabbed her arm long enough to keep her from hitting the concrete floor. A few seconds later, he shoved her back into the storeroom and locked her in.

She all but collapsed in relief because he hadn't noticed that she'd swiped his cell phone. She didn't know D.J.'s number, so she prayed that he was with Cody by now. She dialed Cody's number and hoped he'd answer before her captor came looking for his phone.

Her friend answered on the second ring.

"Cody?"

His voice cracked when he spoke. "Reggie, where the heck are you? We've been so worried."

One of them had to remain calm, and it looked as if it was going to have to be her. "Listen, Cody, is D.J. there with you? I only have a few seconds."

She listened to the sound of the phone being handed off, relieved beyond belief that D.J. had come back. His voice was gruff with worry.

"Damn it, Reggie, I told you to leave well enough alone."

"Yes, you did, but now's not the time to be saying you told me so. You can yell at me all you want once you break me out of this place. I have no idea where I am, so please tell me you can trace this call. After they grabbed me in an alley in Portland, they drugged me, so I don't know how far they drove before we stopped."

"Whose phone are you using?"

"I lifted it from one of the bad guys. He might come looking for it any minute, so work your magic fast."

"Will do. What else can you tell me?"

"They brought me here in a black panel truck. I didn't get the whole license number, but it has an Oregon plate. The three numbers were five-seven-zero. I know that's not much to go on."

"It's a lot more than we had five minutes ago. Leave the phone on as long as you think it's safe. I should get a fix on you in just another couple of minutes. Then I'll be on my way, armed and loaded. Trust me, Reggie. I *will* find you."

Oddly enough, she did trust him. "I know you will, D.J. Oh, and one more thing. There are two guys here with long black-and-silver hair dressed all in black. They look alike enough to be brothers, right down to their boots. I almost escaped but ran right into them. The older one said something about me being promised to them."

D.J. immediately let loose with a furious stream of curse words. Under other circumstances she would've been impressed with his creativity, but right now all it did was scare her even more.

"D.J., stop it. That's not helping."

"Sorry, Reggie. I've almost got you pinpointed. Another few seconds and I'll be on my way. Okay, that's it. Hang up and hide the phone if you can. Set it on vibrate, though, so they won't hear it ring if I call you back."

"Okay. I'm okay, but they're obviously waiting for someone else to show up. I don't know what will happen when he gets here."

"I'm coming, Reggie. No matter what, I'll find you. And no matter where."

Before she could ask what he meant, the doorknob rattled. Damn. She stuffed the phone in a box in the corner and hoped for the best.

Cody planted himself right in front of the door. D.J. knew what he was going to say and couldn't blame the guy. Reggie was Cody's friend and that counted for a lot. However, the last thing D.J. needed right now was this kid demanding to play Robin to his Batman. He also knew a losing battle when he saw one.

The kid had been watching over D.J.'s shoulder while he ran the GPS location on Reggie. If he didn't let him ride along, Cody would find a way to follow. Far better to control the situation. Besides, if everything went to hell, he'd need someone who could call for backup.

"Do we need to stop by your place for anything?"

Not that he wanted to delay another second.

Cody shook his head and opened the door. "I've got my laptop with me, and I don't own any guns."

D.J. grinned at him. The kid knew they were headed into trouble and was doing his best to act like he was down with that. Maybe he was.

"Don't worry, I've got plenty for both of us out in my truck. My only question is if you'd actually know what to do with a gun if I handed you one."

Cody waited until they were outside to answer. "I've done some target shooting using an automatic with Reggie. I did all right, but it's not the same as actually pointing it at a person. Don't know how I'd do if it came to that."

"No one does until the occasion actually arises, but I appreciate the honesty. It's better to err on the side of caution."

He meant it, too, and let it show in his voice. Cocky recruits were always the ones who got killed first. Experience could be a bitch of a teacher, but at least Paladins usually survived the lesson.

Then the kid surprised him. "I'm a fair hand with blades though. I've been taking fencing and sword-fighting lessons at a local martial arts school. I like the discipline required, but it's not as if people actually fight with swords anymore."

Okay, D.J. had to laugh despite the grim circumstances. "You might be surprised about that. I'm partial to blades myself. Here, you drive."

He tossed the keys to Cody. "I'm going to need to make some calls."

He waited until Cody pulled out into traffic and turned south on the interstate. According to the GPS reading they'd gotten, Reggie was being held prisoner in a town a couple of hours south of Portland. It was her description of the two men who'd caught her trying to run away that had him seriously worried.

He needed to contact Devlin immediately. This whole fucking mess was escalating, and it was now officially Paladin business. Ordinarily, he would've found a way to make the call when Cody was out of hearing, but there was going to be no hiding the truth from him now anyway. Not with two Others in the picture. There was no mistaking them for anything else.

"Cody, you're about to hear some serious shit that I'm supposed to keep secret. As long as I'm on the phone, keep your trap shut. I'll answer your questions after I hang up. Got that?"

Cody changed lanes and then shot D.J. a quick look. "More serious shit than you being the Knightwalker?"

He shrugged. "That's more of a sideline. This other business has to do with why I keep a bag full of guns and swords locked up in the big toolbox in the back of my truck twenty-four/seven."

Cody swallowed hard. "I'll be quiet."

"Good."

D.J. punched in Devlin's number and braced himself for a major fight. His friend answered on the second ring.

"Let's hear it."

Leave it to Dev to get right to the point. "Okay, but save us both time by holding off on yelling until I'm through."

"It's that bad?"

"Pretty much."

Devlin's sigh came across loud and clear. "Like I said, let's hear it."

D.J. started at the beginning and brought Devlin up to speed. Lives depended on it. At this point, there was no use in trying to cover his ass.

"Dev, Reggie managed to get a call through to me. I'm heading to the warehouse where they're holding her."

He gave Devlin time to write down the address and directions before continuing.

"She almost managed to escape on her own, but she ran right into another couple of guys. From her description, they sound like Kaliths. I'm thinking there's another hot spot that we didn't know about somewhere in the area."

He had to give Devlin credit. Even though he must be about ready to explode, his voice came across as cool, calm, and collected. It wouldn't last, but D.J. appreciated the effort the man was making.

"What's your plan?"

"I'm going in."

"With no backup?"

"Uh, I'm not exactly alone. I have a civilian with me."

"And you're having this conversation in front of him?"

There was a definite chill coming over the line. Time to explain the situation. "Yeah, I am, but we're going to want to recruit him anyway."

"He's one of us?" There was a new note of excitement in Devlin's voice. "Seriously?"

"Yeah, but he doesn't know. Not yet."

Several seconds passed before Devlin spoke again. "Assess the situation and report in before you do anything. Fill the recruit in on as much as you think necessary. I'll send down some backup for you, but they won't get there right away. The chopper is in use now. If it's not back soon, they'll either have to go commercial or drive."

This was more than D.J. expected. "Thanks, Dev. I'll keep you posted."

"See that you do."

D.J. had lapsed into silence after he ended the call. Despite his promise to answer Cody's questions, it was pretty clear that he wasn't in the mood at the moment. Cody would wait another couple of minutes before prodding him. Hell, he didn't even know what to ask.

Whoever this Devlin guy was, he had to be a serious badass judging by how D.J. had talked to him. He tried to piece together what he'd understood of the one side of the conversation he'd heard.

A couple of things had definitely stood out. D.J. had referred to Cody as a civilian and then said something about wanting to recruit him. What was that all about? Was D.J. in some branch of the military? If so, why on earth would they want him? Yeah, he had some serious computer skills, but that was all he had going for him.

But then there'd been D.J.'s odd reaction to Cody's fondness for swords. He'd definitely found the idea amusing for some reason, which was irritating when he didn't share the joke. Another question to ask.

But right now all that mattered was getting Reggie out of this mess she'd gotten herself into. Hell, it was already late afternoon. If they didn't rescue her before morning, he'd have to let Mr. DeLuca know that Reggie wasn't going to be in. That would lead to all kinds of questions he couldn't answer.

Then the solution came to him. "I'll send him an e-mail!"

"Send who an e-mail?"

Oops, he hadn't realized he'd said that out loud. "I was thinking about our boss, Mr. DeLuca. If he doesn't hear from Reggie by starting time tomorrow, he's going to wonder what the heck's going on with her. If we want to keep him out of this, we'll have to cover for her. I was thinking I could send him an e-mail from her saying she's sick or something."

"Good thinking."

Then D.J. shifted slightly so that he was looking more directly at him. "I didn't mean to zone out on you. I promised you answers. Ask away. I'll tell you what I can."

Translation: he'd hide as much information as he could. Jerk.

"Are you in the military?"

"No."

Cody tried again. "But you carry weapons because you need them close at hand."

"Yep."

Okay, enough was enough. He'd tried to be patient, but this was no game they were playing. His temper, while normally slow to heat up, burned hot when it finally ignited. Frustration had him slamming his fist against the steering wheel.

"Damn it, D.J., just answer the fucking questions! Reggie's my best friend and the closest thing to family I have. If you've sucked her into some kind of criminal shit, I will come after you."

The bastard actually laughed, which just pissed Cody off even more. He cut across three lanes to pull off at the next exit, ignoring the squeal of tires and the blare of horns from other cars. He drove into a service station and parked.

Climbing out of the cab, he stomped around to the passenger side and waited for D.J. to join him. He had no doubt the man could pound him into dust, but he'd get in a few good licks of his own before he was down and out.

To his surprise, D.J. held up his hands in surrender.

"Sorry, you're right. I shouldn't have laughed. But, damn, you remind me so much of myself at times. Let's top off the tank and see if we can get a map of the area. While we're here, we'll pick up a couple of drinks and something full of grease and sugar to eat. Once we're on the road again, I'll start at the beginning."

"Fine, but you better have some damn good answers."

• • •

He was glad they'd bought a sack full of cold drinks and snack food. After all the talking D.J. had been doing, his throat was dust dry and his stomach was growling.

Right now Cody seemed content to mull everything over, but the questions would be starting up again soon. It had taken the kid awhile to get past the idea that D.J. wasn't spinning some yarn straight out of an urban-fantasy novel.

Once that had happened, his questions had been right on target. He now knew more about the world of the Paladins than anyone outside of the organization. All D.J. could do was wait to see what his companion would do with his newly acquired worldview.

Cody polished his second sports drink and shoved the bottle back in the plastic bag. "So I'm really like you?"

"Yeah, you are. I should've picked up on it that first night, but I had other things on my mind."

Like getting naked with Reggie, but he left that part unsaid.

"That stack of papers you shredded was a history of the Paladins."

That answered one of D.J.'s own questions. He'd suspected that Reggie wasn't the only one who'd read at least part of Brenna's report.

"Yeah. I'll give you another copy when we get through all of this."

Now the hard part. "You're not going to like what I say next, but believe me it's for the best. When we reach the warehouse, I'm going in alone."

"But—"

D.J. cut off Cody's protest. "I won't take an untrained Paladin into a situation like this. For Reggie's sake, I can't afford to divide my attention, but that doesn't mean you won't play an important role. Devlin has a couple of my buddies on the way. If all this goes south, I'll need you there to bring them up to speed."

Cody nodded but was obviously not happy about it. "You think things have gotten worse, don't you?"

"She hasn't called back. So either they found the phone or she's somewhere the phones don't work. Neither option is good."

D.J. signaled and moved to the right. "This is our exit. Once we're off the highway, we'll break out the weapons. Then I'll scout out the place so I'm not going in blind. Once I've got the layout and the current status, I'll put in another call to Devlin and the backup team."

"Those bastards better not have hurt her."

D.J. knew just how he felt. It was time to let Cody know how the game was played in the Paladin world.

"Scaring her was enough. They're already dead. They just don't know it yet."

There was a new maturity in Cody's eyes when he looked in D.J.'s direction. "Good. I can't wait for you to tell them."

Chapter 9

*R*eggie braced herself for another confrontation with her captors. She'd thought the guy was back to look for his cell phone, but he hadn't mentioned it.

"You're coming with me. The man wants to see you."

She stayed seated. "Tell him I'm not interested. I've been pretty tied up today and don't have time for idle chitchat."

Okay, smarting off probably wasn't the brightest thing she could do, but it wasn't in her to submit meekly to the whims of her unidentified kidnappers. She half-expected to be smacked for her impertinence, but instead he simply marched in, grabbed her arm, and jerked her to her feet.

She'd have bruises from his grip, but she didn't complain. He dragged Reggie across the warehouse toward the cluster of men standing near the bottom of the stairs. She recognized the two men who'd abducted her and the two long-haired strangers who'd prevented her escape.

But it was the fifth man who really caught her attention. It was clear by the body language of his companions that he was the alpha dog in the group. He wasn't particularly tall or handsome; in fact, at first glance he appeared to be perfectly ordinary. But then he turned his attention in her direction.

Reptilian—that was the only word she could think of to adequately describe his gaze. In that one instant, she felt as if she'd been weighed, measured, and marked as a total disappointment. His lip curled slightly as he took in her disheveled appearance.

She forced herself to stare back, refusing to look cowed or apologetic. Those tailored clothes he wore wouldn't look so hot either if he'd been kidnapped, drugged, and thrown in the back of a truck. She jerked her arm free and threw her shoulders back.

"Who the hell are you?" she demanded. "I want to make sure I give the police the right name when they get here."

The bastard laughed. "No one is coming for you, Reggie. You don't mind if I call you Reggie, do you? We're going to be spending so much time together, it's only right that we use first names. You can call me—"

He seemed to hesitate over what name to give her. "Ray. Just plain Ray."

"Your parents must have really hated you to call you that, Just Plain Ray, but then I can see why they felt that way."

One of the others made the mistake of laughing. She glanced back to see that it was the one whose phone she'd stolen. Ray glared at him.

"Carl, you might want to remember who pays you."

Then Ray's hand whipped out and smacked Reggie's cheek with a loud crack. The pain was instantaneous. She couldn't stop the tears from falling but stood her ground.

Crossing her arms over her chest, she asked the question that had been bothering her since all this had started. "What could you possibly want with me? I'm nothing special. I'm not rich and I have no family to pay a ransom."

Ray studied her for a few seconds before answering. "I like your honesty, but I have it on good authority that you're second to none when it comes to computers."

He edged closer. "In fact, you managed to breach the security of the organization I work for. If it hadn't been for pure damn luck, we'd never have picked up on it at all."

"You work for the Regents?" she blurted out and immediately wished she hadn't. Ray nodded as if she'd just confirmed something for him.

"You slipped in and out, smooth as silk."

She didn't appreciate the approval in his voice. "I didn't do any damage. I was hunting for somebody. That's my job."

"Well, you have a new job now. If you're successful, eventually you'll return home, alive and unharmed."

Ray pegged each of the other men with a hard stare as he said that last part, but that didn't mean they would listen. Right now his men might nod like the dutiful little lackeys they were, but would they keep their hands to themselves when he wasn't around to police their actions?

"What's the job?" Reggie asked.

"You'll find out soon enough. Suffice it to say that I have need of your finely honed computer skills to do a little recovery work for me."

He looked past her toward Carl. "Take her back. We leave in fifteen minutes."

She didn't wait to be dragged back to that makeshift prison, instead walking there on her own. With luck, she'd have time to call D.J. again. She'd try to slip the phone in her pocket when they left, too, and hope her friends could use it to follow.

God, she hoped so. If Ray and company had any intention of letting her live, they wouldn't have let her see their faces. The man hadn't bothered to deny who it was he worked for either. The Regents might be secretive, but that didn't mean they couldn't be found again. She'd already done it once.

"Get in there."

She did as she was told, mainly hoping he'd lock the door and take off again. As soon as he was out of sight, she pulled out the phone and dialed.

D.J. answered on the first ring. "Thank God. Bring me up to speed."

She kept it succinct. "We're leaving this warehouse in fifteen minutes. I don't know where they're taking me, but it's to do some hacking for them. There's a guy here who works for the Regents. His name is—"

Before she could finish her sentence, the door flew

open and Carl stormed in. The first thing he did was knock the cell phone from her hand. Then he shoved her hard, sending her stumbling back into the rusty shelving.

"Stupid bitch, are you trying to get us both killed? Who the hell were you talking to?"

Reggie shot him a smug look, hoping it was convincing. "The police. They're already on their way."

Of course, she had no idea where she was, so even if she had called them, they wouldn't have located her that quickly.

"Yeah, right." He checked the phone to see the last number dialed. Luckily for her, it looked like the phone had broken when it hit the concrete floor.

He cursed and threw it back at her. "Damn it, that bastard is going to kill me for this."

Carl took off at a dead run, yelling for his boss. Reggie straightened up, rubbing her arm where it had collided with the shelving. She checked the phone to see if it was completely dead. Hopefully the impact had only jarred a contact loose.

Quickly prying the back off, she pulled out the battery and reinserted it. Then she checked the hinge. The break must be in there because as she wiggled it, the screen flashed on and off. She tried dialing again.

"Reggie?"

D.J. said more but she was only getting bits and pieces. She tried adjusting the fit of the broken hinge, but with only marginal success. The shouting out in the warehouse was growing louder. Time was definitely running short. Then a shot rang out. A scream was cut off midbreath when the gun fired a second time.

"Oh, God!" Obviously Carl hadn't been kidding.

Reggie instinctively moved farther into the storeroom, trying to put some distance between herself and the horror outside the door. If Ray didn't hesitate to kill one of his own men, she didn't stand a chance.

Ray's voice rang out. "Get the bitch in the truck and take her to the lava caves. Haul ass or the rest of you will join Carl."

Lava caves? That didn't even make sense. But she had mere seconds, at best, to convey the situation to D.J.

"I hope you can hear this. They're moving me now to some caves. The phone's not working right, but I'll keep trying."

Rather than risk losing the phone altogether, she hung up and shoved it in her pocket. Then she picked up a piece of scrap metal and used it to scrape the words "lava caves" in the wall to the left of the door where her captors wouldn't immediately see it.

Then there was nothing left to do but wait.

D.J. slammed the phone down and drove like hell. They were minutes away from the site pinpointed by the GPS chip in the cell phone Reggie had used. At worst, the bastards were already on the run, leaving him no signal to follow.

What the hell had happened? One minute Reggie had been coming in loud and clear. The next, he'd heard a man hollering and then a crash, as if the phone had been dropped, followed by silence. When the phone had rung again, the reception had been piss poor. All he'd caught was something about being on the move.

Ignoring speed limits, he drove like a madman, trying to reach the warehouse in time.

"Turn left at the next corner. The place should be on the right."

D.J. did as instructed, bringing the truck to a tire-squealing halt halfway down the block, near a run-down warehouse. There was no truck in sight. No sign of anyone at all, and the security gate was wide open. Either they were already gone or it was a trap. He was betting on the former, but he drove forward slowly, knowing appearances could be deceiving—and deadly.

Cody crumpled up the map and tossed it behind the seat. "Looks like we missed them."

"Maybe." D.J. considered their options. "Wait here while I scope out the place. I'll wave you in if it's safe. Otherwise, you keep the truck running and your finger on the speed dial on my phone. The first number listed is Devlin Bane. Tell him who you are and what's happening. He won't steer you wrong."

Cody's eyes were huge behind his glasses, but at least he didn't argue. D.J. picked up the revolver he kept under the front seat and stepped out of the truck. There was no cover that would keep his approach hidden, so he took off at a ground-eating lope and hoped he'd make it to the door before being spotted.

The warehouse was dark and empty-looking. He

waved to Cody, who immediately drove into the parking lot, stopping just short of where D.J. stood.

"The place looks deserted."

The kid looked sick. "Then how will we find her?"

"We've managed to get this close. Don't give up yet."

He grabbed two flashlights from the truck and handed one to the kid. "You go right. I'll go left. Then we'll both go upstairs."

Cody pulled himself together and followed D.J. inside the cavernous interior of the warehouse. Each of them swung the narrow beam from their flashlight in wide arcs, looking for any sign of what had gone down.

There! In the back corner there was something too solid to be a shadow and the wrong shape to be part of the warehouse itself. His mind was telling him exactly what he was seeing, even though he wanted to deny it. He could already taste the scent of blood and death in the stale air.

He forced himself to continue forward at a methodical pace. No use in drawing Cody's attention to the problem until absolutely necessary.

As D.J. drew closer, he realized the shape was too bulky to be Reggie sprawled on the floor in a pool of blood. Relief washed through him, but it was mixed with frustration. A live body might have been able to tell him where Reggie was now. A corpse was a complication.

"Hey, over here!"

The excitement in Cody's voice had D.J. running toward the other side of the building.

"What did you find?"

Cody was standing in the glow of light coming from a small room. "I think maybe they kept Reggie in here. There's a half-eaten hamburger and an empty soft-drink cup."

D.J. poked at the scraps from the sandwich. "The bread's definitely fresh. Nice job, Cody."

The kid pushed his glasses up on his nose. "There's more. Somebody scratched something in the paint on the wall behind the door. I'm thinking Reggie was trying to leave us a message where her captors might not see it."

Sure enough, there were two words scratched into the paint, the letters scrawled as if done in a hurry. He didn't give a damn about Reggie's penmanship though. What had him seeing red was the meaning behind the message written there.

"Lava caves? What do you think she means by that?"

D.J.'s blood ran cold and his temper hot. He knew exactly what she meant. He ignored Cody's question as he punched in Devlin's phone number. Son of a bitch, could this get any worse?

"Dev, they've taken her to a lava cave. Check the files and see if we have any record of a crossing point in this area."

It didn't take long. His friend read him the coordinates and then said, "Lonzo and Trahern should catch up with you soon. The chopper dropped them in Medford where they rented a car. I already texted them your location."

"Good. Have Cullen do a search on the ownership of

this warehouse, too. Maybe that will tell us something. Let Lonzo know that Cody will be waiting for them here. They can catch up with me later."

Devlin immediately objected. "D.J., damn it, don't go off half-cocked. Wait for them. No way you're going in alone."

Like hell he'd wait. "And if they suddenly decide that Reggie has become a liability? They've got to suspect we're coming after them."

"So you'll be walking into a trap."

D.J. knew Devlin was right, but he didn't care. He played his trump card. "Did you listen to orders when it was Laurel who'd been kidnapped? Seems like you broke a few rules back then."

"That was different. She was part of our organization."

They both knew Devlin was on the losing end of this particular argument. The Paladin leader would've done anything, no matter what, to save his woman.

"Damn it, Devlin, do you need me to spell it all out for you? You let Barak live, Trahern brought in an outsider without clearance, and then Cullen crossed into Kalithia to bring back Lusahn and the kids. I could go on, but listen to what I'm telling you. I'd go after any woman in this predicament, but Reggie's important to me."

Devlin conceded the battle. "Watch your back. The guys will be right behind you. I'll let them know what's going on."

There was a brief pause. "And if you manage to get

yourself killed, I'll be waiting to kick your ass as soon as you start breathing again."

"Fair enough."

Cody was blocking the doorway when D.J. hung up. "You aren't leaving me here."

"Yes, I am. We've already been over this. I might be willing to get myself killed, but not you. Besides, you'll be coming with the second wave."

"But—"

"No buts, kid. And every second you stand here and argue with me is delaying my getting to Reggie before they take her into that cave."

Cody let him pass but dogged his steps all the way back to the truck. He finally grabbed D.J. by the arm, trying to prevent him from getting into the truck.

"What's the big deal about a cave? Why would they take her there? Who are these guys?"

This was not the time for long explanations. He jerked his arm free and turned the tables on the kid, slamming him up against the truck fender.

"Weren't you listening when I told you about what Paladins do for a living? Two of the bastards who have Reggie are from that other world. The cave must have a stretch of barrier in it. If I reach them before it all goes down, maybe I can get Reggie back before they have a chance to drag her across into Kalithia. She already knows too much for these guys to let her live. If you don't believe we're dealing with stone-cold killers, there's a dead body back in the warehouse that should convince you."

D.J. stepped back. "You *will* wait here. Trahern and Lonzo will be along soon enough. Tell them everything."

Cody looked back toward the warehouse. "There's really a dead guy in there?"

D.J. nodded. "Yeah. He's probably the one whose phone Reggie stole."

"Go get her, D.J., please before they . . ." Cody's voice trailed off, but the misery in his eyes finished the statement anyway.

"I will."

He handed Cody the gun he had stuck in his waistband and then pulled a sword out of the toolbox. "Take these and stay inside and out of sight. I don't know what kind of vehicle my friends will be driving, but they'll recognize my sword. Trahern's tall and has pale gray eyes. He's scary as shit, but he'll take care of you."

Then D.J. got in the truck and drove like hell.

Reggie shuffled her feet, hoping to slow everyone down. All it accomplished though was to force one of the long-haired guys with the odd accents to drag her along by her arm as they traveled over the uneven ground. When she stumbled and fell forward, her escort managed to keep her from hitting the ground. Barely. She didn't bother to thank him.

"Where are we going?"

His pale eyes squinted up against the early evening sun. "Home."

Ray turned around. "Both of you shut up! Jeban, the less she knows, the better."

Reggie gave her companion an incredulous look. "You actually live in the caves?"

At first she didn't think he was going to answer her. When he did, his thick accent made it difficult to understand.

"My home lies beyond the caves. In the land of the dying suns."

She trudged along the barely discernible path. The land of the dying suns? Was that some kind of Native American name for this area? Nothing made sense, but then she was bordering on exhaustion. It had been hours since she'd had anything to eat or drink other than that greasy hamburger and soft drink, neither of which had settled very well.

She prayed D.J. had found her cryptic clue, and that it had set him on their trail. Sure as heck no one else was going to come riding to her rescue. Besides, she'd come to some pretty strange conclusions about what was going on. She couldn't wait to pin him down on some of the finer points to see how close she'd come to the truth.

First and foremost, if the Regents existed, then so did the Paladins. If that much was true, then the next leap in logic was that D.J. himself was a Paladin. Which she really, really hoped meant he rescued the occasional damsel in distress.

They climbed steadily until the trail narrowed enough that her escort had to let go of her arm to squeeze between some boulders. Beyond that point, the trail twisted sharply to the right and then doubled back again. Nestled behind the last outcropping, a rock wall curved around a small, grassy clearing. There were three narrow fissures in the rock face.

Reggie shuddered as she noticed how well hidden they were. Surrounded by solid rock and trees, the openings couldn't possibly be visible from any distance. She watched as Ray and company whipped out flashlights and walked straight into the center one without hesitation. Before following them inside, she dropped down to retie her shoes.

Jeban stopped to wait for her, blocking the way back down the trail. "Come on, woman. Time is running short."

She finished, hoping that she'd managed to leave enough of an impression in the dusty ground for D.J. to see. When Jeban wasn't looking, she quickly marked an X in the dust. Hopefully it would keep D.J. from wasting time checking out the other two openings in the rock.

Just inside the entrance, she found herself in a small cavern barely big enough for the six of them. Okay, this was getting seriously creepy. She fought down the panic creeping up her spine. It didn't make sense that they'd drag her all the way here just to kill her. There'd already been plenty of opportunities without going to this much trouble.

Cold comfort, but she'd take what she could get.

A pair of narrow passages opened out of the back wall. Ray motioned for Jeban's partner to lead the way through the one on the right. They all fell into line, journeying into the chilly depths of the hillside with only the dim flashlights to show the way. It was becoming increasingly difficult for Reggie to keep going. Feeling claustrophobic, the weight of the surrounding rock pressed down on her until she could barely move forward.

Jeban shoved her forward, sending her stumbling into Ray. He turned around to snarl at her. "Watch where you're going."

She bit back the temptation to run into him again. As much as she wanted to resist every inch of the way, right now the man had the power of life and death over her. He'd already demonstrated once that he wouldn't hesitate to kill. She probably shouldn't risk provoking him even if it went against her nature to simply surrender.

That's when she noticed a strange glow coming from just ahead. Either their flashlights had suddenly grown in strength or there was another source of light. The passageway widened out into a large chamber. It would've been unremarkable in itself, but it was the sheet of swirling color that formed about an eight-foot stretch of wall that took her breath away.

She ignored her companions as she approached it. The hair on her arms stood up in response to the buzz of energy in the air.

"What is that?" she asked as she reached out to touch it.

Jeban lunged forward to knock her hand down. "Foolish woman, do you want to die?"

Ray laughed. "That barrier will crispy-critter you in a matter of seconds. Who knows, maybe you'd find that idea more appealing that accompanying my two friends here to their world for a nice vacation."

Was he joking? She looked from man to man, but none of them was laughing. They seemed to be waiting for something to happen.

"Their world? What's that supposed to mean?"

She addressed the question to Jeban, hoping he'd answer her honestly instead of in riddles.

He jerked his head in the direction of the shimmering light and then spoke slowly, maybe so she'd have an easier time understanding him.

"The wall of light divides this world from mine. When it goes down, we'll cross into Kalithia."

Ohh-kay. She really wanted to believe Jeban was as crazy as they come, but he sounded all too matter-of-fact about the whole thing. Her logical mind wanted to deny even the possibility that she was standing but a few feet from an alien world, but too much was starting to add up.

Her control over her emotions had become more tenuous as the day had progressed. It finally shredded completely, and she went on the attack. She directed all her pent-up fury right at Ray. It was his fault she was there in the first place. Time to put her self-defense classes to good use. She didn't stand a chance against five adult men, but she could make sure Ray was hurting before it was all over with.

She stomped down on his instep and then shoved the palm of her hand into the bastard's nose. The resulting crunch of cartilage was most satisfying. Next, she threw him to the floor hard enough to rattle his brain. Before she had a chance to launch an attack on his most vulnerable parts, her original kidnappers had her by the arms and were yanking her back.

"Woman, are you fucking crazy?" one of them demanded. "He just shot a guy for a hell of a lot less than that!"

Jeban and his partner remained impassive, but she was pretty sure that both of them had found the incident amusing. Even so, they helped Ray back up off the floor of the cave. He pulled out a handkerchief to staunch the gush of blood from his nose. When the bleeding slowed, he crossed over to where his two thugs held Reggie immobilized.

He drew back his fist as if to punch her. To her surprise, Jeban blocked the blow. He and his partner had both drawn knives. The blades were long and curved, unlike anything she'd ever seen before.

Ray turned his temper on them. "What the hell do you two think you're doing? Why do you care if I get a little payback?"

Jeban shrugged. "We want her unmarked. Damaged, she is of less value to us."

Ray laughed, his eyes lighting up with a crazed joy. "Well, all right then. We'll send her across to your world unblemished. When I want her back, I'll leave a message here in the cavern. It will probably take a couple of weeks to make sure that no one is still looking for her before I can safely put her to work for me. You boys can enjoy her other talents until then."

The barrier flickered, the colors pulsing bright and then fading. Ray checked his watch. "Right on time. Until I send word, I leave her in your capable hands."

There was nothing Reggie could say to that. Instead, she joined her captors in watching the light show. And when it blinked out completely, she got her first glimpse of Kalithia.

Chapter 10

$\mathcal{D}$.J. was getting close. He'd found the black truck Reggie had described several minutes ago, tucked in a stand of trees. Rather than leave his own vehicle in plain sight, he'd parked it off the road behind some boulders about a quarter mile away.

Preparing for the hunt, he armed himself and picked up his weapons bag. The first thing he did before taking off along the trail was slash the tires on the panel truck. After he was finished, he called Trahern.

"D.J., what the hell are you doing?"

His friend's worried growl had D.J. grinning. "I'm hunting. If you hurry, I might even leave some game for you."

"Can the jokes, you idiot, and tell me what's going on."

Okay, Trahern had even less of a sense of humor than usual. "I've disabled the kidnappers' truck, so they won't be going anywhere soon. Try not to kill them all though. No doubt Devlin has some interesting plans for them."

"Fine," Trahern groused, "but where's the fun in that?"

D.J. could hear another voice in the background. "I guess you've met our newest recruit. He's a good kid."

"Hell of an introduction, don't you think? Nothing like a kidnapping and a dead body to get the new guy off to a good start. Nice that he knows how to wield a sword though."

"Yeah, gotta love that. Where are you now?"

As he listened, D.J. knelt to study the footprints in the dust. After he'd learned all he could, he slung his bag over his shoulder and started up the hillside, talking as he walked.

"Listen, you're only about twenty minutes behind me now. I'll be following the trail these guys left. I count three different male human footprints plus Reggie's. There are also two sets that look like they were made by smooth-soled Kalith boots."

The thought of her alone with those bastards had D.J. moving faster. "Call me when you get here. I parked about a quarter mile west of their truck, near some boulders. I have a seriously bad feeling about all of this. There's no reason for them to drag her all the way out here with them just so those two Kalith can go home alone."

Trahern's silence on the subject was telling. Finally, the man said, "I'd tell you to wait for us, but that's not going to happen, is it? I wouldn't either if it were Brenna up there, but watch your back. Last thing I want to do is haul your dead ass down a mountainside."

D.J. grinned at the rough concern in his friend's voice. "I'll be careful. I'd hate to put you out for any reason. See you soon."

He continued along the trail, stopping every so often to listen for voices and to make sure he was still moving in the right direction. About half a mile farther, he came to a screeching halt, positive he'd heard the angry rumble of a man's voice.

Rather than risk being caught in the open, he ducked behind some boulders and waited. Sure enough, a few minutes later three all-too-human males came hot-footing it down the trail. Two looked like hired muscle, leaving the third man to be the one in charge. He noted the guy's swollen nose. It looked as if he'd just taken a punch and was willing to bet Reggie was the one responsible. He respected her gumption but worried that she might have pushed a killer too far.

He watched the path for another couple of minutes. No sign of the two Kalith or Reggie. Damn it, that couldn't be good. The question now was whether he should risk trying to take these three out himself. Chances were he could, but one might get off a lucky shot. No, he'd leave them for Lonzo and Trahern to deal with.

When they were out of sight, he took off up the hillside at a dead run. A short time later, the visible trail ran out. He lost valuable time when he had to study the rocky ground for what seemed like forever before seeing any sign of where they'd gone from that point.

Finally, after following a narrow, twisting route through some boulders the size of small cars, he found the trail again, which ended in a clearing. Devlin hadn't said anything about there being three different possible caves to choose from. The last thing he wanted to do was waste even more time exploring dead ends.

He studied the ground in front of the first entrance. No sign of entry. He moved on to the second one. Bingo! Someone had knelt in the small patch of dirt right in front of it. Not only that, there was a small *X* scratched in the dust.

"Well, I'll be damned. She did it again."

He peeked into the third one just to make sure, but the cavern inside went barely eight feet before ending completely.

Okay, door number two it was. Time for one last call to Trahern. It went to voice mail, probably because the Paladin was busy rounding up the bad guys. He left a message anyway.

"I found the cave. There are three openings, but it has to be the middle one. I'm going in."

He hesitated, wondering at the wisdom of what he was about to say. Still, unlike Cullen, he wasn't willing to cross the barrier without anyone knowing that was what he was doing. Maybe they could get a message through to that Sworn Guardian friend of Barak's. Unfortunately, there was no way to know where this stretch of barrier was in Kalithia. It could be on the other side of the world from where Berk lived.

"Devlin's not going to like hearing this," he began,

knowing that was why he was telling Trahern instead. "But if they've taken Reggie across, I'm going after her. Ask Hunter to let Sworn Guardian Berk know I might be in his territory."

His decision made, he entered the cave wondering if he'd ever come out again.

The cavern inside reminded him of the one that Hunter Fitzsimon protected north of Seattle. That one warranted a full-time Paladin mainly because of its proximity to civilization. This one, not so much. Hell, considering how well hidden it was he had to wonder how someone had found it in the first place.

He set down his equipment bag and pulled out the backpack he kept stashed inside. It held extra ammunition, bottled water, granola bars, and a spare gun. Next he pulled out his sword. As prepared as he'd ever be, he shoved the equipment bag off to the side, purposefully leaving it where Trahern and Lonzo would find it.

He closed his eyes briefly before deciding which passage to follow to the barrier. Oh, yeah, it was calling to him from the one on the right. He was strongly attuned to the barrier in Seattle as well as the one near Mount St. Helens, but this new stretch hummed softly in the back of his mind.

It was close, too. He turned off his flashlight and moved forward as his eyes adjusted to the darkness. There was a hint of light coming from down the way; that, combined with his Paladin vision, was enough to allow him to walk without hesitation toward where he really, really hoped Reggie was waiting for him.

He stopped to listen just short of the last turn. Nothing except the erratic buzz of the barrier itself. Either they were gone or they were dead. Only one way to find out. Fury burned like acid in his veins, urging him forward.

He slowly coasted to a stop. Nothing. No one.

What now? The barrier was stretched thin in places. Most likely that meant it had recently been down. It clearly wasn't stable yet, but there was no way to know if it would repair itself or go down again.

He studied the floor of the cave, hoping to read some truth about what had happened before his arrival. Reggie had managed to leave clues before. Maybe she had again. The first thing he spotted was a spray of blood, but he figured it belonged to the guy with the injured nose, not Reggie. He ignored it and kept looking. It didn't take him long to find something.

She'd written one word—Jeban—and then an arrow pointing toward the barrier. He didn't know for sure, but Jeban had to be one of the two Kaliths. It sounded right. It also meant his worst fears had come true. Reggie was being held hostage in a world known to be hostile to humans.

No, that wasn't his worst fear—that would have been to find Reggie already dead. As long as she was alive, there was hope. There had to be. He wouldn't have it any other way.

It was time to report in again, not that it would change what he was going to do. Even so, he wouldn't leave Devlin guessing this time about where one of his men had disappeared to. Since cell phones didn't work next to the barrier, he hurried back down the passage.

Outside the cave, he'd started to call when he heard someone coming up the trail and cursing a blue streak. He'd recognize that pissed-off voice anywhere. What was Trahern doing? Why wasn't he dealing with the three humans involved in this mess? Had they dragged them all the way back up here for some reason?

Only one way to find out.

"Trahern, I'm up here," he shouted and then went to meet him.

He rounded the last boulder and found Trahern, Lonzo, and Cody waiting for him. No sign of the three humans.

"Don't tell me you let them get away."

Lonzo looked thoroughly disgusted. "I don't know who you're dealing with here, but they've definitely got some money behind them. Just as we pulled up, a chopper was disappearing over the horizon."

D.J. closed his eyes and fought for control. Once again the bastards had slipped through their fingers. Now how was he supposed to figure out what they wanted with Reggie? He should've shot them when he'd had the chance. He picked up a rock and heaved it at the nearest tree. When that did nothing to relieve the cauldron of fury and frustration burning inside him, he looked around for a more satisfying target and spotted one.

He got right up in his friend's face, both hands clenched in fists. "You said you had my back, Trahern. Fat lot of good that did."

Those cold gray eyes narrowed and Trahern's lips twisted up in a nasty sneer. "Yeah, and if you hadn't gone off half-cocked as usual, none of this would have happened."

Lonzo tried to intervene. He yanked D.J. a step back. "Guys, we don't have time for this shit."

D.J. shook Lonzo's hand off his shoulder. "Stay out of it, Lonzo, or you're next."

Trahern simply smiled at him, the glint in his pale eyes just daring D.J. to try it. It wouldn't be the first time a couple of Paladins went at each other just to blow off steam. However, as satisfying as a down-and-dirty mood adjustment might be, they all needed to focus on getting Reggie back. It wasn't his friends' fault that everything had gone to hell.

D.J. backed up another step, for the first time really noticing that Cody looked pretty damned worried. "Hey, kid, you doing okay?"

He ignored D.J.'s question to ask one of his own. "Where's Reggie?"

There was no use in hiding the truth. "They took her across the barrier."

The kid charged right at him, grabbing a fistful of D.J.'s shirt. "You were supposed to save her, you bastard."

"I tried."

Cody got right up in his face. "Not hard enough. It's your fault she's in this mess in the first place, Knight-walker."

Okay, so Cody had obviously gotten the full complement of Paladin traits, including a hellacious temper. Cody had done nothing to deserve the situation he was in. Neither had Reggie.

"You're right, Cody. That's why I'm going after her."

"If you go, I'm going, too."

That was the last thing D.J. needed right now. "Sorry, but that's not happening. We've already had this discussion. I can't be responsible for your safety when I don't know what I'll be walking into."

"It's not up to you, D.J. I'm an adult. I make my own decisions."

Trahern rejoined the conversation, breaking the kid's hold on D.J. "Listen, Cody. Trust me on this. You don't want to make this any harder for D.J. to succeed. He'll do better working on his own."

Then he turned to D.J. "Devlin's on his way here with Barak. They're bringing you suitable clothing, and Barak will brief you on a few things before you go across. He'll drop the barrier for you, too."

Okay, that was a big plus. D.J. hadn't been sure how he was going to handle that particular problem on his own. Tradition was one of the two reasons the Paladins fought with blades rather than bullets. The other was that bullets could shred the barrier, making it take longer to repair itself. The longer it was down, the more of those crazy fucking Others came pouring across.

But right now, he didn't give a damn if they destroyed this little patch of hell permanently as long as he could get through to the other side. Reggie's safety was the only thing that mattered.

"I'll show you which cave it is, but then I'm going back inside just in case something happens while we're waiting."

The other three followed him around the boulders until they reached the entrance. He pointed to the ground. "Reggie managed to leave her footprints and marked the right one for me."

His friends looked impressed, but Lonzo asked, "Did you check out the other two caves?"

"The far one only goes in about eight feet. I didn't explore the first one."

"I'll take a quick look while Trahern waits for Devlin and Barak. Once they land, we'll catch up with you."

"Sounds good. Cody, you're with me."

D.J. didn't wait to see if the kid followed him. He headed inside and straight back toward the barrier. He paused just before the last turn to wait for his companion to catch up with him.

"Where's that light coming from?"

"You're about to get your first look at the barrier that separates our world from Kalithia. This is just a small stretch. The one that runs under Seattle is much bigger, as is the one in southern Missouri. The damn thing is scattered in bits and pieces all along the Pacific Rim and anywhere else there are major fault lines."

"Seriously? No shit?"

For the first time in hours, D.J. grinned and echoed Cody's response. "Seriously. No shit. This will beat any computer game you've been playing to hell and back."

Then he stood aside and let Cody get the first

glimpse of his new worldview. At least it would give the young Paladin-to-be something to think about other than where the heck Reggie was and if D.J. would be able to pull off a rescue.

The helicopter swooped in low and fast, landing only long enough for them to jump out. Barak hit the ground first, while Devlin followed more slowly, bringing up the rear and carrying the equipment they'd brought with them. It was hard not to laugh at his Kalith friend trying to walk on legs that had turned to rubber.

Although Barak had flown in a chopper before, he'd been badly wounded and hurting at the time. He clearly hadn't enjoyed this experience much more. Judging by the slight greenish tinge to his normally pale coloring, he wouldn't be anxious to try it again soon.

Devlin moved up beside him. "Barak, are you okay?"

The Kalith warrior nodded, although he didn't look convinced. He stumbled slightly, but Devlin caught him before he actually hit the ground. After a few steps, he looked steadier.

He stared up after the retreating chopper. "Even when I lived in my world, I had heard of such things. Back then I never dreamed I would actually have a chance to fly in one. As amazing as it was to see the land from so high in the sky, I would prefer not to do so again."

If the situation wasn't so damn serious, Devlin would've laughed. They were almost to where Trahern stood waiting; he immediately asked Barak, "Do you have any idea why two Kalith males would want to steal a human woman?"

Barak accepted the abrupt greeting with his usual calm reserve. "I have no idea, but it cannot be good."

Devlin couldn't agree more. "Where's D.J.?"

All trace of good humor disappeared from Trahern's expression. "He's inside the cave waiting for us. Or at least I hope he's still there. I don't know who this Reggie is, but she's definitely got our boy tied up in knots. Think she's the reason he's been off his feed lately?"

"Let's keep moving. I'm afraid he'll panic and do something crazy if we don't get back to him soon," Devlin suggested. "But to answer your question, yeah, she is. Seems she's been busting his chops online for a couple of months. Somehow she managed to get past the firewalls he and Cullen installed and was messing around in the Regents' server. D.J. said she found the history of the Paladins that Brenna has been working on."

"Well, that sucks, but it explains a lot."

Devlin studied the area, memorizing the layout in case they had to come back. "Where's this Cody D.J. told me about?"

"He went back into the cave with D.J. to get his first look at the barrier. They've been gone about half an hour. There's no telling how stable the barrier is, but our boy is definitely champing at the bit to cross over."

Knowing D.J. as well as he did, Devlin picked up the pace. "Then we'd better haul ass."

• • •

"Sounds like Trahern and the others are coming this way."

Cody nodded but couldn't tear his eyes away from the barrier. The hum filled his head like a melody he'd heard before but couldn't quite place. And, oh man, the colors! He'd started to take a picture of the barrier with his cell phone, but D.J. almost knocked it out of his hand.

"If you don't want Devlin to stomp your phone into dust, I wouldn't do that."

D.J. went back to pacing. Whoever this Devlin guy was, he must be big-time scary from the respect both D.J. and Trahern had in their voices when they spoke of him. Guess he'd find out soon enough because several people were definitely hoofing it down the passage to the cavern. A few seconds later, they filed in.

Cody reluctantly turned away from the mesmerizing light show to face the newcomers. He nodded at Trahern and Lonzo, but it was the other two men who held his attention.

The one in the middle had to be Devlin. Damn, he'd thought Trahern was big, and Lonzo and D.J. only slightly less so. This guy was absolutely humongous. Heck, his muscles had muscles.

The big man headed straight for him with his hand held out. "Cody, I'm Devlin Bane. It's nice to meet you, although I wish it were under better circumstances. You've certainly managed to dive into the deep end of our little version of reality. You hanging in there?"

"More or less." For some reason he felt compelled to add, "Sir."

Devlin nodded with approval and continued with the introductions. "This is Barak q'Young. He's originally from Kalithia, but he lives here now."

Okay, Cody hadn't expected to actually meet some-one from the other side of the barrier. *Huh, so that's what an alien looks like. So much for all those little green men with big heads and buggy eyes in all the UFO shows on television.*

D.J. interrupted. "Fuck the chitchat, Devlin. The longer we delay, the harder it will be for me to find Reggie. Barak, bring the damn barrier down now."

Devlin crowded closer to D.J. "You don't give the orders around here. Do I need to remind you that if you'd followed protocols, we might have avoided this bullshit in the first place?"

D.J. held his ground. "Screw that, Devlin. You can keelhaul my ass when this is all over, but right now there's a woman's life on the line. Just let me get on with what needs to be done. Every second you waste jawing at me is one more she's spending in hell."

Cody watched the interplay between the two men. He wouldn't have wanted to cross either one of them. Despite the obvious tension in Devlin's stance, his voice was calm when he spoke again.

"I get that, D.J., but you're not going quite yet. Strip off. Barak brought you some of his old clothes to wear so you'll stand a better chance of not getting caught."

Cody watched to see if they'd brought a second set of the alien clothes. Obviously they weren't planning on his going with D.J. To hell with that. Reggie was his friend, not theirs. He eased closer to the barrier and leaned against the wall of the cave. As long as he didn't draw unwanted attention to himself, maybe he could figure out some way to follow D.J. when he crossed into the other world.

Yep, wait and watch, that was the name of the game.

Chapter 11

$\mathcal{D}$.J. peeled off his jeans and shirt and tossed them aside. He yanked the tunic Barak handed him on over his head and then pulled on the black trousers.

Barak held out a pair of boots. "I wasn't sure these would fit you, but it would be better to wear them in my world if you can."

D.J. toed off his running shoes and slipped his feet into the boots. He'd walk on broken glass if that's what it took to find Reggie. He took several steps to try them out. While he did, Barak transferred D.J.'s supplies from his backpack to a smaller one that was similar in design. Both must have come from Kalithia.

He could live with the boots. "They're a bit snug, but they'll do."

"Good, add this cloak and you're all set." Barak stepped back to check him out. "I know you will adapt to the thinner atmosphere in my world as easily as Lonzo and Trahern did. It would be better if you had Berk to act as a guide, but I know you aren't willing to wait for him. I wouldn't be either.

"Hunter promised to get word through to him to be on the lookout for both you and your woman. If possible, Berk will find you and pass you off as one of his men. It's normal for the Sworn Guardian to do all the talking. Once you're with him, keep your mouth shut unless you're in private."

Then Barak knelt down and opened the equipment bag Devlin had carried in. He pulled out a scabbard designed to hold a curved blade.

"Strap this on."

D.J. did as he was told. As soon as he had the leather belt settled around his waist, Barak adjusted it a bit and then held out a Kalith blade.

"Larem sent this to you. It was his, and his father's before him. He hopes it will bring you both luck and success in your rescue mission. He greatly regrets not being able to accompany you."

D.J. wouldn't have asked him to. Larem had just found out he was going to be a father, not to mention that there was a death sentence hanging over his head back in Kalithia.

"He has enough on his plate right now. But let him know I will treat his family's sword with the greatest respect. I understand the honor he has paid me."

After a few practice swings, D.J. nodded in approval at the way the sword fit his hand. "This thing is totally sick. I guess all those lessons you guys gave us in your style of fighting are going to come in handy."

Barak nodded, his expression grave. His own woman had been kidnapped by professional killers, and he had called the fury of a mountain down on his own head to end the threat to Lacey. Like Devlin, Barak knew exactly what D.J. was going through.

"I would come with you myself, but legally, Berk would be obligated to arrest me the minute I crossed into Kalithia. I find myself reluctant to test the depths of his friendship for me."

D.J. had to laugh at that. "Not a problem. Besides, I wouldn't want to face Lacey if I managed to get you arrested in Kalithia. She'd be over there in a heartbeat. The bastards wouldn't know what hit them."

Barak's smile widened. "True enough. My mate has a fierce heart. But back to business. Devlin and I brought enough supplies for me to remain here in the cave for several days. I will check each day at sunrise and sunset to see if you have returned." He paused. "I just wish you knew more about who you were after."

The comment jarred D.J.'s memory. He slapped his forehead. "I'm an idiot!"

Lonzo cracked up. "Tell us something we don't already know."

D.J. ignored him and pointed. "I found a word scratched in the rock over here. I think Reggie was trying to tell me who had kidnapped her."

Barak studied the marking with a grim expression. "Jeban is definitely a Kalith name. Unfortunately, it is common enough that his first name alone won't identify him, but it's a start. We'll share the information with Berk as soon as possible. This woman of yours is clever."

Yeah, she was. Too clever for her own good, but now wasn't the time to think that way. She'd managed to survive so far. Hopefully her quick thinking would keep her alive long enough for him to find her.

"I need to get going."

Devlin had to have the last word. "Don't get yourself killed, D.J. You might be a pain in the ass, but you're our pain in the ass. Besides, I'd like to meet this Reggie. Anyone smart enough to run you around in circles sounds like my kind of woman."

D.J.'s, too, but he hadn't yet earned the right to be thinking that way.

"Barak, do your thing."

The Kalith warrior stood in front of the barrier and held out his hands as he quietly chanted. Almost immediately, the barrier began to fade. As Barak continued to work, D.J. caught a movement out of the corner of his eye. Cody was creeping forward while everyone's attention was focused on the barrier. No doubt he was hoping to jump across into Kalithia.

It wasn't going to happen, although he respected the guy for trying. He caught Trahern's attention and jerked his head in Cody's direction. The Paladin nodded and immediately positioned himself in front of him. There was no way he'd be able to get past Trahern.

Cody knew it, too. He shot D.J. a furious look, but D.J. kept his eye on the barrier as he made his way around behind Barak to talk to Cody.

"I need you to stay here and help Devlin. They're going to need you to track down the guy who did this to Reggie. If we don't find him, he'll go after her again when we get back."

Cody didn't like it, but at least he was listening. D.J. added his last argument for leaving him behind. "You're the only one who can cover for Reggie with your boss. Besides, she wouldn't want you screwing up your classes by missing your finals."

"I'll retake them next quarter if I have to."

"Yeah, but can you afford the extra tuition?" D.J. was grasping at straws, and they both knew it.

Cody could give D.J. a run for his money when it came to sheer cussedness. "That's my problem, not yours."

"Fine, it's your decision, but Reggie will kick both our asses if you have to drop out because of her."

Then he handed Cody the flash drive he'd saved Reggie's files on and the keys to his truck. "Plus, you know how her mind works. My friend Cullen will stand a better chance of finding the bastards behind this with your help."

Devlin had been listening in. "But whether you do this or not, Cody, we'll see that your tuition is covered until you graduate."

Cody's eyes flared wide. "Why would you do that?"

"Because you're one of us now. Now let's get out of the way. Barak's almost done."

Everyone moved back from the barrier except D.J. and Barak. Not knowing who might be waiting on the other side, the Paladins pulled their swords and stood ready to fight.

The swirling energy jerked and twitched as if it were alive. Holes that gradually grew until one blended into the next and the next appeared in the fabric of the energy. Two seconds later the whole thing ripped apart and disappeared. D.J. couldn't afford to hesitate. If he was straddling the line between the two worlds when it popped back up, it would slice him in half.

A voice behind them shouted, "Holy shit!"

Cody's reaction didn't come as any surprise. All of them had stood at the barrier at some point in their lives and caught their first glimpse of an alien world. Although the cavern on the other side was a mirror reflection of the one D.J. had just left, there was an opening directly to the outside that revealed a small glimpse of the twin suns in the sky over Kalithia.

D.J. stopped long enough to look back at his friends. There was no way to know what was going to happen as he hunted for Reggie. He'd find her or die trying. With that thought in mind, he made eye contact with each man in turn, hoping that it conveyed how much they all meant to him.

Barak was showing the strain of maintaining control over the barrier. Even so, he leaned forward slightly as if straining to see past the cave and into the world beyond.

"Once you find your lady, come back here if you can. If not, aim for those low hills you see in the distance. There are caves along the back of the second range. One that holds a small stretch of the barrier hides behind a boulder shaped like an old man's face. I will tell Berk that you know of that cave."

D.J. nodded, feeling better to have two possible escape routes. While they talked, Trahern and Devlin tossed a couple of equipment bags across to the other cave.

"What's that?"

Devlin added one more bag. "Food and water. Basic survival gear. Should be enough to keep you both going until we can get you back across."

D.J.'s throat closed tight with emotion. He could barely choke out a simple, "Thanks, guys."

Then Barak released his control of the barrier. Just that quickly all of his friends disappeared behind the surging colors. D.J. hadn't felt quite so alone in a long time. It took him another few seconds to focus.

Once his pulse had returned to normal, he braced himself for the hunt that was about to begin. He stuck his gun into the waistband of his trousers and sheathed Larem's sword as he stepped out of the cave and into the dim light of a Kalith evening.

God, if he found all of this a bit bewildering, how bad was it for Reggie? He rested his hand on the pommel of his sword, drawing comfort from the familiar feel. Battle fever ran hot in his veins. He'd been at war with this alien world for most of his adult life. The only difference was, this time he was bringing the fight to them.

Reggie stumbled along in between her two captors. Once they'd crossed the barrier, they'd made her put on

a set of clothes and a cloak from the cache of supplies
they'd left in the cave. At least they'd let her keep her
own shoes. Thanks to the oversize pants, her feet barely
showed anyway.

Once they started hiking, it was hard to keep up with
the pace set by Jeban's partner. Obviously they wanted
to put considerable distance between themselves and
the barrier. Judging from the way Jeban kept looking
back, he was worried about being followed.

The thin air left her lungs burning from the effort to
keep up. Despite being physically fit, it was all she could
do to keep putting one foot in front of the other. When
they'd first started out, she tried to take note of the landscape, but eventually gave up trying to make sense of the
endless monotony. The whole freaking world was brown
with the occasional streak of gray. Each step they took
kicked up a cloud of dust, clogging her nose and throat.
Beads of muddy sweat trickled down her face and left
her skin itching.

Would D.J. actually cross into this hellish place to
come after her? There was no way to know for sure that
he'd been able to follow their trail back on earth, much
less track her in an alien world. Her logical mind might
have its doubts, but her heart told her he'd come. Despite having spent only a short time in his company, she
felt a powerful connection to the man.

Hunger and exhaustion were making it much harder
to make sense of everything that had happened in the
past few days, starting with the fight with Big Ed and
then D.J. showing up on her doorstep. Not to mention

how her whole image of reality had been turned inside out and upside down. For now, she just had to keep trudging along. As long as she focused on the simple things, she didn't think so much about why she was there in the first place.

Obviously Ray had his own plans for her. God knows what they were, but he seemed to be waiting for her trail to grow cold before pursuing them. Right now it was Jeban and company who scared her right down to her bones.

"Stop."

The alien in front of her abruptly turned off the trail and waded into the high grass. They'd been walking along a narrow, dusty path that led down a steep hill toward the valley below. Where was he taking her now? She froze where she was, reluctant to go any farther.

Jeban moved up beside her. "Follow him. We're going to stop to rest and have something to eat."

Sure enough, a short distance into the grass, there was a small stream. The two Kalith immediately knelt down and used their hands to scoop up handfuls of water to drink. Reggie didn't even let herself consider what alien microbes might be lurking in the water and followed their example. If these two guys could function back on earth, she had to assume there were enough similarities between the two worlds for her to be able to eat and drink in relative safety.

God, she hoped so anyway. But regardless, she needed to maintain her strength if she was going to escape from these two. How she'd find her way back home on her own was a problem she'd deal with later.

The water was cool and clear and tasted fine. It also felt good to splash it on her face and to rinse the dirt off her hands. When she'd had enough, Jeban motioned for her to have a seat on a nearby rock. Then, to her surprise, he tossed her a couple of granola bars, the same brand she bought for herself.

The little touch of home had her eyes burning with tears that she refused to shed. "So people aren't the only thing you steal from my world."

Jeban's freaky pale eyes narrowed in anger. "I thought you would do better eating your own food."

Darned if she'd feel grateful for anything the guy had done, even if it was thoughtful. She perched on the rock but turned her back on the two men. Neither of them seemed interested in talking to each other much less her. That was fine. She was too tired to maintain a brave front.

She nibbled on the granola bars, hoping to delay their departure as long as she could. Every minute they spent out here on the trail would give D.J. that much more time to track them. Besides, she didn't want to think about what would happen once they reached their final destination.

Footsteps behind her warned that her respite was over. Sure enough, Jeban circled the rock to face her.

"We are leaving soon."

Not knowing when they would stop again, she sipped more of the cool water, enjoying its soothing trickle down her throat. She was about to reach for another handful when the nameless guy stopped her by putting his hand on her shoulder.

"We go *now*."

She nodded but drank anyway. When she stood up, his expression made it all too clear that he'd noted the small rebellion. The chill in his eyes was scary, but she refused to cower.

Once again the other guy took the lead, Jeban following Reggie. It worried her that she was starting to trust Jeban to look after her. That was nothing but stupidity. If he'd really wanted to help her, he would've left her back in her world. Even so, he was far less scary than his partner.

For now she studied their surroundings, trying to memorize the path back to the cave. If somehow she managed to slip away, she'd need a plan. Of course, the cave would be the first place they'd look for her, but it was the only route home that she knew. Besides, it was the first place D.J. would check.

Just past the next rise, they reached the valley floor. The hills behind them looked much like those she could see in the distance. The terrain in between was flat and dry. Most of the plants were burned brown from the dry heat even though the light from the two stars in the sky was far dimmer than earth's single sun. No wonder Jeban had described his home as the land of the dying suns.

The stream ran parallel to the trail until it abruptly disappeared underground. From that point, the path they were following did a ninety-degree turn and headed straight across the valley floor toward the hills beyond.

"How far do we have to go?" she asked.

She'd addressed the question to Jeban, but it was his friend who answered. "Are you in such a hurry to meet your fate?"

There was nothing to be said to that, so she walked on in silence. Despite her two companions, she'd never felt so alone in her life.

Outside the cave, it didn't take long for D.J. to pick up a trail left behind by Reggie and her captors. They were nowhere in sight. Considering the head start they'd gotten, he hadn't really expected them to be. Rather than go charging down the hillside, he went back inside the cave to rummage through the supplies that Devlin had provided.

It was mostly food and water, but his friend had also stuck in extra clips for D.J.'s Glock as well as a first-aid kit and some space blankets, the kind that took up little room but provided a surprising amount of warmth. He'd also included matches, two flashlights, a small backpacker's stove, and even some plastic ties that could be used as restraints.

Yeah, like D.J. was going let the bastards live long enough to need those. Sworn Guardian Berk might have a different opinion on that subject should their paths cross, but he'd deal with it then. Rather than leave the packs in the cave where one of the Others might find them, D.J. stashed them a short distance away from the cave behind some low bushes.

Time to begin the hunt.

He didn't bother with caution. These guys either knew he was coming or they were fools. Whichever it was, he had to make up time if he'd stand any chance of catching them.

Starting off at a trot, he waited to see how the thinner atmosphere affected his stamina before picking up speed. He slowed occasionally to catch his breath as he looked for tracks to verify that he was still following the right trail.

About an hour later, he came to a stop. The grass to the side of the trail looked trampled, as if someone had cut across country. He drew his gun and started forward, worried about what he'd find. As soon as he spotted the stream, his tension drained away. It made sense that they would've stopped here for water and maybe a brief rest.

That didn't keep the fear that 'they'd stopped for much darker reasons from eating at him. He'd feel a whole lot better if he had some inkling of why they'd brought Reggie into Kalithia. It sure as hell wasn't because of her bitchin' computer skills, not in this world where such things didn't exist.

He studied the edge of the stream and could see where three different individuals had knelt to drink. Then he spotted something lying in the dirt beside a nearby rock. Granola wrappers. Okay, so they were feeding her. He had no doubt that she'd left the scraps of paper for him to find. God, he loved the way her mind worked.

Enough time wasted. After a quick drink, he soaked

his handkerchief and wrapped it around his neck. Then he returned to the original trail, picking up greater speed as he ran downhill. Based on what he'd been able to learn from the footprints Reggie and her escorts had left in the dust, they were walking. As long as he maintained a faster pace, eventually he'd catch up with them.

When he did, there'd be hell to pay.

Cody knew he was sulking, but right then he didn't care. In the past two days, thanks to D.J., his whole life had gone straight to hell, starting with his best friend being kidnapped and dragged into an alien world. Not only that, Cody was now surrounded by a bunch of killers armed with swords and guns.

The whole thing read like a bad science fiction movie, the kind where the geeky kid gets swept up in events too big for him to comprehend. Devlin had taken off in a helicopter shortly after they'd left the caves. Lonzo had stayed behind with that Barak guy to wait for D.J.'s return.

Evidently Devlin was going to make contact with someone they knew who still lived in Kalithia. From what they said, this guy Berk was part of some kind of local militia. For Reggie's sake, it was nice to know there were good guys on the other side of that barrier, too.

Devlin was also going to sic D.J.'s friend Cullen on tracking the helicopter that had whisked the human contingent of bad guys off to safety before Trahern and Lonzo could catch up with them. Cody almost wished he'd been invited along for the ride. For one thing, Cullen was the guy D.J. had wanted Cody to work with on the computer stuff.

Right now, though, Trahern was taking Cody back to Portland to pick up a few things before heading up to the Paladins' Seattle headquarters. Rather than think too much about it all, Cody closed his eyes and tried to doze off.

It didn't work. About the time he managed to relax enough, Trahern pulled off the road, jarring Cody back to full alert.

"What's going on?"

"I thought we'd stop and chow down."

Cody wanted to protest. No one seemed to be hurrying enough. Yeah, D.J. was hot on Reggie's trail, but Cody wanted—*needed*—to be doing something soon.

"But—"

Trahern turned his chilly gaze in Cody's direction. "No buts, Cody. None of us can function well when running on empty, and we have a long way to go tonight. Believe me, the first thing you learn in this world of ours is to eat whenever you get a chance. There'll be enough times ahead when you'd give your left nut for even a handful of granola."

Cody hadn't made up his mind yet about whether to throw in his lot with these guys, but for the moment he had little choice in the matter. Once Reggie was back where she belonged and the Paladins had tracked down the guys who'd kidnapped her in the first place, he'd have time to think about it.

The other problem was that he had next to no money. The restaurant didn't look all that expensive, though. Maybe he could afford a bowl of soup; that was usually cheap.

"A little something might be good."

Then Trahern actually winked at him. "Better eat up, Cody. It's not every day Devlin picks up the tab. Personally, I'm going order a big steak with all the trimmings."

Okay, then. Obviously Devlin Bane looked out for his men. That was good to know.

Cody studied the restaurant's sign, which advertised home-style cooking. "Hey, think this place has a good dessert menu? And maybe extras to go?"

"No wonder D.J. took to you." Trahern chuckled as he pulled into a parking spot and turned off the engine. "I like the way you think. You're gonna fit right in with us."

When was the last time he'd fit in anyplace? He couldn't remember, but the idea that these guys actually wanted him to hang with them felt good. As they climbed out of the truck and headed inside, the Paladin clapped him on the back.

"While we're waiting for our dinners, you can tell me all about your fencing classes and what kind of weapon you like best. I'm a broadsword fan myself."

When Cody started talking, it was clear that Trahern was really listening to him and cared about his opinions. Once the food arrived, they both turned their attention to eating.

Hanging with the Paladins felt damn good.

Chapter 12

What was going on? For the third time in the past fifteen minutes, Jeban had paused to stare back up the trail behind them. After the second time, he'd said something to his partner in their own language. All Reggie had been able to pick up was the growing tension in Jeban's voice. That, and his buddy's name: Kolar.

Once Jeban had drawn Kolar's attention to whatever was going on behind them, they'd both started walking faster and looking back more often. Jeban was careful to keep her between them, shoving her forward if she tried to slow down at all. She didn't know what to think. Was help on its way or was something else going on?

Obviously these two were criminals in both worlds. If they were being tracked, it could be that their own people were after them. Only one way to find out. The next time Jeban stopped, she walked back to join him.

If there was something happening behind them, she sure wasn't seeing any sign of it. "What's going on?"

"Perhaps we are being followed," Jeban answered in English as he drew his sword. "Kolar, I'm going to circle back to see for sure."

As soon as he disappeared off the trail into the tall grasses, Kolar caught Reggie by the arm and dragged her along in his wake. She fought to pull free of his grasp. He only tightened his grip, hard enough to leave bruises, making her wish that Jeban had been the one to stay with her.

"Any idea who it might be back there?"

Kolar stopped to answer. "Does it matter? If it is one of our people, he will be enjoying your company along with us."

As he spoke, Kolar's eyes traveled from her head to her toes, pausing along the way to let her know exactly what he was thinking. She glared at him, but it had no effect.

His smile made her skin crawl. "Of course, it could be someone from your world coming to retrieve you, but that will not happen. Either he will die or you both will. That would be a shame. I have such interesting and pleasurable plans for you. Pleasurable for me, anyway."

He moved in closer, his intent to kiss her obvious. Reggie turned her head to the side so that his lips landed on the side of her head. In response, he caught her chin in a painful grip and positioned her face right where he wanted it.

"You should be careful, pretty little human. I like it when women resist my attentions. Punishment offers its own pleasure."

Then his mouth crushed down on hers as he used his other hand to grope her breast, hard. When he deepened the kiss, she retaliated by biting down on his tongue.

Kolar howled in pain and jumped back. He spit a mouthful of blood on the ground, his furious expression promising retribution. She immediately retreated, preparing to bolt if he took one more step toward her.

Instead, she backed right into Jeban. It didn't take him long to size up the situation. He looked at each of them with equal disgust. When Kolar tried to grab her, she used his partner as a shield.

"Get out of the way, Jeban. She needs to learn some manners. I shall greatly enjoy teaching them to her."

Jeban kept himself firmly between her and his friend. "Now is not the time. There will be plenty of time later for us to school her in the proper behavior for a slave."

Her stomach plummeted. So much for Jeban being the nice guy. When he reached out to take her hand, she jerked it back out of his reach and marched off down the trail ahead of them both.

Reggie ached straight through to her bones. Despite being physically fit, she'd been too long without sleep or enough food. Breathing was rapidly becoming problematic, thanks to air that was too thin on oxygen and too thick with dust. The legs of her black trousers were coated with the stuff; even her teeth were gritty.

A drink of water would taste good about now, but she was in no hurry to stop for the day. As tired as she was, she wasn't sure how much longer she could keep moving. For certain, she didn't want to give Kolar an excuse to begin the training session Jeban had mentioned.

Barbarian bastards.

What passed for daylight in this world was almost gone by the time they'd traversed halfway across the valley. Finally, Jeban called a halt. After a brief discussion with Kolar, he switched to English for her benefit.

"Our regular camp lies in that direction," he said, pointing toward a clump of scrubby trees a short distance off to the right. "There we will stop for the night and wait for our partners to join us late tomorrow."

He paused to look back the way they'd come. "Kolar, I'll start the fire and the evening meal. Why don't you circle back this time? I still sense someone behind us."

Kolar nodded. "If I find it is a human, should he die?"

Jeban looked at Reggie before answering, a cold gleam in his pale eyes. "If you can capture him, do so, but it will be no great loss if he dies. Enough of our people have been murdered by human hands. Balancing the scales would be satisfying."

Reggie shivered. These two talked of killing as if a life held no worth at all. Maybe for them, humans were disposable. If that was indeed D.J. or one of his fellow Paladins behind them, she could only pray that they stayed safely out of sight. Then there was the whole other problem of more of Jeban's gang being on their way to meet them.

She slowly followed Jeban to the campsite. She knew she should fear what these alien bastards had planned, but right now all she could do was collapse on the ground. Drawing her knees up to her chest, she wrapped her arms around her legs and made herself as small as possible.

Jeban ignored her while he started a fire and then filled a kettle with water from a nearby spring. While he took care of the chores, Reggie prayed harder than she had in years.

God, I don't want my life to end here, but please don't let D.J. die because of me.

As she waited to see what would happen next, she stared into the fire and let her head fill with images of D.J. From what she'd read about the Paladins, he and his friends were certainly the stuff legends were made of: warriors with a code of honor so profound that they sacrificed their lives over and over again to protect ordinary people like her.

She really wished the two of them had had more time together. Rather than think about the potential horrors that might await her, she thought about the amazing kiss they had shared and drew comfort from the memory.

Todd did his best to ignore the argument occuring just outside his office. He didn't know what it was about and didn't care.

Then the door to his office slammed open with no warning. What the hell? He'd told his assistant Melinda to hold his calls and fend off anyone who wanted to see him so he could get this damned report done.

She hovered in the doorway, waiting for him to acknowledge her. Behind her stood Ray, obviously back from his trip to the coast. What the hell had happened to him? Rather than acknowledge him, Todd concentrated on soothing his assistant's ruffled feathers.

"Yes, Melinda, what is it?"

"I'm sorry, sir. I told Mr. Pine here that you weren't to be disturbed, but he wouldn't listen." She shot the other man a nasty look. "Shall I call security?"

He forced a smile to hide his irritation

"That won't be necessary, Melinda. I should've told you that Ray might be stopping by today."

Her relief was obvious as she backed out of the office, shooting one last look at Ray before pulling the door closed. When she was gone and safely out of hearing, Todd leaned back in his chair and glared at his unwanted associate.

"Ray, what the fuck happened to your face and why are you here? I thought we'd agreed that we wouldn't meet at work."

The other man ignored him. Instead he helped himself to a cup of coffee before settling into the chair facing Todd's desk. He looked like hell. If Todd had to guess, Ray hadn't slept much in the past two days. He was also sporting a pair of world-class shiners and a nose swollen to twice its normal size. And the man looked thoroughly pissed off.

Todd couldn't resist tweaking the guy's already bad

mood. "Tough day at the office or are you going to a costume party as a raccoon?"

Ray glared at him over the rim of his coffee cup. "Fuck you, Todd. I told you I didn't want to make that trip. Now look at me."

Todd studied his friend's face. "Looks painful."

"It is, and what's more, I'm going to need surgery to put my nose back together. Tomorrow, as a matter of fact, so I'll be out of commission for at least a couple of days. That little bitch you wanted picked up did this to me. I hope those two Others I left her with—"

When Ray's voice got louder with each word, Todd cut him off in midsentence. "Shut the fuck up right now. This is not the time or the place for this conversation."

Ray glared right back at him. "Yeah, well, tough shit, Todd. Why don't you explain to my wife how I ended up like this after a business trip?"

God, he hated placating the peons. "Fine, I get it. You're hurt. You're mad. She's mad."

Damn it, he should've handled the situation himself to make sure it was done well right from the start.

"I suppose it never occurred to you that by heading straight here you've led a trail right to my door." He rose to his feet. "Let's go."

"Where?"

"Someplace where we can talk without being overheard."

• • •

Twenty minutes later they were sitting on a park bench
with a couple of sandwiches and cold drinks. Todd had
lost his appetite when Ray walked into his office, but
appearances were everything. If anyone was paying any
attention, it would look as if two friends were taking ad-
vantage of their lunch hour to enjoy a sunny afternoon in
St. Louis.

"Okay, start to finish, fill me in."

He took a bite of his sandwich while Ray explained
what had happened. The more Todd listened, the more
he wanted to choke the bastard.

"Any chance the dead guy can be traced back to you?"

Because if he could, there just might be another
corpse in the making. At least Ray had been smart
enough to use local talent in Portland. One Regents
employee making a trip to the area might go unnoticed.
Sending four but having only three return would be
harder to hide.

"No way. We kept it to first names only. I paid cash
and used burn phones."

Ray paused to take a long swig of his iced tea. Then
he cleared his throat. "There's more."

"I figured there was."

Todd stared out across the grassy slope and waited
for the shit to hit the fan.

"Someone is already hunting for her. I don't know for
sure, but I think it might be the Paladins from Seattle."

Todd snorted his soft drink, nearly choking in the
process. "Are you sure?"

"No, but one of the guys thought he overheard her

call someone D.J. It would be too much of a coincidence for it to be some other random guy by that name."

"Did he hear anything else?" One look at Ray's face told the story. "Don't tell me, he's the one you shot."

"He let her steal his cell phone. It was his fault that things got this screwed up. I'm telling you right now, if the Paladins are really on the hunt, I want out."

Yeah, like that was going to happen. But before Todd explained the facts of life to his good buddy Ray, he had to ask one more question.

"How the hell did you manage to drag those bastards into this? It was supposed to be a clean snatch-and-grab. You were to let the Others have some fun with the bitch, so that when we drag her back across the barrier she'd be more cooperative."

Not that it would save her life in the long run.

"I don't know how they caught wind of what was going on. All I know is that someone followed us to the caves. We never saw them, but whoever it was sliced the tires to the truck. If I hadn't had a helo on call, we'd have been screwed. As it was, we'd barely gotten off the ground when another truck drove up."

"Did you get a good look at them?"

"Three guys got out of the truck. One was tall and blond, the other two were shorter, with dark hair. We were too high up to pick out details."

At least that meant it was unlikely that the guys on the ground could see Ray any better in the helicopter. Okay, maybe Ray could live awhile longer.

Todd pondered the situation. "Okay, I'll do some

checking and see if I can pick up any chatter from out
west. If necessary, I'll do some damage control. Right
now I've got to get back to work."

He wadded up the rest of his lunch, no longer hungry. "Go get your nose fixed."

Wouldn't want the man to look bad for his own fu-
neral.

In the distance, a flare of light and a wisp of smoke
caught D.J.'s eye. If he had to guess, someone was setting up camp. Good. If his quarry had stopped for the
night, this would be his best chance to catch up with
them. With his night vision, he could keep moving even
if both of Kalithia's cursed stars disappeared behind the
horizon.

He kept a wary eye on his surroundings. There was
no way to know if he'd managed to hide his presence
from Reggie's captors. If he were them, he'd have one
guy set up camp while the other hung back to watch the
trail just in case someone had crossed over into Kalithia
intent on rescuing Reggie.

As he walked, he studied the terrain ahead. If he
were setting the trap, he'd be waiting just past where
the trail wound up and over the side of the last hill over-
looking the valley beyond. The trail ran along the edge
of a rocky drop-off that would funnel him right toward
where he hoped they were resting.

Options. He needed options. His Glock would allow
him to kill from a distance. The downside was that the

noise would alert any other Kalith in the area. A knife would be silent, but he'd have to get within cutting distance of the enemy.

He opted for skirting around the back side of the hill even though it would take him some distance off the trail. If he was reading the terrain correctly, he'd come out behind where they might be waiting. With luck, the enemy would be too intent on watching for him on the trail to notice that he was staging a little trap of his own.

The hike took him over some rough ground, leaving him breathing hard. When his pulse slowed to normal, he drew his Glock and crept forward to where he could look down on the trail. At first glance, he didn't see any hint of the enemy, but his instincts were screaming that someone was out there.

The night settled around him, the darkness getting thicker with each passing minute. A movement in the grass caught his attention. He continued to stare at the spot, trying to decide if the shadows there truly did have more substance than the surrounding ones.

Oh, yeah. The bastard was there all right, the blade of his weapon catching the faint glow of the moons rising in the sky above. D.J. resisted the temptation to use his gun to blow the Other to hell and back. If he could actually capture the guy, maybe he'd be able to learn more about the situation he'd be walking into before he reached the campfire in the distance.

D.J. bent low and started forward, his gun in one hand, sword in the other. The blade would be his first choice of weapons, but he couldn't risk the Other getting the upper hand with Reggie depending on D.J. to rescue her.

The Other rose up to look around. Had the guy decided that he'd only been imagining someone dogging his footsteps? Maybe, because after ducking down briefly, the Other stood again to stare up the trail. After a few seconds, he started forward, his sword at the ready. D.J.'s prey moved slowly, his head sweeping from side to side, testing the night air and hunting using his sense of smell.

It was easy to know the instant the male picked up D.J.'s scent. The Other froze in midstep, slowly bringing his sword up into attack position. From where D.J. stood, he could take the Other out with a single shot. Tempting as it was, D.J. holstered his gun and followed the Kalith, Larem's sword in his hand.

He was able to get surprisingly close before the guy realized he was no longer alone. He'd started backing up, only to realize that his prey stood right behind him.

D.J.'s predatory nature had him smiling. "Looking for me?"

The Other didn't hesitate but spun and charged forward, swinging his sword in an arc designed to slash D.J.'s head from his shoulders. He blocked the blow with his own blade and shoved the bastard back a few steps.

D.J. taunted his opponent. "Tsk, tsk, is this how you usually greet guests in Kalithia? I didn't see any of us trying to kill you while you were in my world."

He went on the attack as he spoke. "Of course, I

would've skewered both you and your buddy had I gotten the opportunity."

The tip of his blade sliced open the Other's cheek. Blood flowed in dark contrast to his pale skin, but the wound was more painful than serious.

"Did I mention that was my woman you kidnapped?" D.J. danced forward and marked the male's other cheek the same way. "Tell me who has her and why, and I promise to ease your passing."

The Other rejoined the battle, doing his own fair share of taunting in heavily accented English. "You will die screaming in my world, Paladin. I will celebrate your death by taking your woman to my pallet. I have already tasted her kiss and held her body against mine."

D.J. fought to control his burning fury, knowing cold hate served him better in a battle to the death. He studied his opponent's technique. The Other was good, but not great. No way this guy had the skills of a Sword Guardian. He might get lucky, but he'd never defeat D.J. on skill alone.

One thing was clear. The Other wouldn't offer any useful information, not unless D.J. subdued him long enough to use some creative interrogation techniques. There wasn't time for that, and it was doubtful the information would be reliable anyway.

But from the increasing panic in the guy's fighting style, the dance was about to turn lethal. So far, D.J. had managed to stay out of striking distance, but it was going to come down to stamina or bad luck.

With a bellow loud enough to wake the dead, the

Other charged one last time, nicking D.J.'s sword arm and then shoving him backward. D.J. ignored the stinging pain and pushed back, causing the Other to lose his footing right at the edge of the drop-off.

For a handful of slow-motion seconds the Other hovered there, his arms pinwheeling until he finally lost his balance and went flying backward over the edge. His scream echoed through the valley, only to be cut off in midnote when his body crashed into the rocks below.

D.J. peered over the edge in a futile attempt to determine if the Other was still breathing. All he could tell was that the Kalith wasn't moving. Rather than wasting his time climbing down to make sure, D.J. opted for retrieving his pack and taking off down the trail after Reggie.

If the Other's dying scream had carried as far as the campfire, his partner might panic. At the very least, he'd be waiting for D.J. now, most likely armed and ready to use Reggie as a hostage.

This time, D.J. wouldn't hesitate to use the Glock. He ran full out, grateful for the boots that Barak had loaned him. They made little noise as he tore through the darkness. As he ran, he ignored the pain in his arm, his near exhaustion, and his lungs' struggle to filter enough oxygen from the thin air.

All that mattered was getting to Reggie.

Chapter 13

*H*er captor was practically twitching with nerves. So far, Jeban had been the calm one, but with Kolar gone so long, he paced restlessly, stopping every so often to listen to the night.

She knew the instant he sensed something because he turned in her direction, his pale eyes reflecting the flames of the campfire. His hand hovered over the pommel of his sword, as if unsure about drawing his weapon. What had he heard that had him so freaked out? Rather than sit there on the ground, she rose to her feet, not sure what she intended to do. But whatever was about to happen, she'd face it head-on.

"What's wrong, Jeban?" she asked, even though she doubted he'd actually answer. "Are your friends coming?"

He shook his head. "They aren't due until late tomorrow afternoon. Kolar went hunting. It appears he found something."

No, not something. Someone.

The two of them stood staring off into the darkness. She didn't know about Jeban, but she couldn't see much of anything beyond the circle of flickering light cast by the campfire. She tried closing her eyes, hoping that she'd be able to hear better that way.

After a few seconds of continued silence, a horrifying scream ripped through the night, only to be cut off abruptly, unfinished. The night grew quiet again, but this time with a feeling of building tension. Jeban didn't hesitate. He drew his sword and then yanked Reggie close to his side, the blade at her throat.

"I would guess the hunt has ended," he whispered near her ear. "The question is, which hunter was successful?"

With the cold steel against her skin, Reggie could neither talk nor even swallow for fear the sword would draw blood. Her instincts told her that someone had died up there on the trail. There was nothing to do now but wait and pray that the footsteps running through the night belonged to D.J. and not Kolar.

Time came to a screeching halt. For an eternity, it was just her, Jeban, and the pounding of her heart. Her captor had turned to stone, his body stiff with anticipation. His gaze remained trained on some invisible point in the impenetrable darkness beyond. What was he sensing that she wasn't? Wave after wave of chills washed through her, fear quickly eroding her self-control.

Please, God, she didn't want to die alone in this alien world, but neither would she go down without fighting.

Calling upon all her years of training, she yanked her focus away from the anxiety churning in her chest and on to the externals.

She could hear her sensei's gravelly voice in her head. *Breathe in and breathe out, slow and steady. Control yourself even if you cannot control the situation.*

Good advice. As she gradually calmed down, she realized there was now a hairbreadth more room between her neck and Jeban's blade. If he so much as flinched, she'd go on the attack, using her bare hands if necessary.

Suddenly, she could make out the vague shape of someone coming toward them. One minute the trail was empty, and the next, as if forming from the darkest of the shadows themselves, a man stepped into the farthest reaches of the firelight. He wore all black and a Kalith cloak, the hood pulled down close to his face.

Her heart sank as he calmly strode toward them, everything about him screaming that he didn't doubt his welcome. At first glance, she assumed it was Kolar. But then she looked again. After hours of trailing the Kalith, she knew how Kolar moved. And this wasn't him. She was sure of it.

The weight of the silence pressed down on her, making it hard to breathe and even harder to hope. If something had happened to Kolar, it didn't necessarily translate to this guy being on her side.

Jeban shifted his weight, the first movement he'd made since he'd grabbed her. She leaned in the opposite direction, but he only tightened his hold.

Then he rattled off something in his native language. Whatever he said, it clearly wasn't meant to be friendly. The newcomer showed no reaction at all, instead continuing his approach without a break in his step. If he was at all worried, it sure didn't show.

Jeban spoke again, this time clearly in warning. He was growing more agitated by the newcomer's refusal to answer because he once again pressed the blade of his sword against Reggie's neck.

"I *will* kill her." This time he spoke in English.

The hooded figure paused a short distance away and tossed the edge of his cloak back over his shoulders as he drew his weapon. A Kalith sword. Then she saw the gun in his other hand.

For the first time the new arrival spoke. "If she dies, so will you, and it will be a death without honor. You will die screaming for mercy, just as your buddy did."

"Who are you?" Jeban demanded as he dragged Reggie back a few steps.

The stranger followed them, step for step. Then he tipped his head back and let the hood drop onto his shoulders. He was no stranger after all, at least not to her.

"Reggie, has this bastard or his dead partner hurt you?" D.J.'s dark eyes met hers, promising retribution if they had.

"I'll be all right now," she whispered around the pressure of the blade on her throat. "I knew you'd come."

Her captor didn't like that remark one bit. His hand

dropped from her throat to her breast. "Tell me, human, is she really that good that you risk dying for the chance to have her underneath you again?"

Did Jeban see his own death reflected in the Paladin's angry gaze? Reggie hoped so. She might not survive the night, but at least the two men who had dragged her into this hellish world would pay for their crimes.

Then she realized that Jeban was now pointing his sword toward D.J. rather than at her. This might be her one chance to break his hold on her. She slowly blinked three times right at D.J. and then slowly tilted her head to the side, trying to convey her intent. The corner of his mouth twitched up in a small smile.

"So, tell me, Other, do you prefer death by bullet or blade? This sword was loaned to me by a Kalith friend, if you're curious. Didn't want you to think I stole it off your dead friend."

As soon as Jeban started to respond, Reggie lunged to the side, dropping to roll out of his reach and leave him an open target for D.J. The Kalith charged after her, his sword raised and ready to slash down in a lethal arc. She had instinctively held up her arm to block the blow when a series of shots rang out. Jeban's murderous fury evolved into a look of stunned surprise as his life ended in a burst of blood and brains.

Pure panic took over as Reggie stared at the aftermath. Jeban lay sprawled on the ground, crumpled and broken. His unseeing eyes stared at her in dead bewilderment as someone screamed loud and long. Even when she realized that she was making all the noise, she couldn't seem to stop. It went on and on, ripping her throat raw.

Damn, D.J. hadn't meant for Reggie to catch the brunt of the Other's death. But if he'd delayed even a second longer to see if she could get out of range, the Other could've gutted her with his sword. Why the fucker had gone after her instead of D.J. was a mystery, unless he thought to hurt D.J. in the worst way possible by taking her life.

If Reggie had to end up covered in gore, at least it was the Other's. D.J. paused to cover the body with the guy's own cloak before kneeling down to wrap Reggie in his arms. She buried her face against his chest, still keening her pain and fear.

"Shhh, honey, it's over for now. I've got you. You're safe."

Slowly, her sobs slowed down and then stopped. But when she tried to wipe away the tears on her cheeks, her hands came away covered in blood.

She held out her bloody palms, her hysteria ramping up again. "Get it off! Please get it off!"

He'd love to accommodate her, but he had to priori- tize what came next. He caught her hands in his as he looked around the Kaliths' camp.

"I will take care of this, but it will have to wait until I make sure there aren't any more of these bastards in the immediate vicinity. By the looks of things, this place was set up for more than just the two of them and you."

Reggie looked back toward the shrouded figure on the ground with a shudder.

"Jeban said the rest would be here late tomorrow." Her words came out in hiccups as she fought to control the sobs.

"Good. That's real good, Reggie. Okay, I'll go back and get some water. The creek I passed is some distance away, but I promise I'll haul ass. Will you be all right alone while I'm gone?"

"No, wait." She held out a shaky hand to point in the opposite direction. "Past the tents. There's water that way."

Better yet. "Good, we'll go wash all of that off you."

He picked her up and carried her over to the side of a quiet pool of water that fed into a narrow stream. After setting her back down, he rooted through his pack for something Reggie could use to clean up with. A spare shirt would have to do. He tore off a strip to use as a washcloth while keeping the rest for a makeshift towel.

Then he tested the temperature of the water with his hand.

"The water is clear but a little cold." He considered their options, none of them good. Best to just get on with it.

"Reggie, your clothes are covered in blood, so I need you to strip them off. Afterward, you can cover up with my cloak and sit by the fire while I wash out your clothes and hang them up to dry."

She nodded, but her hands were shaking too hard to manage by herself. D.J. reluctantly took over, starting with her shoes and then working his way up to her tunic and trousers. Yeah, he'd been wanting to get Reggie naked, but not like this.

For both their sakes, he left her bra and panties in place for her to deal with. He did his honorable best not to notice how her nipples pebbled up in the evening chill or the way her narrow waist gave way to the gentle flare of her hips. God, he was a bastard for even thinking about such things.

He held out the pieces of his shirt. "You're good to go. Use these to wash up."

Then he noticed a dark streak caught up in the curls of her hair. When he touched it, his hand came away bloody.

"Uh, looks like you need to wash your hair, too."

Her eyes widened in horror as the implication of what he was saying sank in. "How am I going to do that from the edge of the water?"

She was right. "Maybe a quick rinse won't get the job done. Maybe you should just go for broke and take a quick bath."

Reggie studied the dark sheen of the water suspiciously, but finally she nodded. "All right, if you think it's safe."

"It should be," he assured her, mentally crossing his fingers. "Give me a second so I can see what kind of supplies I have that you can use."

He dumped the pack out on the ground and studied the contents: shampoo, a toothbrush, a bar of soap, and even a spare tunic. Damn, Devlin and Barak had thought of everything.

He arranged the items on a flat rock next to the edge of the water. "Here you go, Reggie. I'll turn my back, but I'll stay close by in case you need me."

He did as promised, but listened to make sure she was doing all right. The rustle of fabric sliding down skin, the almost silent plop of something dropping on the ground, and then the splash of water, followed by a bloodcurdling squeal.

What the hell? He spun back around, gun in hand and ready to defend her against all comers. Except no one was there except a totally nude Reggie, standing thigh deep in the water and glaring back at him.

"I thought you said the water was just a little cold!"

He tried not to laugh, he really did. But she was so cute, standing there naked and absolutely furious. She had no idea how clearly he could see in the dark, so she wasn't trying to cover up. At least the little lost girl was gone, momentarily replaced by her usual feisty nature.

"Yeah, I may have exaggerated a bit on that point," he said, trying to sound apologetic and failing miserably.

"You think, you big jerk?"

She gave him a disgusted look and then gingerly waded out farther into the water. "Remind me to get even with you for this."

"Yes, ma'am." He turned his back again, more to keep her from realizing that he was having a hard time not laughing rather than from any sense of decorum.

It didn't take her long to bathe. When she started to wade back out of the water, he backed toward her and held out his cloak. "Dry off with the shirt as best you can. I found a spare tunic you can put on and then you can wrap yourself in the cloak."

"Thanks."

More rustling, then she said, "I'm freezing, but at least I'm clean."

"That's the spirit. We'll get you to the fire, and then I'll come back and rinse these out."

"Before you go to all that trouble, let's check the supplies Jeban—"

As soon as she said the name, her eyes shot past D.J. to the dead Other's body. She swallowed hard and tried again.

"They had supplies we can look through."

He nodded. "Let's get you situated first."

Then, before she could protest, he swept her off her feet again to carry her across the camp, setting her down so that her back was to the body. He ran over to his pack and brought back one of the space blankets. He peeled open the package and unfolded the silvery fabric.

"This will help keep you warm."

He waited until she was settled and then added additional wood to the fire. He'd have to find more before turning in for the night.

But first he had to get rid of the body. He probably should bury the Other, but he wasn't going to waste the energy. Right now, he had more important things to do. Grunting from the effort, he hefted the Other up and over his shoulder and carried him off into the darkness.

He set the corpse down in between a cluster of rocks and some scrubby trees. Would anyone miss this guy?

Maybe. Once they were back across the barrier, he'd get word to Berk so that he could locate the two dead Others if he wanted to retrieve the bodies.

Satisfied that he'd done as much as he could for the dead, D.J. walked away. Time to focus on the living.

Chapter 14

"*H*ey, kid, time to wake up."

A big hand landed on Cody's shoulder and shook it. Awareness came rushing back as he fought his way up from oblivion. He wished he could've stayed there. Lately reality sucked. Blinking sleepily, he peered out into the darkness, trying to see where they were.

On the outskirts of Portland. Okay, he hadn't been asleep all that long.

"You back with me?" Trahern's voice rumbled in the cab of the truck.

"Yeah, I'm getting there."

Cody stretched to work out the kinks in his neck and get his blood flowing again.

"Sorry to conk out on you like that."

"Not a problem. I'd have let you sleep longer, but I need directions from here."

Cody glanced at the street sign on the side of the highway. "Two more exits north, go east."

Now that he was awake, he felt guilty. He was full, warm, and safe. Could the same be said for Reggie? Fear for his friend settled like a gray fog in his mind.

"Do you think she's okay? Reggie, I mean."

The Paladin glanced over at him. "Do you want the truth or platitudes?"

"The truth." He kept his eyes pointed toward the windshield, not wanting the big man to see his fear.

"I keep wondering how long a human can survive in that alien environment."

Trahern spoke in a matter-of-fact tone, but then evidently he'd been dealing with weird for a long time. "The air is thinner than ours, but breathable. The ecology is all fucked up because their suns are burning out, so the whole place is dim. Dusty and dry is how I would describe it."

"Sounds like you've spent time there."

Trahern's smile gleamed in the flash of another car's headlights. "I did. One of my buddies crossed over and met up with Barak's sister. She's what they call a Sworn Guardian, a warrior who polices their world with a squad of assistants. Everything went to hell in a handcart from there. Cullen helped her smuggle her two adopted kids back across to our side, but Lusahn got captured along with Larem, one of her Blademates. They were sentenced to die for betraying their kind."

Trahern quit talking while he cut across two lanes to the exit ahead. "Where to next?"

"Drive straight for the next ten blocks and then hang a left."

"Got it. Anyway, Cullen, Barak, Lonzo, and I crossed back into Kalithia to rescue Lusahn and ended up dragging Larem back here, too. It was quite an adventure."

He paused as if considering his next words. "I have no idea why those two Others wanted to drag your friend into their world, but it can't be good. And why wait until now instead of when she first started playing cybergames with D.J.?"

Okay, that was a shocker. Reggie had been in contact with the Knightwalker for *months* and hadn't said anything? Right now he was too worried about her to be pissed that she'd been keeping secrets, but they'd definitely have words when she got home.

If she got home.

Trahern was waiting for him to speak. "She wasn't *playing*. We work for a company that does internet security for other companies. Someone just hired us to track down a hacker known as the Knightwalker."

"I take it that's D.J.'s alter ego?"

"Yeah, the Knightwalker is a legend among hackers, but Reggie never said she already knew who he was. I do know she hacked into the Regents' server and printed out a history of the Paladins. Maybe that's why."

Trahern looked disgusted. "I swear, every time we think we've cut the head off the snake, it grows two more."

What did that mean? Before Cody could ask, Trahern started talking again.

"We've had some problems in the organization lately. Greedy bastards robbing both worlds, that kind of thing.

As soon as we caught wind of it, we started hunting for everyone involved. Obviously, we've missed a couple. They may have wanted to stash Reggie over there where no one could find her until the heat dies down. That would make sense if somebody on this side is calling the shots."

Trahern's answer was no help at all. It just meant Reggie was in danger, but they already knew that. Frustration had Cody pounding his fist on his thigh.

"Damn it, I should've gone with D.J."

Trahern's big hand caught Cody fist in midswing. "No, you shouldn't have. To be brutally honest, until we get your fighting skills up to par, you'd be more of a hindrance than a help out in the field. It's damn hard to be stuck on the sidelines, but that's the hand you've been dealt. Believe me when I say that if I were Reggie, there's no one I'd rather have hunting for me than D.J. The man's fearless, and there aren't many who could best him at either tactics or weapons."

That might be true, but it didn't make it any easier to swallow. Glad for the excuse of giving directions to change the subject, Cody pointed out the windshield.

"That's my building over there."

Trahern parked the truck and climbed out, obviously planning to go inside with him. Cody really wished he wouldn't. His apartment was barely one step up from living on the streets, furnished with stuff he'd picked up at yard sales or sitting by Dumpsters.

"If you'd rather wait in the truck, I'll just take a minute."

Trahern shook his head. "Sorry, no can do. I prom- ised Devlin I'd stick to you like a tick."

The big man stopped inside the door of the building and looked around. "Cody, just so you know, a lot of us started off with nothing. Hell, I was living on the streets in St. Louis until I got lucky and ended up in the right judge's courtroom. Turns out he was a Regent and rec- ognized what I was.

"I'm not the only one either. D.J.'s story is his to tell, but it's not much better. Bottom line, you've got no rea- son to be embarrassed by where you live. Hell, you're going to college and have a good job. That's more than I was doing at your age. I'm impressed and I know Devlin is, too."

What could Cody say to that? It was hard to talk around the big lump in his throat.

"Then come on in. I'll throw a few things in my pack, and then we'd better get over to Reggie's place."

Half an hour later they were inside Reggie's apartment. Trahern had the same totally sick lock-picking skills that D.J. had. Cody couldn't help but admire the talent.

"Is breaking and entering a standard part of the Pala- din training?"

Trahern chuckled. "Actually, I learned it on my own, but it still comes in handy once in a while. I'm sure we'll manage to squeeze it into your curriculum at some point."

"Cool."

As much as Cody had been looking forward to graduating, the future stretched out before him had looked pretty empty. Now it seemed as if the Paladins and the Regents might just fill in the gaping holes in his life. It felt damn good to hear Trahern, Devlin, and even D.J. talking about his future with them.

But now wasn't the time to be thinking about anything except getting Reggie home safe.

"I'm going to log into Reggie's e-mail and contact our boss. D.J. wanted me to pretend to be her and tell Mr. DeLuca she's sick and will be working from home for a few days."

"Good thinking, but what about you?"

"I'll tell him I've got finals. He won't question it unless I'm gone too long."

"When you're done, pack up her laptop to take with us. Meanwhile, I'll see if I can't forward her phone numbers to our Seattle office so Cullen can monitor them."

It didn't take Cody long to send the e-mails. It almost felt as if he was turning in his resignation rather than just asking for a few days off. Who knew, maybe he was.

Trahern turned off the sole light they'd used. "Okay, I'm done. Let's hit the road. We still have a long way to go."

Not as far as Reggie did, but Cody kept that comment to himself.

Just as they reached the truck, Trahern's cell phone rang. After answering, he listened for several seconds.

"Yeah, Dev, we just finished up. We can be there in half an hour or so."

As he spoke, he stared over at Cody. Where would they be in half an hour? The last Cody had heard, they were heading back to the Paladin headquarters in Seattle, at least a four-hour drive.

"See you soon. Yeah, I'll tell him." Trahern disconnected the call. "Hope you're not afraid of heights."

"Not as far as I know. Why?"

"Dev pulled some strings and we're hitching a ride back to Seattle in a helicopter."

"Seriously?"

"Yeah. Are you down with that?"

Cody grinned. "Oh, yeah."

"Too bad it's dark out. The view of the Cascades and the volcanoes is seriously bitchin' from a chopper. But hang with us and eventually you'll get to see the mountains up close and personal from the air."

"Sounds like fun."

The other man's face turned grim. "I wish it was, Cody. I really wish it was."

When D.J. returned from disposing of the body, Reggie took one look at his empty hands and seemed to shrink in on herself. At least the horror in her eyes had faded to a more manageable level, leaving her looking washed out and tired. And so damn sad. When had she last slept?

At least she didn't ask him what he'd done with the Kalith's remains. Maybe she didn't care. More likely, she was just relieved that any reminders of what had just happened were now out of sight. Speaking of which, he headed back to the stream.

Kneeling down in the grass, he dumped all of her clothes into the water and let them soak for a few minutes. She was right about how cold it was. By the time he finished rinsing out her underwear, tunic, and pants several times each, his hands were damn near too numb to move.

He spread her clothing over some nearby bushes, but doubted they'd dry by morning. When he had them all arranged, he wiped his hands on his pants and looked around for something else to do. With a maelstrom of emotions churning in his chest, he didn't trust himself around Reggie right now. Part of him wanted to wrap her up in his arms, do his best to soothe her fears, and then kiss her until this nightmare was only a dim memory.

His other half wanted to shake her until her teeth rattled for getting herself mired in his world. Damn the woman. If only she'd listened to him. But she hadn't.

He skirted the edge of the camp, gathering some more firewood and at the same time acquainting himself with their surroundings. Rain must not be a problem because the Others had laid their pallets out on the ground with no shelter of any kind. How would Reggie react to sleeping in a dead man's bed? It wasn't like they had a lot of choice right now.

Here they both were, trapped in Kalithia and hoping like hell they lived long enough to tell the tale. Even if Reggie had the strength to hike her delectable ass back up to the cave tonight, it would be hours before Barak dropped the barrier again.

Nor would she be out of danger once they crossed back into their world, not if the humans involved were still flying under the radar. Besides, she lacked his night vision and moving in the dark increased the risk that she might stumble and fall. The whole situation made him crazy. Once again his eyes automatically sought her out.

Damn it, she was shivering again. He had to do something about that. Neither of them had eaten anything and keeping up their strength was important. He'd brought just a few things in his pack, but it would have to be enough to see them through until morning. After dropping the firewood in the pile, he sorted through their options for dinner. At least the dead Kalith had put water on to heat. That would help.

Oh, goodie. There was powdered chicken broth and freeze-dried stew. At the bottom of the pack, he found his own personal favorite, dried eggs. It was better than starving—maybe.

Ripping open a packet, he poured the bouillon into a cup of hot water, stirring as he carried it over to where Reggie sat. The whole time, she watched his every move with wary eyes, as if poised to run should he make a single wrong move.

Did she think he was going to come after her next? Yeah, sure, seeing someone shot to death was probably a new experience for her, but it was either kill the bastard or watch her die. She'd seemed awfully damn glad to see him earlier.

Had something happened to change that or was she just now really seeing him for what he was—a stone-cold killer? Maybe it was better if she was scared. Maybe then she'd listen the next time he told her to stay the fuck out of his life.

"Here. It's just chicken broth, but at least it's hot and will hold you until the stew is ready." He shoved the cup at her and then stalked off.

Reggie watched D.J. walk away as she wrapped her hands around the metal cup. The oppressive silence was getting to her. She'd never been one for camping, but back home, back in her real world, even the night had its own sounds.

Right now all she could hear was the crackle of the fire and the small noises D.J. made while fixing their meal. Intellectually, she knew the valley and hills were still out there beyond the firelight, but she couldn't see them; she couldn't even feel their presence. A city girl at heart, she was used to being surrounded by thousands, even millions, of souls.

Here in this alien place, there was just herself and D.J. From the way he was acting right now, she suspected he'd just as soon be alone. That hurt, but then she hadn't even thought to thank him for the things he'd done. Granted, her head was all muddled from everything that had happened, but at least he'd cared enough to come after her.

Would he forgive her for putting him in a position

where he had to kill two Kaliths? Personally, she'd been too busy freaking out to think about good manners. Hopefully, better late than never.

"D.J.?"

She waited for him to look at her before continuing.

"What?"

"I wanted to thank you for everything you've done." Then she held up the cup. "By the way, this broth is helping. You may have noticed that I'm pretty much a mess."

His dark eyes stared at her, his mood unfathomable from across the fire. His voice was gruff when he finally answered. "Not much of a surprise considering all you've gone through in the past twenty-four hours."

She wasn't alone in that. After all, he'd been caught up in the ugliness of the situation, too. "I'm not the only one. I'm so sorry you had to kill both of those guys."

He flinched as if she'd hit him, his jaw clenched tight. "I'm not."

"Not what?" Although she knew.

"I'm not sorry." He came closer. "I won't lose a single minute's sleep over those two dying. Good riddance, if you ask me."

"But—"

By now he was standing over her, his face a series of sharp angles and fury. "No buts, Reggie. Remember how curious you were about what a Paladin does? Well, now you know. We kill vermin like those two. Day in and day out, year after year, I wade through buckets of blood to protect our world from the crazy fuckers from this one. My friends and I fight with swords or axes or even our bare hands if it comes to that, but we get the job done."

He knelt down to stare right into her eyes. "And the funny part is, modern science says we share their DNA. That's why I can see in the dark."

Her mouth dropped open in shock. "But that means—"

He cut her off in midsentence. "Yeah, that means you've shared ice cream with someone who isn't completely human."

Then his gaze zeroed in on her mouth. "Not to mention that you actually kissed a freak."

She couldn't listen to this. "No matter what you say, you're nothing like them."

"Lie to yourself if you need to, Reggie, but don't say I didn't warn you."

He rose back up and grabbed the pommel of the sword he wore at his side. Then with a look of total frustration, he shoved it back down in the sheath and walked away again.

"D.J.?" she whispered, his words still battering her mind like heavy fists.

He looked back at her. "Look, just forget I said anything."

Heck no. Despite his claim to the contrary, it was clear that the deaths had affected him whether he admitted it or not. So did his supposed alien DNA. Also obvious was the fact that someone in the past had rejected him for that very reason. Sure, she was shocked by his revelation, but who wouldn't have been? It wasn't as if she'd even heard of this world before yesterday.

No matter how tired she was, he wasn't going to get by with convicting her of crimes she hadn't committed. She gathered the cloak around her and followed D.J. over to where he bent down to stir the pot he'd scavenged from the Kaliths' supplies.

When her shadow fell over him, he looked up. "What do you want now?"

"An apology."

He dropped the spoon in the pot as he jerked back upright to tower over her. "Just how the hell do you figure I owe you an apology? I'm not the one who got herself kidnapped and dragged into an alien world. You should be grateful that you're not currently sharing one of those pallets with those two aliens."

Okay, if he wanted to be a jerk, fine. She didn't back away an inch.

"You're right, and I already told you that I was grateful. But for the past hour you've been acting like I just kicked your puppy or stole your lollipop."

She tightened her hold on the cloak. "I am sorry that I ever tried to track you down, and I'm sorry I didn't listen when you warned me off. But don't accuse me of crimes I didn't commit. Kiss or no kiss, yes, it came as a shock that you *might* have some alien DNA. Considering that I didn't know it was even possible until five minutes ago, maybe you could cut me some slack."

"There's no might about it, Reggie."

She poked him in the chest with her finger. "But I'm

guessing you're jumping to conclusions about how I'd react based on someone else's sins, and I don't appreciate it."

Maybe she was mistaken, but the gleam in his chocolate brown eyes had taken on a whole different meaning. Maybe a tactical retreat was in order. At this point, she wasn't sure what they were really fighting about or why. But their tempers were both definitely running hot, maybe because focusing on D.J. kept her from thinking about anything else.

He matched her retreat step for step. "Where are you going, Reggie? I thought you wanted an apology."

"I changed my mind."

His eyes flicked past her to where Jeban had spread out pallets on the ground. "I wouldn't want us to go to bed mad at each other."

The image of the two of them sharing a bed popped into her head. Okay, she was not going there. "Look, I'm not mad anymore. Besides, I think maybe the stew is burning. You might want to check on it."

"I can always make more."

He wasn't so much walking as prowling, and there was no doubt who was his prey.

"D.J." She used his name as a warning, holding up her hand to stop him.

"Reggie." He made hers sounded like a purr, warming up the night—and her—with his deep voice.

"There's no time for this."

That was a lie. They had all night. As crazy as it was, she wanted his touch to drive away her fear and to hold her nightmares at bay. She stopped retreating.

"Tired of running?" D.J. sounded disappointed as he twined a strand of her hair around his fingers. "Or are you planning on using some of your fancy martial-arts moves on me?"

Her sensei would be bitterly disappointed to find out that the thought hadn't even occurred to her. But then, alien blood or not, the threat D.J. posed to her wasn't physical, but emotional. She had no moves, fancy or otherwise, to protect herself from that.

"Not unless you force the issue."

Okay, his smile was driving her crazy. This time his fingertips followed the curve of her throat, down and down, to lightly trace the valley between her breasts. The ache that followed in the wake of his touch melted the last bit of her resistance.

She held the cloak closed with one hand and used the other one to do some touching of her own. Ever aware of the difference in their heights, she rose up on her toes to brush her fingers over his sexy mouth. "Are you going to kiss me?"

He nipped at her fingertips, his smile heating up yet another notch—or ten. "Got a thing for aliens, do you?"

That again? "Yeah, D.J., I just love little green men."

His breath teased her skin as he leaned down close to her ear and whispered, "Sorry to disappoint, but you can see I'm not green, and I'll be happy to prove to you that I'm not little."

Now there was an image guaranteed to fry her brain. For the first time in hours she was warm. Hot even. Feeling alive.

The rough fabric of the cloak chafed her skin. Even the night air felt heavy.

She leaned into D.J.'s strength, drawing in the scent of his skin. In the past, she'd always been cautious around men, reluctant to trust and even more reluctant to surrender. But here, in the small circle of light from the fire, they lived in a world of two. All that mattered were their rules, their choices, their needs.

And right now, she needed this man to help ground her, to stop the fear of what lurked out there in the shadows.

"Kiss me."

Chapter 15

*R*eggie wasn't asking him a question, but issuing an order. It was a shame she hadn't yet met Devlin because the big guy could tell her all about how well D.J. took orders. He always got the job done, but he did it in his own time and in his own way. Guess she'd have to learn that lesson on her own.

First things first. Where should they stage this little party? The handful of pallets were scattered around the clearing.

He kissed her cheek. "Hold that thought. I'll be right back."

He dragged two of the makeshift beds close together near the fire and then spread the third and fourth on top for good measure. With each only little better than a couple of thin blankets, they wouldn't offer much by way of cushioning. Under the circumstances, he'd play the gentleman and make sure he was the one who ended up with rocks digging into his ass.

Next, he took the blanket Reggie had dropped and used it to cover the nest he was building. He turned back the top edge, hoping it would look inviting. Then he pulled the stew off the fire but left it where it would stay warm. For later. A lot later.

Okay, back to Reggie. With luck she hadn't changed her mind, although he wouldn't blame her if she had. A woman like her deserved to be courted and then seduced, not subjected to a quick tumble only hours after she'd been kidnapped and threatened with far worse.

D.J. made his approach slowly, watching her for any hint of reluctance. The final decision would be hers, even if it killed him. Considering how hard he was at the moment, it just might. Hot damn, she was so perfect and petite. With her hair tumbling down her shoulders in soft waves and her pretty bare feet peeking out from the bottom of the cloak, she was temptation itself.

Her eyes stared past him, right at the bed he'd made, her normally expressive face impossible to read. He coasted to a stop just out of reach.

"Should I make another bed for myself?"

He was impressed with how calm he sounded. The thought of sleeping alone made him want to howl with frustration, but she'd already had enough of men dragging her around. As he waited for her answer, all he could hear was the snap, crackle, and pop of the fire. Well, that and the pounding of his heart.

"You'd really do that, wouldn't you?" she murmured.

He nodded, although she'd sounded as if she were talking more to herself. At long last, her eyes sought his. The heat in their depths had nothing to do with the fire, her smile a funny mix of caution and fearlessness. In a move that stunned him stupid, she let the cloak slide to her feet. Then she shimmied out of the tunic, leaving her wearing nothing but the dim glow of moonlight on her skin.

"You still haven't kissed me."

It was hard to talk with his tongue dragging on the ground. "Sorry, my bad."

Then he leaned toward her to correct that omission.

As soon as D.J. touched her, she melted. The man was big and powerful and scary, but she'd never felt so safe, so cherished, as when he folded her in his arms. His mouth took hers in a simple kiss. A claiming, to be sure, but so gentle.

Who would've thought a man who charged through life at a dead run could slow down to linger over a moment like this one?

His hands worshipped her as they skimmed across her shoulders and down her back. The sweet sensation made her sigh, and D.J. deepened the kiss. The tip of his tongue staged a foray between her lips, sampling a quick taste before retreating.

She smiled against his mouth and did some exploring of her own. The play of their tongues stoked the growing heat, first in her breasts and then deep in her belly and at the juncture of her thighs.

"Hold on," he breathed between kisses.

Then his hands cupped her bottom, lifting her up high against his chest. She dug her fingers into his shoulder muscles and wrapped her legs around his hips. The soft fabric of his trousers did next to nothing to disguise his impressive desire for her.

She wanted his clothes off. She tugged at the hem of his tunic. "Get rid of these. Now, D.J. Sooner if possible."

He grinned. "Mind if I put you down first?"

"I thought you'd never ask."

He kicked the silver blanket back and then settled her down in the bed he'd prepared. Then he yanked off his tunic, followed by the T-shirt he wore underneath it. Reggie propped herself up on her elbows to enjoy the view. It was flat-out amazing, and not just because the man was seriously ripped under all those clothes.

Her past experience, limited as it was, had always been indoors and under the covers. But here they were, outside, under the moons of this alien sky, surrounded not by walls but by a circle of firelight. Its soft dancing glow highlighted the lean lines of D.J.'s body, showing off his sculpted muscles.

And he hadn't been bragging. There was nothing small about him. Anywhere. In fact, impressive didn't do the man justice. Imagine, all that scrumptiousness just for her. Oh, yeah, this was going to be good.

When every stitch of his clothing was gone, D.J. picked up his wallet and pulled out a single foil packet.

Looking disappointed, he dropped it beside the pallet. "I'll be back in a minute."

The view of him walking away made the delay almost bearable. He dumped his pack out again and rooted through the stuff scattered on the ground. Then he grinned at her and held up three more packets before starting back over to her.

She tried to keep her eyes focused on his, but finally gave in to the temptation to check him out from top to toes. When he realized what she was doing, he slowed down and then did a slow turn just for her benefit.

It felt good to laugh. It would feel even better to get her hands on him. "Stop preening and get back here."

"Hey, now, Paladins don't preen."

"Yeah, right. I know preening when I see it."

He looked mildly insulted, which made her giggle again. Finally, he gave in and grinned back.

"It's nice to see you smile again, Reggie."

The packets joined the other one where they'd be within easy reach. D.J. stretched out beside her.

His smile faded as he cupped her cheek with his hand. "You still all right with this?"

Darn him, he was making her think—the last thing she wanted to do right now. Yes, she still wanted him. The question was, why? Was she using him just to buy a few hours of oblivion? Not entirely.

Whatever he was seeing in her eyes had him sitting up and reaching for the boxers he'd tossed in the dust. She caught his hand in hers. He tugged it free.

"Reggie, I'm not going anywhere, even if all you need is for me to hold you all night long. But if that's what you want, I'm going to need something other than just my good intentions between us unless you want me to sleep somewhere else."

He really was a hero, one she craved right now with an amazing intensity.

"I want you right here, right now." She captured his hand again and pressed a kiss to his fingertips. "Yes, in part because you—this—will drive away all thoughts of what's happened. If that was all it was, though, I'd take you up on the offer to cuddle."

"But?"

She straddled his lap, opening herself up to him in more ways than one. Running her fingers through his thick hair, she smiled into his dark eyes.

"As long as we both know going in that what we share is just for tonight—no questions, no promises— then I want this."

Before he could marshal any more arguments, she kissed him again. And again.

It was as if she'd touched a spark to dry tinder. D.J. claimed her mouth with a searing kiss as his hands roamed over her body, touching, testing, teasing. She loved the tickle of his chest hair against her already sensitive breasts.

He thrust up against her, rubbing his erection against her core, the friction making her beg for more as he palmed her breasts. She broke off the kiss and arched back to offer him easier access.

"Like that, do you?" he asked just before he captured her nipple with his lips.

"God, yes."

He chuckled, the vibration echoing through her body. He took his time, making sure each breast got equal attention. As much as she loved it, she needed more. If he didn't lay her down and take her fast and hard and soon, she wouldn't be responsible for her actions.

To focus his attention in that direction, she wrapped her fingers around his shaft and slid her hand up and down slowly. When he closed his eyes and groaned, she did it again, this time picking up speed and using her other hand to cup his sac.

"Hey, lover, guess what I want?"

He didn't bother to answer, but stretched out on his back, carrying her with him. She pushed herself back upright, loving the feel of her body centered right over his. It still wasn't enough. She wanted him in her. On her. Now.

"D.J., please."

She rolled to the side and tried to take him with her. Considering the difference in their relative sizes, she should've known better. They ended up laying on their sides, facing each other.

The heat in his expression gave her the shivers, especially when he lifted her leg up over his hips so his wicked, wicked fingers could slide over her damp folds. When one slipped deep inside her, her muscles clamped down hard, the tension building. Once again she tried unsuccessfully to pull him over her.

He pressed a kiss against her damp skin. "Hold that thought."

• • •

In his hurry to get back to Reggie, he fumbled with the packet, dropping it twice before he finally managed to handle the situation. Thank goodness it was a warm night. He hadn't made love in the great outdoors since he'd been a randy teenager with no better place to take his girlfriend.

And he should be kicked for thinking about anyone other than the beauty waiting for him to come back to her. Reggie was propped up on her elbows, waiting and watching him. She smiled and held out her hand in clear invitation. The skin-to-skin contact was electrifying as he joined her on the makeshift bed. Damn, this was going to be good.

When she laid back, he had to ask, "Are you sure you don't want to be on top? These blankets won't offer much of a cushion."

Her smile would've put the sirens to shame. "I'm betting you'll make sure I won't even notice."

Well, all right then. "I'm always up for a challenge."

He placed her hand right where it needed to be to prove his point. Her eyes twinkled.

"Braggart! You're definitely up all right, but let's see some action."

He liked that she wasn't afraid to make her own demands clear. But that didn't mean he was in a big hurry to meet them, not when there was so much more to learn about her. He caught her wandering hands in his as he made a slow journey down her body, starting with kissing that sassy mouth. He worshiped her sweet breasts with soft flicks of his tongue, pausing to blow gently on them and smiling as the tips pebbled.

Moving down, her stomach was soft and warm. He rested his face there briefly, memorizing the scent of her skin. He parted her legs as he stared up into her pretty eyes, before slowly lowering his mouth to learn her most intimate secrets. She whimpered. He smiled and tasted her again.

"D.J.!"

There was a husky note in her voice that hadn't been there before, a hunger that rang out as he drove her on and on. He stopped just short of the finish line, wanting to share that first moment of triumph with her.

He settled into the cradle of her body, careful to take most of his weight on his elbows. He loved the way they fit together despite their differences. Or maybe because of them. It didn't matter why this was so perfect, just that it was.

He rocked against her, preparing to go deep. "Honey, you'd better hold on tight."

She immediately brought her legs high up around his hips as he thrust forward, seating himself in her slick heat. Reggie immediately arched up, taking him even deeper. God, it felt like heaven, like home. He shuddered with the need to cut loose, but he wanted to give her a chance to adjust to his abrupt invasion.

When Reggie trailed her fingertips down his back to dig into his backside, his restraint shattered. Plunging deep, again and again, until all he knew was motion and heat and the need to claim this woman completely, making her his own.

D.J. was all sleek power as he drove her on relentlessly. Her control was shot and her sanity gone. All that was left was this burning need to take what he gave her and give it back tenfold. Despite his overpowering strength, he didn't use it against her but gave her his best.

His face was set in harsh lines, the red-gold light of the fire reflected in his eyes. She reached up to cup his face, coaxing him down for a kiss, their tongues mating in counterpoint to the rhythm of their bodies.

Then he swiveled his hips hard. Once, twice, three times, until she was conscious only of where their bodies were joined and the powerful storm building inside her. With a shout like a crack of thunder, D.J. pounded harder, pouring everything he was into her. Her own climax rolled through her, starting deep inside and spreading outward in a cataclysm that left her unsure of where she left off and D.J. began.

D.J. yelled her name. She whispered his. And then silence.

Hours later, the sky was growing lighter. D.J. wished like hell it wouldn't. Normally, he wasn't much for sleeping in, but then it wasn't every day that he woke up with a beautiful woman curled up beside him.

A *naked*, beautiful woman.

There were good reasons for that. He never knew when he'd get called out, which raised questions he couldn't answer. Like all Paladins, he had a cover story to explain what he did for a living, not to mention his frequent disappearances. Missing a date because he was dead wasn't something he'd ever wanted to tell someone. Besides, the effort it took to maintain the lies was exhausting, and most of the women he'd met weren't worth it.

Now that he thought about it, Reggie was his first lover who knew what he was, even if she didn't quite believe the whole alien DNA thing. He hated that she'd actually seen him in action. She was a kick-ass woman in her own right, but she didn't deserve to be ensnared in the violence of his world. If she'd had any romantic illusions about what the Paladins did for a living, they were well and truly shattered now.

If only he could erase those ugly memories for her. Last night, he'd done his best to give her better things to think about. Despite the less than stellar accommodations, making love to her had been spectacular. Afterward, he'd slept better than he had in ages. It wasn't just the sex either, although that had certainly helped. Reggie not only challenged him on every level, she also soothed him.

But now wasn't the time to linger, not with the possibility of a passel of Kalith crazies heading right for them. They needed to get moving and soon. It was the smart thing to do, even if it was a crying shame.

Reggie stirred a bit as if trying to snuggle closer. Her

head was already tucked in under his chin, her soft-as-silk hair spread out over his chest and her leg flung over his, making him her willing prisoner. God knows, he didn't want to move.

If they reached the cave safely, they could easily be back in their own world by nightfall. That meant this might be the only moment they shared like this. If that were the case, he wanted to make sure it was memorable for both of them.

He eased Reggie over to the side, grinning when she frowned in her sleep and tried to climb right back on top of him. That would be fine if only she were awake enough to take charge of the situation.

When he trailed his hand down her spine to squeeze her adorable ass, her eyes popped open. She blinked several times, as if unsure of what she was seeing.

"D.J., what are you doing?"

He kissed her forehead. "If I have to explain, I must not be doing it right."

She yawned until her jaw cracked. "Sorry, but I'm not much of a morning person."

"Maybe that's because no one has ever shown you how much fun mornings can be with the right person."

Her eyes narrowed in suspicion. "And you're an expert on such things?"

Reggie deserved his honesty. "No, actually I'm not. I can't remember the last time I spent an entire night with a woman. Life doesn't lend itself to long-term commitments when you have to hide what you are. It's always easier to leave than to lie."

"Good answer, big guy. But tell me, do we really have time for this?"

Once again he settled for the truth. "Every minute we're here, the more likely we'll be discovered."

"Rain check then?"

Her obvious disappointment left a warm spot in his chest. "You got it. Now, we'd better get a move on."

He mustered up all his good intentions and extricated himself from the warm cocoon they'd shared. He snagged his boxers and pulled them on, the whole time eyeing the one remaining foil packet with regret.

After gathering up the rest of his Kalith clothing, he smiled down at Reggie. "I'll check on your clothes."

One touch and he knew he'd have to find her something else to wear with the tunic she'd worn the night before. Her underclothes were dry enough, but the pants she'd been wearing would make for a miserable day.

They'd take the clothes with them, though. No use leaving clues behind. He rooted through the supply cache that the Others had left behind. Score! He shook out the pants and held them up.

Looking over toward Reggie, he tried to gauge how they'd fit and had to laugh. Considering how petite she was, they'd have to cut them off at the knees.

He handed her the clothes he'd gathered. "I'll fetch some fresh water while you get dressed. We'll have to hack a couple of feet off the bottom of those pants before you put them on, though."

She looked insulted. "Very funny. I am not that short."

Yeah, she was, but he was smart enough not to argue the point. "I'll be back in a couple."

She waited until D.J. was out of sight to toss the covers aside. It was one thing to prance around naked in the darkness, daylight was quite another. At least her bra and panties were nearly dry. The tunic she'd tossed aside last night was covered in dust, but a couple of good shakes took care of that. And one look at the pants D.J. had found convinced her that he was right about cutting them off.

Yeah, she was on the short side, but those pants could've been made for an NBA star.

While she waited for D.J. to return, she made use of the comb he'd left out for her. Bless the man—he was doing his best to take care of her, a rarity in her life.

So was sleeping so soundly, especially considering the hell she'd been through the past couple of days. She was normally a light sleeper and didn't like sharing a bed with anyone. But right after they'd made love a third time, D.J. had kissed her good night and tucked her close to his side. That was the last thing she remembered until he'd coaxed her awake at first light.

But now the memories were flowing back, dark and ugly. With the suns coming up, there was no way to ignore the outside world. The interlude she and D.J. had shared had calmed her, even helped her heal, but suddenly she needed to be moving. Right now, before the Kalith came and found them.

D.J. was back. He took one look at her and frowned. "What's wrong?"

She crossed her arms over her chest, hoping to control her shaking hands. "We're running out of time."

"Yeah, we are, but I promise we'll be gone soon. I want to fix us a quick breakfast because we won't have another chance to stop before we reach the cave. While I do that, you can put the pallets back where we found them. Once we've eaten, we'll police the area to make sure we aren't leaving anything behind."

She loved a man with a plan. Especially this man. They both started in on the list of chores he'd outlined. She gathered up what trash she found and left it in a pile by the fire. Then she dragged the pallets back to their original positions. When she was done, D.J. held out a cup with a clump of something yellowish in it.

"Dried eggs," he said, answering her unspoken question. "Not exactly my favorite meal, but we need the protein."

She sniffed the cup and wrinkled her nose. "Uh, yum?"

He laughed as she choked it down. When they were both done, she held out the pants.

"Can you cut about a foot and a half off these? They must be extra, extra tall."

D.J.'s dark eyes twinkled, but he wisely said nothing as he pulled out a Swiss army knife. After holding the pants up to her to measure, he made a quick cut through the fabric and then ripped it the rest of the way. He added the leftover material to his pack.

She pulled the pants on. "How do I look?"

"Stunning," he said with a grin. "I can honestly say I've never been quite so attracted to anyone who was wearing Kalith clothing."

"Thanks, I think."

"It was meant as a compliment." He settled the pack on his back and then added the cloak. "Why don't you wait over on the trail itself while I do one last check. If the rest of the gang shows up here, hopefully they'll wait awhile before they start hunting for their two buddies."

Five minutes later, she fell into step behind D.J. and prayed they made it to the cave before anyone in this world spotted them. She hadn't hiked this much in years, or maybe ever. But at least D.J. adjusted his own stride so that she didn't have to struggle to keep up.

At first the going was pretty easy because the valley floor was fairly flat. As soon as they started toward the top of a small rise, D.J. stopped. He opened his bottle of water and offered her a drink.

"Wait here a minute."

Then with no further explanation, he walked a little farther ahead to peer over the edge of a sharp drop-off to the valley below. He frowned as he walked along staring at the ground. Watching him stroll along the edge gave her the heebie-jeebies. One false step and he could go plunging off, especially the way he was concentrating on the ground far below and not where he was walking.

She moved closer, careful not to startle D.J., who was growing more agitated as he paced back and forth.

Finally, he stopped long enough to look back the way they'd come, running his hands through his hair in frustration. "Damn it, this has to be the place."

"What place? What's wrong?"

Rather than answer right away, he bent down to study the ground. He trailed his fingers in the dust, frowned, and then moved on a few more steps.

"Damn it, this is bad. In fact, it's really bad."

He looked at her. "We need to move out. Now."

Reggie scurried to catch up with him. "Fine, but explain to me what's going on."

His head was swiveling from side to side like crazy, his energy level ramping up big time. "Last night, before I reached the camp where you were, the second Kalith was waiting over there to ambush me."

She nodded, trying not to think what would have happened to her if the ambush had been successful. Well, and to D.J., too.

"You told Jeban you'd killed his partner last night."

"Well, that's the problem. He actually fell over the cliff. I saw him go flying off, flapping his arms like wings as he fell."

Okay, too much information. "So?"

"So there's no sign of a body down there. Either someone found it or the bastard got up and walked off."

"You're sure this is the spot."

He nodded. "I had a feeling they'd try something of the sort, so I circled around behind this hill and spotted where he was hiding. We were fighting when he went over the edge."

He sounded disgusted. "It was too dark to see how badly he was hurt."

As the trail curved, she looked back. "No one could survive a fall like that."

D.J. got an odd look on his face. "I wouldn't bet on that, but whether or not he died is beside the point. Either he's up and moving or someone else found the body."

"So we could be walking into a trap?"

He nodded. "I'll look for someplace to stash you while I check out the trail. We have an alternative route we can use if we have to, but it's a lot farther and would mean we'd have to get by the Others your kidnappers were expecting."

She didn't like the sound of that idea. "I'd rather stay with you than get left behind."

The fact that she was sweating had nothing to do with the temperature of the air. Fear was eating big holes in her control.

"I'd rather keep you with me, too, but I don't want you to get caught in the middle of a swordfight if I can help it."

She was huffing pretty hard now. "Seriously? I'd rather neither of us got caught up in a swordfight."

He abruptly slowed his steps and looked back at her. "If I'm going too fast, say something. Why don't you wait here while I scout up ahead. Once I know it's clear sailing, I'll wave to you."

She didn't want to agree, but she definitely needed a moment to catch up on her oxygen supply. "Go ahead. I'll be fine."

Before he left her, he pulled out an automatic and handed it to her. "Don't hesitate to use this if you need to. I know you don't want to kill anyone, but trust me. These crazies won't hesitate to return the favor."

The metal surface of the gun was cold and smooth to the touch, and the grip fit her hand as if it had been custom-made for her. She hated that. Despite her self-defense training, she had no desire to use lethal force against anyone. Could she bring herself to even pull the trigger? For both their sakes, she hoped so.

D.J. disappeared around a bend in the trail. He'd told her to wait for him to signal, but she found herself creeping forward, hating that she couldn't see him anymore. She was on the brink of charging after him when he reappeared and waved.

Relieved, she picked up her pace. He was alternating between watching the valley below and the trail above as he waited for her.

"See anything?"

"Not yet. The dust in this place covers up trails pretty quickly, but I haven't seen any clear sign of anyone having gone up the trail recently."

"Clear sign? Does that mean you might have seen something?"

He shrugged. "It's hard to say. I saw some footprints pointed in that direction, but they didn't keep going."

That made sense. "Maybe they're from when Jeban backtracked to see if someone was following them. Us, I mean."

"I hope that's it." D.J. continued to stare up the trail.

"But if it is Jeban's buddy between us and the cave, there's no telling what he has planned. Regardless, we either need to get into the cave so we can cross into our world or we need to retrieve the supplies I left stashed up there."

He pointed back across the valley. "My friend Barak is from this world. He said there's another crossing point beyond that second ridge of hills across the valley. He also sent word to his Kalith friend Berk to be on the lookout for us."

"Can these guys be trusted?"

"Barak, absolutely, and Berk is a Sworn Guardian, which means a lot in this world. He's worked with us a couple of times and hasn't screwed us over yet. If he ever does—"

D.J. flexed his right hand on the pommel of his sword; his left held a gun that was the big brother to the one he'd given her. His stance positively shouted *God help anyone who crossed him.*

It was hard to see her gentle lover from the night before as the hard-edged man standing beside her now. The metamorphosis disturbed her on several levels, even though she'd seen this same side of him right before he'd killed Jeban. The question was, which was the real D.J., the killer or the lover? His seamless change from one to the other bothered her more than she cared to admit.

"Let's keep going. As I remember it, there aren't any good hiding spots for some distance up the trail."

With an increasing sense of dread, she nodded and started walking. She just wished she knew if they were headed for salvation or slaughter.

Chapter 16

$\mathcal{D}$evlin set a cold can of pop down on the desk along with a sandwich and a bag of chips.

"Here, Cody, take a break and eat. We try not to starve our people if we can help it. Are you and Cullen hitting it off okay?"

Cody grinned. "Oh, yeah. He's already taught me a few new tricks."

As he unwrapped his sandwich, he looked up at the clock. God, where had the time gone? Devlin had met him and Trahern at the local airport sometime in the early morning hours. They'd dropped the other man off, and then Devlin had taken Cody to his house. After they'd each grabbed a few hours of sleep, he'd brought Cody to Paladin headquarters in the Seattle Underground. Almost seven hours had passed since then.

The Paladin leader perched himself on the corner of the desk. "So how's the hunt going? Any progress?"

Cody nodded as he washed a bite of his sandwich

down with a swig of pop. "D.J. had already found an e-mail someone sent Reggie offering to meet up with her in Portland. Whoever it was promised to answer her questions about the Regents and the Paladins."

"Which means it's an inside job."

"Yeah, that's what D.J. thought, and Cullen agrees. We've been tracking the e-mail back to its origin. As far as we can tell, it came from—"

Cullen finished the sentence for him as he walked back over to the desk. "Headquarters in St. Louis. I swear, we'd be better off nuking the whole damn building."

Devlin grinned at his friend. "Tell you what, I'll light the fuse if you two build the bomb."

A female voice entered the conversation. "Mind if I give my dad enough warning to get away from ground zero?"

Both Cullen and Devlin winced as a woman about the same size as Reggie joined them.

Devlin turned to face her. "Sorry, Sasha. You know we don't mean it."

Surprisingly, she just laughed. "Oh, yeah, you do. However, I assume you have good reasons since you called me here to meet you."

When she spotted Cody, she came around the desk and held out her hand. "Hi, I'm Sasha. I don't believe we've met."

He looked to Devlin for guidance, who nodded. "I'm Cody. I'm, uh, new here."

Cullen and Devlin immediately moved to flank him.

Hopefully it was a gesture of support. What was it about this woman that had both men acting so weird?

She raised her eyebrows at their action. "Nice to meet you, Cody. I wasn't aware that we had a new recruit."

Okay, what was he supposed to say to that? Luckily, Devlin stepped in.

"He's actually more of a consultant at this point. He's been working on a special project with Trahern and Cullen."

"Really? Am I to assume this special project is why I'm here?"

Devlin nodded. "Why don't you come into my office so Cullen and Cody can get back to work? I promise to explain everything."

"Good idea. I'd rather hear what's going on from you than be blindsided by St. Louis." She turned her attention to Cullen. "Would you let Larem know where I am and bring him up to speed on the situation with D.J.?"

"Sure thing."

She smiled at Cody again. "It was nice to meet you. I hope to see more of you."

Cody waited until she and Devlin disappeared into the Paladin's office before asking Cullen, "Okay, so, who is she? And who is Larem?"

Why did that name sound familiar?

"Sasha is the Regents' representative in our area, and her father serves on the Board of Regents back in Missouri. Larem is, uh—"

"Standing right behind you."

Cody jumped about a foot at the deep voice coming from over his shoulder. That was the first shock. The second was that Larem had the same distinctive look as Barak. His hair was long and dark but mixed with silver. His pale eyes were sort of freaky, too, but he was an alien after all. The whole idea of people coming and going from another world was beyond weird, although the Paladins he'd met so far obviously had no problem with it.

To be polite, he rose to his feet and held out his hand. "Hi, I'm Cody."

"I've heard good things about you, Cody." Larem gave his hand a firm shake and then stepped back. "Trahern said you're handling all the stuff that's been thrown at you with the strength of a Paladin."

"I'm trying."

Then Cody got a clear look at Larem's companion. Holy hell, was that a white wolf? Probably not, but that was one huge, scary animal. When the dog started forward, Cody instinctively backed away. Unfortunately, the desk prevented him from putting any real distance between himself and the dog.

Larem caught his pet by the collar. "Chance, that's enough. That sandwich belongs to Cody."

The dog shot his owner a disappointed look and sat down with a big sigh. Okay, so maybe Chance wasn't all that scary after all.

Evidently satisfied that the dog was going to behave, Larem turned his attention to Cullen. "I assume it's too soon to have heard anything back from D.J. and his lady."

Cody wasn't sure how he felt about their assumption that Reggie somehow belonged to D.J. Yeah, it turned out that she'd been playing cybergames with the man for a couple of months, but she'd met him in person only a few days ago. How did that translate into D.J. having any claim to her?

Cullen was shaking his head. "Lonzo checked in earlier to say that Barak took the barrier down first thing this morning, but there was no sign of D.J. as of yet. They'll try again tonight. How about Berk? Was Hunter able to get word to him?"

Larem's pale eyes stared into Cody's briefly, as if unsure about how much to say in front of him. "Hunter left a message in the usual place. It's not Berk's regular day to make contact, but he sometimes checks in more often than that. Hunter will let him know what's going on. I'm sure the Sworn Guardian will assist D.J. in any way that he can."

It was so hard to trust strangers to keep Reggie safe. Cody sat back down at the desk using the excuse of finishing his sandwich to avoid more conversation. Aware that a pair of brown eyes watched his every move, he broke off a corner of his sandwich and held it out to Chance. The dog's tail wagged wildly as he gulped down Cody's offering.

Chance plopped his big head on Cody's lap with a contented sigh. As Cody brushed his hand over the dog's fur, it finally hit him where he'd heard Larem's name before. He'd been the one to lend his father's sword to D.J.

He kept Chance happy with ear scratches while he

waited for a lull in the conversation. "That was your sword that D.J. took with him."

"Chance, will you quit that?" Larem glared at his dog, who'd gone back to eyeing Cody's sandwich, before answering. "Yes, it is my family's sword. I thought D.J. might prefer a weapon that wouldn't immediately brand him as human."

"He was glad to have it. He said he was honored."

Although Larem didn't exactly smile, there was a softening in his solemn expression that made Cody think he was pleased.

"I know you are concerned about your friend, but D.J. will do everything possible to bring her back safely."

To hide his worry, Cody went back to petting the dog. "I'll just be glad when Reggie is back on this side of the barrier."

Cullen patted Cody on the shoulder. "With that in mind, we'd better get back to the hunt. Where were we?"

The Paladin knew exactly where they'd left off, but Cody appreciated the excuse to concentrate on something he could actually help with. It was hard to sit still though. He picked up a pencil and began tapping it on the desk in counterpoint to the rhythm of his foot kicking the leg of his chair.

After a few seconds, Cullen shook his head and grinned. "It's easy to see why you and D.J. hit it off. That man has more pent-up energy than any three people combined, but you run a close second."

"My bad." Cody dropped the pencil back on the desk

and tried to stay still. "Seriously, the only reason Reggie can stand to share a cubicle with me is because she's almost as bad. When I'm bothering her too much, she throws one of her desk toys at me."

He'd been eyeing the collection of toys on a nearby desk. "I'm guessing those belong to D.J."

Larem picked up one of the balls and tossed it to Cody. "You guessed right. I see he's gotten new ones since the last time I was here."

He actually smiled. "Chance stole a couple of the balls and chewed them up. D.J. pretended to be mad about it, but then gave him two more to play with."

The Kalith's cell phone rang. After a brief conversation, he clipped Chance's leash back on his collar.

"It seems like Sasha's meeting with Devlin is going to take longer than expected. I'm going to make a coffee run. Cody, would you like to take a walk with me and Chance?"

Cody looked to Cullen for permission, who spoke without looking away from the computer. "Go ahead and go. Bring me back one, too. Larem knows what I like."

"Okay. Be back in a few."

As Cody followed Larem and Chance to the door, he had to smile. Who knew aliens liked lattes?

The dust hung in the air and clumped on D.J.'s sweaty skin, making the day feel even hotter. His head felt like it was mounted on a swivel as he tried to keep one eye on the trail in front of them and one on Reggie. She'd yet to complain, but breathing the thin air was harder on her than it was for him, no doubt thanks to his mixed DNA.

He forced himself to slow down despite the growing sense of urgency that had him wanting to hoof it up the hillside full-speed ahead. It wasn't fair to Reggie with her shorter legs. Besides, if things did suddenly go to hell, he wanted her to have enough stamina to make a quick run for cover.

When the path leveled off a little, he stopped by a cluster of scrubby trees that would afford them a little shade and at least minimal cover. He pulled a bottle from his pack and took a long swallow.

Reggie reached him a few seconds later, looking tired and a bit frazzled. He smiled at her. "I thought you might like a short break. God knows I could use one."

She sank down on a nearby rock and shuffled through the Kalith bag she'd taken for water and a granola bar. While she caught her breath and refueled, D.J. returned to the edge of the path and stared back down the hillside. What—or who—was out there setting off all his alarms?

He wandered the trail for a short distance in each direction, trying to find a vantage point that gave him a clearer view of what lay ahead. Nothing. Not even a bird or a bug or any kind of local fauna moving around, just the rolling grassland in the valley below and the stunted trees jutting out of the hillside.

Reggie joined him. "What's wrong? Well, other than the obvious, us being stuck in Kalithia."

She squeezed his hand and looked up at him with a smile. He couldn't believe it. A little thing like her, she had to be exhausted, yet *she* was supporting *him*. He hoped like hell that the time she'd spent with him last night hadn't added a whole new layer of complications for her.

It sure had for him. No matter what happened from this point on, the memories of what they'd shared would be a bright, shining moment in the endless bloodbath of his life. Reggie deserved better.

The kindest thing he could do would be to take her back home, make sure the assholes within the organization left her alone, and let her get back to her real life. That's exactly what he planned on doing, even if the mere thought of letting her disappear from his life made him want to scream.

He forced himself to step away from her, staring down into the valley as a pretext.

"No sign of anyone following us yet."

She shaded her eyes and surveyed their surroundings. "That's a good thing. Maybe our luck has taken a turn for the better."

"Let's get moving before it changes back. I'll check the trail ahead again. Just give me a second."

He walked away before she could say anything, but he felt her confusion. The last thing he wanted to do was hurt her feelings, but her life depended on their making it back across the barrier. Each step away from her felt as if he was walking through sludge.

Focus, damn it!

Just around the next turn, he noticed something odd—a heel mark in the dust. It looked too fresh to have been from the day before. He might be wrong, but he didn't think so.

Kneeling down, he studied the print, looking for others. They weren't hard to find, and they were definitely headed in the same direction as he and Reggie. He backtracked a short distance until he found where they'd started. Someone had climbed up to the trail from right below where he stood. He stood at the far edge and looked down at the ridge. No sign of anyone now, but he could see where a few rocks had been disturbed, marking the Other's route to where D.J. now stood.

Great. As far as he knew, the only thing of note located along that trail was the cave and the barrier inside. This couldn't be good. Not at all.

It appeared the prints belonged to one individual, which didn't particularly worry him. In this world, no one was armed with anything other than blades. *That* he could deal with. The real question was what the guy was up to. Was he hoping to make contact with someone from Earth?

That didn't feel right. No, it had to be another trap. Not all Kalith had the healing capabilities the Paladins had inherited but some had it in spades. If this was the guy who had plummeted off the cliff the previous night, he'd had plenty of time to recover from the experience, provided he'd survived at all. For sure, he'd be carrying one heck of a grudge against D.J. for damn near killing him. If the Kalith had found out that D.J. was responsible for the death of his partner, that would only compound the problem.

Should he and Reggie continue onward and upward? Shit, what choice did they have? No matter what, it was still their best option. The straightest route to back home was through that cave. If nothing else, their supplies were stashed only a short distance from the entrance.

God forbid they'd have to hike their asses back down the trail and across the valley to their fallback position on the other side. But if that's what they had to do, they'd need the food and supplies in that pack. He hustled back to where Reggie was waiting. She looked relieved to see him but then frowned.

"D.J., what's wrong?"

There was no use lying to her. "I think someone has been up here today. It might be the guy I fought last night."

"Kolar? The one you thought died when he fell off the cliff?"

"Yeah, but it almost has to be him. No one else has passed by us, and this trail comes to a dead end just past the cave."

Reggie backed away a few steps. "How is that even possible? Even if Kolar survived the fall, he'd be injured too badly to hike this far."

Now wasn't the time to discuss the full capabilities of the Paladins or their alien counterparts. She'd already learned more than she should have about his world. Okay, that was a lie. It wasn't his world he was trying to protect. He didn't want her to find out how much of a freak he really was.

"Trust me, with these guys almost anything is possible." He shouldered his own pack, but drew Larem's sword. "Keep your gun aimed down and to the side. Stay behind me as much as possible."

He made sure she was following his directions before starting up the hillside. They had less than half a mile to go. Once they drew closer to the entrance, he'd find somewhere to stash Reggie while he investigated. When they reached the cave safely, he should be able to defend them both until Barak opened up the way home.

Home. He couldn't wait. No doubt Reggie felt the same way to the power of ten. Had she stopped to think that getting back across the barrier was only the first step in returning her life to normal? Until he and the Paladins managed to track down the bastard who had ordered the kidnapping in the first place, she'd have to be under armed guard.

She'd hate that, but one step at a time. Right now he needed to concentrate on the immediate problem of getting them both safely inside the cave.

There was another cluster of trees and rocks just ahead, the perfect place for Reggie to wait while he scouted. In the time it took for her to catch up, he'd dropped his cloak and pack on the ground. He'd move more easily without them.

She came puffing her way up the trail a few seconds later. "Why are we stopping here? Isn't that the cave entrance just ahead?"

"It is, which is why you're going to stay here. If someone has laid a trap for us, I'll need room to maneuver. I can't do that and protect you at the same time."

Reggie took a deep breath and then planted herself right in front of him, blocking the trail. "Hold up just a second."

He tried to get around her but ended up just slide-stepping as she kept pace with him. Short of mowing her down, he'd get nowhere.

"Come on, Reggie, no arguments. If this turns violent, I don't want you caught in the middle."

For such a tiny thing, she sure was stubborn. "Hold still, for Pete's sake. I'm not trying to stop you from going, just stop you from going *yet*."

Her smile was a bit ragged as she reached up to capture his face in her hands. "I'm scared, and I want to give you a kiss for luck before you go up there."

He stared down into those eyes that read him like an open book. She was worried, but mainly about him, even though they were both at risk. For a brief second he knew what it was like to be Devlin and Trahern, having women in their lives who sent them off to battle knowing that they were loved.

He kissed her with everything he had. It might've been a bit awkward, holding her close with his hands full of weapons, but that didn't detract one bit from the sweetness of the moment. Standing there on the hillside in full view of the whole world was insanity, but he desperately needed this little bit of craziness in his life.

A trickle of gravel slipping down the hillside was his

only warning. D.J. managed to shove Reggie out of the way just in time to block the charging Other's blow with his own weapon.

"Reggie, get back!" he bellowed as he forced the enemy to retreat one step, then a second.

He could hear Reggie scrambling for cover. The previous night he'd never gotten a clear look at his opponent, shrouded as he'd been in his cloak, but the Other's fighting style was unmistakable. The bastard was good, but then desperation often took a fighter to a new level.

They were going at it too fast, too up close and personal for D.J. to get off a clean shot with his gun, especially when he wasn't quite sure where Reggie had gone to ground. He tossed the gun aside, freeing up his second hand to grasp the pommel of Larem's sword. The two-handed grip gave him that much more control and power.

"You have any last wishes, Other?" D.J. taunted as he charged the bastard, forcing him to give more ground. Their blades clanged together, the two men ending up pommel to pommel and smelling each other's breath.

The Kalith smiled, sweat and dust streaks on his pale face only emphasizing the insanity in his eyes. "Human, I'm not the only one who will die this day. You and your woman both will breathe your last here in Kalithia."

D.J. didn't waste precious energy responding to the smug bastard. He jumped back, only to rebound with a series of fast and furious blows intended to wear the Other down. Maybe the previous night's injuries had yet to heal completely, because the man's defense was rapidly weakening.

D.J. finally caught the Other on the upper leg, the curve of his blade slicing straight through flesh until it hit bone. D.J. jerked the sword free and danced back a few steps. Blood gushed from the wound as the Other screamed in agony, retreating back uphill toward the cavern entrance.

D.J. followed slowly. Given the rate the guy was leaking oil, he'd be dead within three minutes, maybe less. And D.J. planned on making sure there'd be no coming back this time. Back home, he'd shoved his share of wounded Others back into their own world, seeing no need to finish them off as long as they stayed on their side of the barrier.

Not this time. Not after what this pale-eyed bastard had done to his woman.

Damn it, he'd forgotten all about her. The last thing Reggie needed was to witness another bloodbath. He looked around for her. Smart woman that she was, she'd found a good-size boulder to hide behind. She still held the gun in her hand, but she was shaking so hard he hoped like hell that she had the safety on.

A soft moan snapped his attention back to the matter at hand. By now, the trail of blood left by the Other had almost reached the cave. He had collapsed in the dirt, the stream of blood flowing more slowly than it had been a few seconds before. Death had its hooks in the male and wouldn't be letting go.

Still, the wounded man kept dragging himself closer

to the cave. He'd abandoned his sword, using his one hand in a futile attempt to staunch the bleeding as he limped along leaning against the rocky wall with the other. Finally, he slumped down to sit in the dirt right outside the entrance and reached for something on the ground.

What the hell was he up to now?

D.J. ran forward, ready to end it once and for all. But then he saw what the Other had clutched in his bloody hands. Two wires. What the fuck?

Oh, hell, no! He backed away, slowly at first but then faster.

"Run, Reggie, run!" he shouted, knowing they'd never get far enough away in time.

Kolar looked up at D.J., the fading light in his eyes triumphant as he touched the wires together. The two pieces of metal sparked and sizzled. Turning his back on the dying man, D.J. hauled ass down the trail, hoping like hell Reggie made it out of the blast zone.

A deep rumble shook the ground beneath his feet, almost sending him skidding to his knees. He managed to keep his balance right up until the hillside erupted in a blast of heat and fire. Rocks and burning ash rained down. Ahead, the shock wave sent Reggie pitching head-first to the ground. D.J. dove to cover her body with his, ignoring the pain as the rocks and dirt pelted him.

He wrapped his arms around her and held on with all his strength, waiting for the world to right itself. As bad as it was, at least they were both still breathing.

With luck, maybe they'd both survive this.

Chapter 17

*D*evlin's door slammed open. Cody jumped about a mile as the big man stormed out of his office looking royally pissed off. What had happened? Everyone in the area froze in midmotion, no doubt wondering the same thing.

For several seconds, all Devlin did was curse as he abused the furniture in the area. A wastebasket bounced off the wall. A second one followed the first, throwing up a cloud of trash and sending it fluttering through the air. When Devlin picked up the nearest desk chair, Trahern and Cullen bolted across the room to gang-tackle him. They might have knocked the wind out of him, but it didn't last. Within a heartbeat, he'd almost succeeded in bucking them off, screaming threats at the top of his lungs.

"Let me the fuck go!"

Trahern bellowed, "Help, you idiots!"

Larem and a couple of young Paladins immediately

joined the party, aiming for Devlin's arms and legs. It took all of their combined efforts to pin the man down, a tribute to his strength and fury. Even then, the mass of big bodies writhed across the floor.

Trahern gripped his friend's face with one of his big hands. "Damn it, Devlin, quit this shit."

Cody stood up, and was considering adding his weight to the pile when Trahern rose up long enough to belt his friend. Abruptly all the fight went out of Devlin.

One by one, the combatants peeled off the heap until only Trahern and Cullen remained kneeling beside their friend. From where Cody stood, it was impossible to see how much damage Trahern had done with his fist. After a few seconds, the two men helped Devlin sit up.

The Paladin leader shook his head as if to clear it and rubbed his jaw with his hand.

"Damn it, Blake, I forgot just how hard you can hit."

Trahern flexed his hand and laughed as he got back up to his feet. He and Cullen pulled Devlin upright before shoving him into the same chair he'd threatened to demolish. He happened to look in Cody's direction and cursed under his breath.

"Sorry, Cody. Didn't mean to go ballistic in front of you. Normally, I have better control."

"No problem."

Then Cody asked the question he knew they were all wanting answered. "How bad is it?"

Devlin pushed himself to his feet and looked around the room. "Barak just called. He and Lonzo were still camped out and waiting to bring the barrier down for

ALEXIS MORGAN

D.J. and Reggie. About half an hour ago, all hell broke loose. One second the barrier was at full strength, and the next it basically imploded. They only got a brief glimpse through to the cave on the other side, but it appears that someone blew it all to hell and back."

His already grim expression worsened. "They couldn't tell if anyone was inside the cavern on the other side. Lonzo and Barak had to take off running before the aftershocks rolled through to our side. The whole fucking place collapsed only seconds after they got out. That's all we know for now."

The walls started closing in on Cody, and the temperature bounced from hot to cold and back again. Maybe it was the waves of tension coming off every man in the room.

"How soon can Barak find out what's going on?"

Devlin shifted his gaze to a spot on the wall behind Cody's head. "They can't go back in, even through one of the other caves. The whole area is too damn unstable now. Not that it matters. With that part of the barrier destroyed, no one will be coming through there anytime soon. All we can do is wait until D.J. and Reggie find another way home."

The Paladin leader looked straight across to where Cody stood. As the man's words sank in, Cody's lungs forgot how to work and his pulse raced out of control.

"I've told Barak and Lonzo to head on back. There's nothing more to be done there."

Cody needed to sit down. Now. Evidently someone else thought so, too, because a chair hit him in the back of his legs and a hand shoved his head between his knees.

"Breathe, damn it."

Even through the dizziness, Cody felt the rough concern in Trahern's voice, reminding him that he wasn't alone in this. Reggie was his friend, but D.J. was theirs. Well, maybe his, too.

A minute or two passed before the spots in front of his eyes faded. He stood slowly once the fog started lifting. As soon as he was upright, Cullen stuck a bottle of water in his face.

"Drink this and then we'll go eat. Don't want you to starve to death before we have a chance to nail the bastards."

Although the water helped, Cullen's barely controlled anger was what actually made Cody feel better. At the very least their cyberhunt would give them something to concentrate on other than worrying.

Devlin was back to snapping out orders. "Larem, get Hunter on the horn and have him send a followup message to Berk. Tell him what's happened. Maybe he can send someone to check out the cave and see if they're . . ."

He stopped talking and pinched the bridge of his nose. "Look, just tell him we need to know one way or the other. Maybe he can split up his men and have some check out this area and send the rest to watch for D.J. and Reggie heading toward their secondary target."

Larem was already dialing the phone. While he talked, his dog ignored everyone else in the room and headed straight for Cody. Scratching the dog's head, he smiled a little when the dog groaned and closed his big brown eyes. For a moment, Cody concentrated on making the dog happy, the only thing in his control.

Cullen walked over to where he was sitting, twirling his key ring on his forefinger. "You ready?"

"Yeah, sure." Reluctantly, Cody nodded and pushed the dog back so he could stand up. He wasn't particularly hungry, but right now getting out of there for a while sounded damn good. His own mood was bleak enough, but being surrounded by a bunch of guys whose moods were even darker wasn't helping. He waited until he and Cullen had put some distance between themselves and the rest of the crew.

Keeping his voice low, he asked, "Devlin thinks they're already dead, doesn't he?"

Before Cullen could answer, Devlin's voice rang out over the distance. "Hell, no, I don't think that! Never underestimate D.J. He's one tough son of a bitch, and no fucking Other is going to get the better of him. You just watch. He and Reggie will come strolling back across the barrier in a day or so. When he does, I'm going to kick his ass just for worrying you this much."

Cody looked at Cullen. "I thought I whispered that."

The Paladin smiled at him. "We all have exceptional hearing, but his is better than most."

Evidently Devlin wasn't done horning in on their conversation. "It comes from years of riding herd on this bunch of idiots. Now, go eat and then get your asses back here. There's work to be done."

Then Devlin walked back into his office, abusing his door once again as he slammed it behind him. Once he was out of sight, everyone else scattered. Cullen gave Cody a slight push toward the door at the end of the hall.

"So what sounds good for lunch?"

"I'm not picky, but I could go for Italian."

Before they reached the door, an obnoxious horn blasted up and down the hallway. The racket was unbelievable. What the heck was that? Obviously something bad because Paladins came pouring out of nearby offices and hallways at a dead run, most carrying swords.

"Cullen, what's going on?"

The Paladin was already walking back the way they'd come. He had the same fierce expression on his face as the others. Gone was the affable hacker and in his place a stone-cold killer, his expression hard and brittle.

"Listen, Cody, that alarm tells us the barrier below has gone down. Chances are there are a bunch of crazies from Kalithia foaming at the mouth to escape into our world. I'm going to have to join the rest of the guys to make sure that doesn't happen. Go with Larem. He'll stay with you until we get back."

"How long will that be?"

"There's no telling. Could be fifteen minutes or two days."

Larem stood in the middle of the desks watching the Paladins rush by. Cody waited for a break in the crowd to join him. If he'd thought the Kalith's face had been difficult to read before, it was impossible now. When the last of the Paladins disappeared from sight, Larem finally acknowledged Cody's presence.

"Did you need something?"

"Cullen and I were on our way to grab a bite to eat, but obviously that's not happening."

Larem continued to stare down the hall as if seeing something other than elevators and office doors, his hand rubbing his upper thigh. His demeanor had taken on the same hard edge as Cullen's. When he didn't immediately respond, Cody took a step back, a little leery of bothering him.

As if breaking free of his mood, Larem shuddered slightly before turning to face Cody.

"I didn't mean to ignore you. I find it difficult to stand here and do nothing when my friends are fighting for their lives."

"I'm sorry." What else could he say?

Larem's pale eyes looked so sad. "Me, too. As my friend Hunter reminds me, we can only play the cards we are dealt. Why don't we both get out of here for a while? We'll have to take Chance with us, but I know a place with great takeout. If you don't mind, we'll take it to the animal shelter where I volunteer. Maybe you can help me there until Cullen is back."

Cody nodded and followed Larem out.

Todd studied the printouts Ray had slipped to him before leaving for the day. The man was still bitching about the Morrison woman punching him and the revenge he was planning when she returned. Personally, Todd figured spending time as a plaything for their Kalith allies was punishment enough, but then it hadn't been his nose she'd broken.

If Ray's nose surgery went well, he'd be back in a few days. Until he returned, though, it was up to Todd to monitor what was going on out in Seattle.

Rumor had it that one of the Paladins had gone missing. A couple of them had been away from the Seattle office briefly. No one seemed to know where they'd been, although Todd had his suspicions. Wherever it was, they'd evidently returned with a new recruit in tow. Great. Just what the world needed—another loose cannon trained in the fine art of killing everything in sight.

Okay, maybe that was cold, but it was true. No one he knew ever claimed Paladins were all that stable, just that they were the most capable means to prevent an all-out invasion of alien crazies.

Todd had dedicated most of his working life to providing the supplies and equipment needed to keep the whole organization running smoothly. So what if he'd siphoned off a few bucks here and there for his own use? He deserved some compensation for having to deal with the freaks.

Flying under the radar while he did it was the hard part. With that in mind, he'd better spend some quality time with those printouts. If Devlin Bane's boys were hot on Todd's trail, maybe it was time to take that vacation his wife had been nagging him about.

Too bad he'd be going without her.

• • •

Reggie's ears were ringing, and she couldn't catch her breath. Everything ached. Absolutely everything. She really, really hoped that last problem was due to the fact that D.J. was on top of her. When he didn't immediately roll off, she felt the first stirrings of panic setting in.

"D.J., are you okay?"

Still no response. She waited another heartbeat or two, and then tried to wiggle out from underneath him. As soon as she moved, he spoke, his voice a rough whisper.

"Hold still, Reggie, and give me a minute. The side of the trail has given way. We're poised at the edge, and I'm not sure how stable it is."

He shifted a little to her right side, his weight grinding her farther into the rocky ground. She wasn't about to complain about the pain, not when he was trying to keep her alive. If she didn't trust him by now, she never would.

"On a count of three, I'm going to roll to the right and take you with me. Once we're on more solid ground, we'll assess the damage."

His hold on her tightened as he counted off in a quiet murmur. Then he abruptly rolled to the side, jerking her off the ground and literally tossing her about a yard to his right. She landed in a painful heap against the base of a tree. D.J. scrambled after her.

When she pushed herself up, she got her first look at their world postexplosion. All around them trees were uprooted and boulders shattered. The cave entrance was gone, buried in a tumble of dirt and rocks. There was no sign of Kolar. Considering that he'd been at the center of the blast, that came as no surprise.

It had only been by sheer blind luck that a rocky shelf had shielded D.J. and herself from the worst of the blast. A few nicks and bruises weren't much in the grand scheme of things.

"Are you all right?"

She suspected she'd yelled the words because of the way D.J. flinched before he nodded.

"Sorry about that," she mouthed. "My ears are seriously screwed up."

"Not a problem."

He stood and took a couple of steps, not looking all that steady himself. At least he had the good sense to stay in one place until he was sure his legs would support him. That's when she noticed the trickle of blood pouring down his arm.

"You're hurt!"

Okay, she hollered that, too, but who could blame her? He actually looked puzzled until she pointed at the gash on his forearm.

"Let me check you over."

"I'm okay." He swiped at the blood with the hem of his tunic. "It's nothing."

Oh, brother. "I don't need that macho crap from you. Now let me clean that up before it gets infected."

"Trust me. It won't."

She ignored his protests as she took hold of his

arm and turned it around to get a better look at the wound. There was a large sliver of wood embedded in the cut.

She needed more than just the hem of his tunic to clean the wound. Looking around, she spotted the strap of her pack peeking up from out of the rubble.

"Stay here a minute."

He sighed but did as ordered. When she unearthed her meager store of supplies, she pulled out her water bottle and soaked a piece of the fabric he'd cut off her pants to use as a washcloth.

"This is going to hurt."

"I'll try to be brave," he promised even though his dark eyes showed more amusement than pain.

"Smart-ass."

She tugged the splinter free and let the wound bleed itself clean. After a few seconds, she washed the area as best she could with the cloth. Then she used a strip of the other piece of fabric to bind the gash. He also had a scattering of smaller cuts on his cheek and the back of his neck. She wiped them clean of dust and blood.

"I wish I had some antibiotic ointment to put on those."

"I'll be fine, Reggie. Now, if you're done playing doctor, I need to check on something. I'll be right back."

He started clambering over the rocks up toward where the cave had been. She wanted to make him come right back, not risk it. With each step, he moved farther from her across the slippery slope of loose rock. The heartbeat that had barely returned to normal picked up speed again. She was relieved when he finally dropped down to scramble on all fours.

With a shout of triumph, he pulled a sword out of the gravel. She had no idea if it was the one he'd been fighting with, but he seemed sure of it. He laid it to the side as he continued on his way.

Just before he reached the crest of the slope, he paused to call back to her. "I'll be out of sight, but I'm not going far. The damage past here isn't as bad. I'm hoping to retrieve the supplies I stashed."

"Be careful."

"Believe it or not, I usually am." He grinned at her just before he vanished from sight.

While he was gone, she did some cautious exploring of her own. She did a quick survey of the contents of her pack. It had been pretty squashed, but at least granola-bar crumbs were still edible.

She located D.J.'s other pack and his cloak. She was accruing a small pile of treasures. Where had their guns gone? It was hard to orient herself because the landscape had changed so drastically, but she thought D.J. had tossed his over near the base of the bushes above her.

She climbed up, sliding back one step for each three she went forward. Success! She checked the safety before making her way back to her cache of supplies.

D.J. crested the hill with a large duffel slung over his shoulder. He showed the good sense to sit down and cross the last distance in a controlled slide.

When he reached her side, he nodded toward the pile beside her. "I see you've been busy, too."

She held out his gun. "Sorry, but I'm afraid mine is buried under all that mess."

"Don't sweat it." He checked the gun over with quiet efficiency and then tucked it back in his waistband.

He stood up again to look around. "We should really get moving again, but if you need to rest a bit longer, say so. We've got a little time."

Or not. From the way his eyes kept fanning the area, she suspected he was only saying that for her sake. Sitting there on the hillside, they were both too exposed. The last thing she wanted was to see D.J. fighting for both their lives—again. She closed her eyes, wishing her memory came with a Delete button to clear away those horrific images.

"I'm fine." Not really and maybe not ever.

He knew it, too. After setting his duffel aside, he offered her a hand up off the ground and immediately wrapped her in his arms. He rested his chin on top of her head as his hand stroked her back in slow, gentle circles.

"I bet you're counting the minutes until you get home and can forget all about me."

What could she say to that? Yes, she hated his world, his life, but she didn't hate *him*. Far from it, even if she couldn't decipher exactly what she did feel for him, not with all of her emotions tangled up in one big knot with a bow made of fear.

"I'll never regret meeting you, D.J."

Evidently he wasn't buying it. "Give it time, Reggie. Right now you need me, and I get that. But once this is all over, you're going to want a big dose of normal back in your life. You'll never have that hanging around with me."

Before she could think of what to say to that, he pressed a soft kiss to the top of her head and stepped back.

"We'd better hit the road. I don't know how well noise carries in this thin air. But if Kolar's buddies are anywhere in the vicinity, they're bound to have noticed the dust cloud from the explosion."

"Okay, I'll be right behind you."

D.J. shouldered his duffel and adjusted his sword in its scabbard before walking away. As he did, she finally realized what she should've said to him: that normal was seriously overrated if it meant that a man like D.J. had to be on the outside looking in.

Chapter 18

*C*ullen leaned back in his chair and rubbed his eyes. "I don't know about you, Cody my man, but I'm dead on my feet."

No arguments there. "I'm pretty sure my brain shut down an hour ago."

"Let me go see what Devlin's plans are for you."

Earlier, Cody had hung out at the animal shelter with Larem for about three hours before Cullen had called them back. Playing with the puppies had been a nice distraction. All the fur balls had asked of him was a good scratch and a couple of treats.

Larem and Chance had walked him back to headquarters before taking off to meet up with Sasha. Turned out there were other people from Kalithia who'd hooked up with people in the Seattle area. Aliens with human lovers. Cody wasn't sure how he felt about that. Still, he'd met two of the three and liked them both. Not to mention that the third one lived with Cullen. So maybe it was okay, if a bit weird.

On the way back, Cullen had met them in the alley outside headquarters, making Cody feel rather like a baton being handed off in a relay race. He wondered whose turn it was next and how long the race was going to last. If it felt like forever to him, how much worse was it for Reggie?

That is, if her race hadn't already ended with that explosion. No, damn it, he wouldn't—couldn't—think that way. She was fine. She had to be. D.J. was with her, and they were on their way home.

He rubbed away the sudden burn in his eyes. He was exhausted. Part of that was simple lack of sleep. The other was having his normal life ripped out by the roots to be replanted in the world of the Paladins. Even if this all worked out in the best possible way, he couldn't go back to his old life knowing what he now knew.

Right now his thoughts were whirling in circles and getting nowhere, an indication of how burned out he was. He forced his eyes open to see that Cullen was on his way back.

Cullen dropped down in his chair. "I'm going to shut down for now and head home. We'll pick up again first thing in the morning. Devlin wants to see you in his office."

Did that have an ominous sound to it? No, there was no reason to get all paranoid. So far, all these guys had been nothing but nice to him. Besides, if there'd been news of any kind, Cullen would either be celebrating or seriously pissed. Right now the man was calmly finishing up the task he'd been working on so he could leave. No reason to think anything else had gone wrong.

Cody shoved his own laptop back in his pack along with Reggie's. "Okay, I'll see you tomorrow."

Cullen's fingers flew across the keyboard with enviable skill. He shot Cody a quick grin without missing a beat. "Sure thing. Just so you know, under other circumstances, this would've been fun. Other than D.J., I don't often get to play with someone who has such serious talent."

The compliment made Cody smile. "Wait until you meet Reggie. She makes me look like a rank amateur."

"Yeah, I've heard that. Seems she's been running my buddy around in circles for a while." Cullen's grin widened considerably. "That certainly explains the two laptops that met their demise slamming into the wall over there."

Cody had been wondering what had made the big gouges in the drywall. There'd been times he'd been tempted to do the same thing, but he couldn't afford to replace his computer just because of a temper tantrum.

He deliberately walked by the damaged wall on his way to Devlin's office. To be honest, it worried him. He hoped D.J. was holding it together for Reggie. It would take more than a hair-trigger temper to get them both back home safely.

Devlin's door was closed. Cody raised his fist to knock just as it opened. Trahern stood inside, looking every bit as tired as Cody felt.

"Hey, kid, how are you holding up?"

"Fine."

"Well, you look like hell. I was just coming to see you. Barak and Lonzo caught a commercial flight back from Portland, and I need to pick them up at Sea-Tac. Thought maybe you'd like to ride along. Afterward, you can crash at my place tonight."

Devlin joined in. "If you're not up to it, say so and you can come home with me again. Your choice."

He looked from Trahern to Devlin and back again. "I'd like to hear what they have to say about the explosion, if that's all right, sir."

Trahern jerked his head in a quick nod. "Yeah, I don't blame you. Besides, this way you can meet Brenna. She's the one who wrote that history of the Paladins Reggie found."

That bit of fishing combined with her hunt for D.J. had caused Reggie all this trouble, but it wouldn't be fair to hold that against Brenna. Besides, he was curious about Paladin history himself.

"Call if you hear anything, Dev, or if you need me. Okay, let's hit the road."

Before they closed the door, Trahern whispered, "By the way, Brenna can cook. Laurel, not so much."

Devlin hollered after them, "Damn it, Trahern, I heard that. Quit insulting my wife."

"It's not an insult when it's the truth. You just feel obligated to defend her cooking because you're married to the woman."

The other man glared at his friend. "Oh, just shut up and go. And, Cody, don't let him be a bad influence on you. The last thing I need around here is another guy with attitude."

Cody wasn't sure whether to laugh or duck for cover.

He gave into the urge to grin when Trahern winked at him.

"Yes, sir. No attitude, bad or otherwise."

As the two of them headed toward the exit, he was pretty sure he heard Devlin laughing.

D.J. was pushing them both hard. Time was ticking by, and the suns were about to set. They needed to reach the flatlands below where they'd stand a better chance of hiding in the deep grass than they would perched here on this fucking hillside.

Reggie was a real trooper. Although she didn't hesitate to ask for a short break when she really needed one, she'd kept delays to a minimum. Even when they did stop, she spent most of her time fussing over him and the minor injuries he'd gotten in the explosion. What was she going to do come morning when they'd all but disappeared?

Another point for the freak score.

The trail up ahead looked all too familiar. It was a sad state of affairs that he'd spent enough time in this hellhole to already know the terrain. Right now they were only a short distance from where he'd thwarted the Other's ambush the last time he'd passed this spot.

Should he check the place out the same way he had last time or charge through and hope for the best? No contest. He might put himself at risk, but no way in hell he'd let Reggie go waltzing into a possible trap.

No sooner had that thought crossed his mind than he

caught the faint sound of voices on the wind. Turning his head to the side to catch the sound more clearly, he cursed under his breath. If he hadn't stopped when he had, the two of them might have stumbled right into the Others' waiting arms.

Reggie quietly moved up beside him. "What's wrong?"

She pitched her voice just loud enough for him to hear. The woman sure had the right instincts. He hoped like hell she survived this adventure and never had to put her hard-earned experience to practical use again.

He whispered the answer near her ear. "Someone's coming. We've got to get out of sight."

There wasn't anything he could do about the trail of footprints they'd left behind in the dust. At least it was getting dark enough that eventually the Others would have trouble reading their tracks.

Which way to go? There was really no choice. He led Reggie around to the far side of the hill, following the same route he'd followed scouting out the earlier ambush. Had that been just the night before?

He pulled Reggie closer to explain the plan. "I want you to stay out of sight in the shadows under those trees up ahead."

"Where will you be?"

He pointed to a nearby cluster of boulders. "I'll stay there. Once they're safely past us, I'll join you."

She slowly nodded, her eyes telling him without words that she thought his plan sucked. Yeah, it did, but it was the best one they had at the moment.

He waited until she'd safely disappeared into the trees before ducking behind the rocks. Just in time, too, because their enemy was almost upon them. There were seven that he could see in the group. From what he knew of Kalith culture, it was unlikely that this was a Sworn Guardian and his Blademates because they traveled in multiples of four.

They also lacked the militaristic discipline that was second nature to Larem, Barak, and even Lusahn. No, he was willing to bet this mob were the buddies Kolar and his friend had been waiting for. Their voices carried clearly in the early evening silence. That didn't mean he understood a word they said.

He kept his Glock in hand as he held his breath, hoping like hell they'd just keep going. Just when he thought they were going to pass by, one of them came to an abrupt halt. He held up his hand, the universal signal for his companions to stop and shut up. Then he tipped his head back and drew in a slow, deep breath.

Son of a bitch, had the bastard caught their scent? After a few seconds, the Kalith crept forward, his hand reaching to draw a long knife from his belt. He was headed in Reggie's direction. D.J. flicked off the safety on his gun, ready to start picking off the Others one by one.

The Glock held more than enough ammunition to kill them all. But it didn't mean a fucking thing if he couldn't take them all out. The chances were close to nil that he'd get the job done before one reached Reggie's hiding place.

He'd die trying though.

He was about to rise, to draw their attention, when the Other flicked his wrist, sending his knife flying toward the ground a short distance away. One of the bushes erupted in a flurry of action as a small animal charged out, limping badly. The Other shouted in triumph as he finished off the poor critter with a second blade.

After picking up his knives and cleaning them, he retrieved his kill and held it up for his buddies to admire. As they moved off, he carried the carcass with him, obviously pleased that fresh meat was now on their dinner menu. That in itself was odd. The three Seattle Kaliths were all vegetarians. Fresh game sure sounded better than the MREs Devlin had packed for D.J., not that he was complaining. Right now, all food meant was maintaining enough energy for the two of them to keep moving.

He waited impatiently for the Others to leave. The need to put some distance between themselves and that bunch was riding him hard. He'd look for a place he and Reggie could stop to get some much-needed rest. Tomorrow, they'd resume their charge toward the distant hills and hope they found the barrier before the Others found them.

"Just a little farther."

That had to be the fourth time D.J. had made that promise, but Reggie didn't have the energy to call him on it. She understood that he was worried about those guys circling back, but seriously, if they didn't stop for the night soon, she'd drop right in her tracks.

Rather than think about that, she cast about for something else, something positive, to think about. Like last night. The feel of D.J. moving over her, moving in her. Oh, yeah, those were definitely happy thoughts. She normally didn't go for big men—and he was definitely big *all* over—but there was just something about D.J.

Intelligence was high on her must-have list when it came to men. Check. So was a sense of humor. Double-check. A considerate lover. Check—in fact, triple-check that one. He definitely subscribed to the "ladies first" theory.

She was so focused on her list that she didn't notice D.J. had stopped walking. When she ran right into him, he reached out to steady her.

"What's up?"

"I was thinking this looks like a good place to stop for the night. I can hear a stream, so it can't be far. We can't risk a fire, but at least we'll be able clean up a bit and get some sleep."

He didn't wait for an answer, but simply stepped off the trail and left her to follow as she would.

Half an hour later, she was sitting on the edge of the creek, soaking her feet in the surprisingly warm water. After their makeshift meal, she might just do more than dip her toes. She didn't know about D.J., but she'd sleep better if she shed about ten pounds of dust and dirt before turning in.

"Here's your dinner, fresh from the foil pouch."

D.J. smiled at her as he sat down on the bank beside her. She started eating, but he set his own meal aside to peel off his boots and socks. He eased his feet into the water and sighed happily.

"Oh, yeah, that's good."

Between bites, she asked, "How is your arm doing?"

"My arm?" He seemed genuinely puzzled by the question.

God save her from macho men who wouldn't admit to a little pain. She pointed at the bandage on his arm with her plastic fork. "That cut. You know, the one that had a chunk of wood stuck in it earlier today."

"Oh, that one. It's fine. Seriously, it wasn't nearly as bad as we first thought."

"I'll be the judge of that. After we finish dinner, I'll take a look at it."

He didn't argue, but she suspected it would be a fight to get him to let her doctor his wound. Also typical of D.J., he was keeping time to a rhythm only he could hear, kicking his feet in the water.

When a few droplets hit her, she did a little kicking of her own, paying him back with interest. He wiped his face dry with the sleeve of his tunic.

"You like to live dangerously, lady. Did I happen to mention that one of my mottos is that I don't just get even, I get ahead?"

He gave the deep pool of water a pointed look. "Looks plenty deep to drown one little woman."

She snorted. "Try it, big guy, and I won't be the only one wearing wet clothes tomorrow."

Despite the darkness, she could sense the intensity in his gaze and the temptation in his smile.

A few seconds later, he finished his dinner and set it aside. Then he stood up, peeled off his tunic, and tossed it on the grass behind them.

When he reached for the clasp of his pants, she scooted away. "D.J., what's going on in that mind of yours?"

"I decided you were right about not getting my clothes wet."

She should be doing something besides staring, she really should. However, she couldn't seem to get her eyes to look anywhere else but at all that luscious man-flesh kissed by the faint moonlight.

When he'd shed everything except his boxers, he started toward her. She scrambled to her feet and backed away.

"D.J., don't you dare! You stop right there."

"I didn't start this, Reggie. You did." He took another baby step toward her. "I am, however, going to finish it."

He folded his arms over his chest. "But to show you just what a nice guy I am, I'll give you one minute to take off whatever clothes you don't want to get soaked before I drag you into the water with me."

"You wouldn't!"

But she hoped he would. After all the horrible stuff

they'd been through, maybe a little playtime was in order. Anything to hold the ugliness at bay.

The grass felt cool against her bare toes as she faced her would-be tormentor. All right, the game was on. She reversed the order that D.J. had used, disposing of her trousers first by turning her back and taking her time to slide them off, bending over as she did so.

Her panties were simple white cotton, but the sharp intake of D.J.'s breath hinted that he didn't mind at all. Next, her tunic went sailing over her shoulder straight at him. She felt perfectly decadent standing outside under alien stars and pale moons wearing nothing but her bra and panties.

The shiver of goose bumps tickling her skin had nothing to do with the warm night air, and everything to do with the weight of her lover's gaze as she slowly eased her panties off. Her fingers fumbled with the catch on the back of her bra, making her feel awkward and clumsy.

"Let me." D.J.'s voice sounded deeper, huskier.

Cocooned in the darkness, hidden from the rest of creation, she nodded and turned around. She wanted, needed, his hands on her. With a quick flick, her bra came undone and fell away, only to be replaced by the warmth of D.J.'s palms. He pressed her back against his chest as he nibbled his way along the curve of her neck, the whole time kneading her breasts with his powerful hands. She closed her eyes, shutting out everything except his touch.

When she was about to melt into a little puddle of

need, he swept her up in his arms and waded into the stream. Instead of dunking her as she expected, he slowly sank into the water and took her with him.

"Thought we'd play some before things get too far out of hand."

With that comment, he abruptly dropped her. She slipped completely under the surface and came up sputtering and furious. Talk about ruining a beautiful moment! Okay, two could play that game.

She twirled in the water. Where had that jerk gone? Then he surfaced right in front of her and lay a hot kiss on her lips before once again disappearing beneath the dark surface.

He swam past her legs a few seconds later, his hand touching and teasing on the way by. Reggie dove after him, managing to land on his back. She held him down briefly before making her own escape. His wicked grin promised retribution when he came up for air. She turned her back to him and tried to escape, but stood no chance against his long reach. When he flipped her around to face him, she wrapped an arm around his neck and held on. Her other hand slid down between them to capture his, um, attention.

She didn't know what he'd planned to do next, but as her fingers worked their magic, he froze and let her have her way with him for several strokes. His mouth sought hers, the warm brush of his tongue a sweet contrast to the cool water against her skin.

When his hands cupped her ass, she wrapped her legs around his waist. Being pressed against his powerful chest did little to assuage the ache in her breasts. She needed more.

As if reading her mind, he waded toward the shallows and then sank down into the water as she straddled him. He bent her back enough that his mouth found her nipple, sucking to just the right side of painful. He turned his attention to her other breast, at the same time slipping his hand down between her legs. One finger tested her passage, working her gently, then with a stronger rhythm. The splash of the water, the heat of his mouth, the thrust of his fingers—it all suddenly became too much to bear.

She wasn't sure whether to beg him to stop or to beg for more. He took the decision away from her. Once again he lifted her in his arms, but this time he laid her down in the grass along the bank of the stream. Before she could catch her breath, he parted her thighs and used his tongue to quickly drive her over the edge.

She might have screamed his name. She didn't know for sure. It was all she could do to remember how to breathe. She was dimly aware of him leaving her briefly, though she protested. Without his heat to keep her warm, she shivered. Where had he gone? She rolled over to see.

He was already on his way back. Unless she was mistaken, that was an empty foil packet he dropped in the grass as he knelt beside her. When she would've turned onto her back, he stopped her.

His hand rested briefly on her lower back before wandering to her backside and then back up. The long, slow strokes relaxed her, and at the same time slowly built up the fire again. Gradually, his caresses drifted to her legs, finally spreading them apart and staking his claim there. He grasped her waist and pulled her back toward him and up onto her knees.

He leaned out over the length of her back. "Is this okay?"

She dropped her head down to her arms and tried to frame an answer to his question. Never before in her life had she made love outside with nothing but the heat of a man for a blanket. It was intoxicating. Primitive. Perfect.

Then she looked back over her shoulder at the man poised there, ready to take her soaring again.

"D.J., this is so much more than just okay."

Chapter 19

Breakfast consisted of drive-up cuisine, heavy on the caffeine and cholesterol. Cody downed three sandwiches in rapid order and was in the process of finishing off a fourth. He'd have apologized for pigging out, but Trahern had ordered three dozen. With Devlin, Trahern, Lonzo, and Cullen in the room, the food disappeared quickly. Even Barak had consumed his fair share.

They'd all gathered in Devlin's office, which evidently often served as a hangout. As soon as everyone finished stuffing their faces, Devlin cleared his throat. The room got quiet, the mood suddenly grim.

"Okay, here's where we are. First of all, the crossing D.J. used is officially dead and gone. We won't be monitoring it any longer because the barrier vanished with the explosion. Second, Hunter finally heard from Berk. The Sworn Guardian has sent word to other Guardians he trusts, and their Blademates will be on the lookout for D.J. and Reggie. He'll notify Hunter with any news on that front."

Cody leaned forward with his elbows on his knees and stared at the floor. If that was their entire rescue plan, it sure wasn't much. No matter how you looked at it, Reggie and D.J. were still trapped in the alien world. At least everyone was assuming they were both still alive. Okay, he got that. No one wanted to be the one to even hint that they weren't.

Did these guys really trust a bunch of aliens to scour the countryside to find Reggie and D.J.? Why weren't they mounting an invasion to go on the offensive?

When Cody looked up, Devlin caught his eye. "I understand you and Cullen made some progress yesterday. Where do we stand on that end of things?"

Cody let his cyberpartner fill Devlin and the rest in on the trail they were following. Cullen's summary was dead-on. Cody swallowed hard. He had something to add to the report but wasn't sure how they'd react to what he was about to say. What was the worst Devlin could do to him? Well, maybe shove him across the barrier the next time it went down.

Cullen was winding up. "So that's where we'll start today."

Cody raised his hand and then realized his mistake when Devlin's eyebrows shot up. Then the Paladin leader grinned.

"See, you bunch of bozos, that's how you indicate you have something to add to the conversation. A nice, polite raised hand."

While Lonzo rolled his eyes, Trahern muttered something about teacher's pet.

Devlin cut them off cold. "Okay, you two, let him talk."

At the moment, there was nothing Cody wanted more than to crawl into a hole. He kept his eyes on Devlin and tried to get his mouth to work.

"Okay, well, you see, I had trouble sleeping last night."

He shot a quick look in Trahern's direction. The man nodded, encouraging him to continue. "That's okay. Just spit it out."

"Since I was up anyway, I decided to hack into the Regents' server, hoping I could pick up where Cullen and I left off. But I found a new trail to follow. A guy named Ray Pine from St. Louis flew into Portland and then back to St. Louis. Since he got back, he had to have surgery on his nose. Seems it was fractured while he was traveling."

Okay, now the room was quiet again, but it felt different this time. More like the calm before the storm and he was sitting right where the lightning was about to strike. Shit, he should've kept his mouth shut.

No, that wasn't true. He'd face down a whole lot worse than a room full of Paladins and their allies if that was what it took to make this world safe for Reggie again. That didn't mean he wasn't fighting the urge to bolt and run.

It was Cullen who spoke first. He looked totally incredulous as he demanded, "Seriously? You managed to break through the new firewalls I installed?"

No use in lying. "Yeah, I did. Sorry if I bent the rules, but—"

Cullen's mouth broke into a wide grin. "No apologies needed. Damn, I'm proud of you! That's great work."

Then the Paladin gathered up the trash from his breakfast and headed toward the door. "Come on. Let's go fire up the system so you can show me what you found and how you got in. D.J. and I will have to fix that after he gets back."

Cody looked to Devlin and then Trahern, unsure if he should follow Cullen. Both men looked more thoughtful than angry.

Devlin made a shooing motion. "Go ahead. See if you can figure out who else was involved in this guy's travels."

An hour later, he and Cullen were high-fiving and hooting up a storm. When Devlin poked his head out of his office to see what the ruckus was about, Cullen waved him over.

"Okay, you already know the guy with the broken nose is Ray Pine from the Technology Department. We found where he most likely picked up on Reggie's incursion into the Regents' files. We're sure he knew about her downloading Brenna's history of the Paladins."

Devlin leaned against the door frame. "Okay, so besides his name and what he knew, what else can we learn about him? Was he working alone?"

Cody let Cullen field the questions. "I can't imagine

him being a lone wolf. He's middle management. His employee reviews indicate a certain lack of drive, adequate, but not top drawer. I'm reading between the lines here, but it looks as if he was passed over for a promotion about six months ago. The guy who got the job was younger and had less time with the organization. That's bound to have pissed him off."

Devlin wandered closer. "Does he have any special connections within the organization that stick out?"

Cullen elbowed Cody. "You found it. You tell him."

Cody would rather Cullen did it, but gave it his best shot. "I reviewed all of his phone records. Most are pretty routine—his home number, others within his department, et cetera. However, there's this one number he called only twice. The first time was right before Reggie was abducted. The second was the day after he got back from Portland."

Cody didn't know what Devlin was thinking, but he sure hoped that scary look was aimed at Ray Pine and not at him. He rubbed his hands on his jeans, hoping he didn't look as nervous as he felt.

Devlin gave Cullen a thoughtful look. "What do we know about this other guy?"

"Not much so far." Cullen pointed toward the information displayed on the computer screen. "We were just getting started on him. His name is Todd Bedford. He's higher up in the organization, and from the outside looking in, it's doubtful their jobs are connected. I'm going to do some checking into Todd's finances and see where that gets us."

"Good job, guys. Keep me posted. If it seems likely these two are involved, I'll be scheduling a road trip. In the meantime, I'll check in with Jarvis back in Missouri and see what the scoop is on these guys."

Cullen looked up from his screen. "How about asking Sasha what she knows? She has better connections within the Regents than we do."

"I'd like a little more solid intel first. But as soon as you get me some hard data on these two, I'll give her a head's-up. Maybe her father will want to join the hunt. Nice job, both of you. D.J. will appreciate all your hard work when he returns. I'm guessing he'll want to be in on it when we go after these guys."

Devlin started toward his office, but then stopped and turned back. "Cullen, keep an eye on this Todd guy. If he feels threatened, he might try to bolt. We don't want to lose him."

"Will do, boss," Cullen said as he started to reach for the keyboard. "Okay, it looks like we still have work to do."

Cody cleared his throat. "Um, before we get started, is it all right if I check on Reggie's e-mail from work and make sure the boss isn't looking for her? It would be nice if she still has a job to come back to."

Then he forced himself to ask, "Do you really think D.J. and Reggie will make it back?"

Cullen didn't answer right away, clearly giving the matter some thought. "Yeah, I really do. I know you didn't spend much time with D.J., but he's the smartest man I've ever met, and he's relentless when he wants to get something done. He'll bring her home."

Or die trying.

Cullen never actually said the words, but Cody heard them anyway.

D.J. couldn't sleep, not with Others out there wandering around. Chances were that they'd found the cave-in by now. The only question was what they'd do about it. By the time they reached the top of the trail, the suns would've disappeared over the horizon. Like the Paladins, they had better night vision than most humans, but that wouldn't help them much when it came to tracking an enemy.

Come sunrise, though, they'd be hauling ass back down the trail, on the hunt. Granted, they wouldn't have found their buddy Kolar, but there was a damn good chance they'd found the dead body back at their camp.

All of which meant that he and Reggie needed to be up and moving as soon as it was light enough for her to travel safely.

He wandered closer to where Reggie lay curled up in the bed he'd made out of their cloaks. He'd held her close until she drifted off. For a long while, he'd simply enjoyed watching her sleep. It would be all too easy to get used to doing that. Finally, he'd eased away from her, mainly to avoid the building temptation to make love to her again. They were out of condoms, and getting her pregnant would be a mistake of epic proportions.

Although the thought of her carrying a child, especially his child, made him wish he was a different man living a different life. The kind of life that could offer a woman like Reggie everything she deserved—a comfortable home, a loving husband she could depend on, safety.

With everything that had happened, she'd never settle for someone like him and shouldn't have to. Right now, circumstances forced her to depend on his strong sword arm to get her back across the barrier. Even his alien DNA was an asset if they were going to make it home, but she still didn't know the full extent of what that DNA meant. How could she be anything but horrified that she'd slept with him once she did find out?

Maybe he was underestimating her ability to look past all of that. Certainly there were women who'd proven to be able to accept the truth of what it meant to be a Paladin: Laurel, Brenna, and Jarvis's Gwen, for starters. But unlike them, Reggie made her living hunting down cybercriminals like D.J. Oh, yeah, there were all kinds of reasons for her coming to regret their brief fling.

Deep down, he didn't want what they'd shared to be just a fling. But with Reggie, he'd take what he could get.

An hour later, the distant horizon was tinged with pink. Time to get Reggie up and moving. The Others would be on the prowl soon.

He walked over to where she still slept soundly. As tiny as she was, only the top of her head showed above the covers. He smiled when he spotted the toes of her right foot peeking out at the bottom. If they weren't pressed for time, he'd give some serious thought to starting with those toes and kissing his way up her compact body to wake her.

Oh, yeah, that would certainly work for him. But then they might never get started on their trek in time to avoid their pursuers. He settled for bending down to shake Reggie's shoulder.

She came awake slowly, but smiled when she opened her eyes to see him hovering over her.

"Come on, lazybones, time to get moving."

He'd gathered her clothes up for her just as he'd done the day before. "With luck, we'll make the hills today, but we need to hustle."

Her smile dimmed. "You think those guys we saw last night are headed this way."

It wasn't a question, but he nodded anyway as he stood up. "Yeah, I do."

She reached for her underclothes. "I'll be ready in five minutes."

A couple of granola bars might be good for her, but without a cup of strong coffee, it didn't feel like breakfast. Most of the time, a cup of coffee *was* her breakfast. As they hiked along the trail toward the hills, she entertained herself by making a mental list of everything she was going to do when she got home.

Drinking a gallon of hot coffee was at the top of the list. Taking a long, hot bubble bath was running a close second. Chocolate, clean clothes, and a manicure were absolute necessities. Add in some fast food and a marathon of her favorite movies—sans the ones involving aliens or sword fights—for the perfect end to her first day back in her apartment.

Which made her think of Cody. How was he doing? Knowing him, he'd be feeling guilty for not being right here in this dusty hell with her. Was he back at work? She hoped so. It would be nice if one of them was still employed after all of this was over. When her life went back to normal, living alone with her laptop and some African violets.

She looked up from the trail to study the man in front of her. Maybe there were a few other things she'd like to do at the end of the hedonistic day. She even knew the perfect person to do them with, if he was still interested that is.

D.J. had been most considerate since waking her up, but there'd been a certain distance in his behavior. She wasn't exactly sensing any regret, just a more business-like attitude that didn't encourage any of the secret smiles and shared laughter they'd enjoyed the night before.

She'd like to chalk it up to his concern that they make good time across the valley. That was certainly part of it, she was sure. Yet she was just as certain that there was more to his change in attitude.

It was starting to irritate her a bit. Of course, all of her feelings for D.J. were a jumbled-up mess, partly because she'd seen too many different facets to his personality to get a solid feel for who he really was, starting with the whole hacker extraordinaire thing he had going on. She'd have to find some way to deal with that particular problem; her job could very well depend on it.

Then there was the playful lover. She could honestly say that she'd never even come close to enjoying sex as much as she had with D.J. Heck, she even liked the dark shadow of beard that only added to his roguish good looks even if it had left her skin feeling pretty tender in certain places.

He was funny, considerate, and on top of all that good stuff, he was a warrior. She tried not to think about all the horrific violence she'd witnessed the past few days, but she suspected when it came to D.J., it was more than just his job. It was an integral part of his makeup.

Yes, she understood that he'd killed Jeban to save her, but he'd shown absolutely no regret then or since. Kolar had brought the mountainside down on his own head, but D.J. had nearly killed him, too. No one wielded a sword with such proficiency without years of practice.

To be fair, part of what bothered her wasn't even D.J.'s reaction, but her own. She was secretly glad those two men were dead, not to mention the one back in the warehouse. In all three cases, it had come down to her life in exchange for theirs. A fair bargain as far as she was concerned. How was she going to live with feeling that way? Right now, with the continuing threat of more attacks, she was doing her best to hold everything at bay.

But when they got back home, she feared it would all come crashing down on her. Somehow she'd have to put the whole experience into perspective and come to terms with all that had happened. She had to believe she could. After all, what choice did she have? It wasn't as if she could go to a therapist and talk about murderous aliens, let alone about being trapped in their world.

Eventually the memories would fade, but not if she continued to see D.J. He'd be a constant reminder.

As if sensing her staring at him, D.J. glanced back at her. "You doing okay? Need a break?"

"I'm fine," she lied.

He started to say something, but then he stopped to stare back at the way they'd come, frowning big time. She tried to pick out whatever had caught his attention, but it was either too far away or she was too short to see it clearly.

"What's wrong?"

"I thought I saw some movement on the trail behind us, but it's gone now. Either I imagined it or maybe it was just an animal that's gone to ground. It's probably nothing."

Then he abruptly turned around and moved off at a faster pace than before. Yeah, right, it was nothing. He'd seen something all right. She ran a few steps to catch up with him, but made no effort to slow him down.

"What did you see? And don't bother lying to me. I can tell."

His expression was grim. "There's a sizable dust cloud down near the bottom of the trail right before it hits the valley floor. Like I said, maybe it's nothing, or it could be those guys coming after us full-speed ahead. Either way, it doesn't change our plan. We keep moving toward the other side of the valley as fast as your little legs can get there."

He sounded as if he was teasing her, and she hoped he was. Just last night he'd been singing in praise of those very same legs, especially when they were wrapped around him with her heels digging into his ass.

Rather than belabor the point, wasting breath she really couldn't spare, she kicked it up another notch and breezed right by him. Her small victory didn't last for long, thanks to the thin air and his long legs.

He planted those big feet of his right in her path and wouldn't let her go another step. "Reggie, what the hell are you trying to do?"

"I was walking. I didn't want my little legs to keep you from getting where you wanted to go. Now get out of my way."

He didn't move an inch. Neither did she. Stubborn deserved stubborn. She smiled when he broke first.

"Reggie, we don't have time for this."

She shrugged her shoulders. "I'm not the one blocking the path. If you'll kindly get out of my way, I'll start walking again. You can do what you want."

He cocked his head to one side as he looked down at her. "It's not walking we don't have time for."

"Then what?"

"This."

In an instant, she went from standing on her own

two feet to have them dangling in the air while D.J. kissed her as if his life depended on it. Oh, yeah, this was what she'd been missing since they'd broken camp and started this never-ending hike across hell.

His kiss tasted so unbelievably good. Hot and all male. Then abruptly he broke it off and slowly set her back down. His dark eyes reflected a mix of emotions, the chief one being either anger or frustration. She understood that last one.

Then he looked past her. "That dust cloud is definitely moving this way. Let's go."

Her heart did a stutter step or two as she hurried after him. But whether it was in response to D.J.'s kiss or to the aliens in fast pursuit behind them, she simply didn't know.

D.J. scanned the landscape in front of them, turning occasionally to see if the bastards behind them were closing the gap. So far he and Reggie had been able to maintain a steady pace and were making good progress on their way to the hills ahead. He'd feel a helluva lot better about the situation if he actually knew where they were headed. Barak's directions had been pretty vague.

It was all well and good to know there was a stretch of barrier that could be used to return home, but they couldn't afford the time to wander aimlessly hoping to get lucky and stumble across it. This entire mission was a fucked-up mess. Well, not all of it, but the whole rescue part of it sure wasn't playing out the way he'd hoped.

What was Reggie thinking about so hard? Most of the time she just kept picking them up and putting them down even though she had to be exhausted. But every so often, he sensed her staring a hole right through his back. Was it anger or passion that had her pretty eyes sparkling, full of emotion?

Time to scan the horizon again. He blinked twice and even leaned forward to get a better look. The twin to the dust cloud behind them had just appeared at the base of the hills they'd been aiming for. So far their luck had been running bad, worse, or totally fucked. Guess which this was.

"Reggie, we've got to get off the trail right now."

The only question was which direction offered the best shelter. On the left, the stream seemed to roughly follow the trail heading toward the hills. The ground to the right was more rugged thanks to large expanses of rocks, making it harder to traverse but also harder for their enemies to track them.

If he had to face off with these bastards, he'd much prefer to be standing at the barrier and swinging his favorite ax. At least there the goal was clear: stand with his brothers-in-arms to keep the enemy from getting anywhere near the rest of humanity.

Here, the slightest mistake in his calculations could end in death—or worse—for both him and Reggie. He might survive a lethal wound. She wouldn't.

He picked the rougher terrain to the right. The going would be more difficult than if they took to the water, but they'd stand a better chance the Others would lose their trail on the harder ground.

In addition, it was higher than the trail. Hopefully it would afford them a clearer picture of what they were walking into. He waited until they reached a stretch of trail that was rockier so that their footprints didn't show before veering off the trail.

The ground climbed steadily the farther off the trail they got, to the point that he was huffing and puffing almost as badly as Reggie. After they'd safely traversed a particularly steep incline, the ground flattened out for some distance. At the far side, a small creek trickled through the grass. Perfect. If they stayed low and quiet, no one should be able to spot them.

"We'll stop here to catch our breath."

Once again Reggie didn't say a word. She simply dropped to the ground and started tugging off her boots. He started to tell her that they weren't stopping that long, but then he saw the blood. Damn it all to hell, why hadn't she told him that she was getting blisters?

Because she knew it didn't matter. Hurt or not, they had to keep going. At least he could doctor her feet for her before they had to start walking again. He set down his packs and started digging through them for the first-aid kit.

"Let's get those cleaned up for you."

"I can take care of myself," she said but without any real heat.

"I know you can." And he did. "But this one time, why don't you let me help?"

She laid back in the grass and put her feet in the

creek to let the water wash them clean. "All right, but next time we get stuck in an alien world, I get to be the hero."

"Fair enough."

Damn, he loved her spunk. Might even love her. And wasn't that a hell of a shocker?

Chapter 20

*T*odd gripped the phone in a stranglehold, wishing his hand was wrapped around Ray's throat instead.

"I don't give a flying fuck who you think is after you! I told you not to call me again. Ever. Now forget you ever knew my number or even my name."

Todd slammed the phone down in the cradle, fighting the urge to jerk the damn thing from the wall and heave it out the window. With his luck, it would land on somebody and they'd sue him.

Well, only if they could find him. Good luck with that.

It would be nice to believe that it was Ray's pain medication making the stupid bastard so damn paranoid. For sure, it was making him careless enough to call Todd's direct line. Last night he'd even left a rambling message on Todd's home number. It had been pure luck that he'd been able to erase it before his wife heard it.

Unfortunately, Todd had a horrible feeling that Ray

was right, and the Paladins were in fact breathing down the man's neck. Drugged or not, Ray had always had a sixth sense when it came to saving his own ass. If those sword jockeys did get their paws on the coward, he'd cave in a heartbeat, and they'd be beating on Todd's door in the time it took to drive from Ray's house to his.

He could kick himself for not emptying his safety deposit box on the way home just in case everything went south. Now he'd have to wait until morning to access his stash of money and passports. After that, he'd fly out of town under his real name.

Then he'd become Justin Camp.

It wouldn't be enough to head to a country the U.S. didn't have an extradition treaty with because there were Paladins stationed all over the globe. He had a sick feeling they'd have the attitude that a threat to any of them was a threat to all of them. If Devlin Bane put out an all-call on Todd, those deadly bastards would come after him with weapons drawn no matter where he went.

Again, but only if they found him. In the next two days Todd Bedford would simply cease to exist.

He'd already told his wife he was leaving town on business. She was too caught up in her little charities to notice if he packed more clothes than usual. How long would it take her to figure out that he wasn't coming back? He wished he could be a fly on the wall when she realized her meal ticket had been canceled.

Prince that he was, he wouldn't completely clean out their bank accounts, but only because he was afraid it would send up too many red flags. She'd have enough to live on until she got a divorce and found some other poor bastard to support her.

For now, though, he had to maintain appearances. They were scheduled to have dinner with one of the Regents tonight.

With luck, by tomorrow evening he'd be winging his way to someplace with sunny beaches and beautiful women. As long as he concentrated on the good things maybe he wouldn't worry so much about waking up with a sword at his throat.

With that chilling thought, he poured himself another stiff scotch. It was hard to swallow around the solid lump of fear in his throat, but he drank it anyway.

If the terrain didn't get easier to cross, they might have to give up and head back to the trail they'd been following earlier. With all the damn boulders and vertical drop-offs, they'd walked twice as far to get half the distance. If D.J.'s legs were aching this much, he could only imagine how Reggie was feeling, but she kept trucking right along.

He slowed down a bit, hoping she wouldn't notice. The last time he'd tried to accommodate her shorter gait, she'd ripped into him but good. She sure was a fierce little thing, the kind of woman who'd make some lucky guy one hell of a life partner.

Okay, Reggie with another man was an image he didn't want to think about. Especially her getting naked with someone else, even if it was some nice guy who lived a normal life. Hell, no, he'd gut the bastard before he'd let him touch her. D.J.'s hand had strayed to the pommel of his sword and pulled it halfway out of the scabbard. He shoved it back in and jerked his hand back to his side.

Unfortunately, Reggie had noticed.

"D.J., what's wrong? Did you see something?"

Damn it, D.J., get your head in the game.

"Uh, no. Just checking my weapons."

That was his story and he was sticking to it. At least Reggie seemed to accept his explanation. He stopped and waited for her.

"Why don't you take a break while I see what's over that next rise?"

It was a testament to how tired she was that she simply nodded and leaned against a nearby rock with a heavy sigh. When he looked back from the cover of the trees, she was sipping her water, her face a study in pain. Damn, maybe they should stop for the night even though they still had hours of dim sunshine in which to travel.

He'd been slowly working their way back toward the trail for the past hour. If he could determine where the Others were, it might be worth the risk to use the trail long enough to reach the hills. They'd definitely make better time that way.

It took him about fifteen minutes to reach a point where he could see the trail below. For the moment, there was no one in sight, not even the telltale sign of dust floating in the air. He retreated down the slope and took off running back to Reggie. He'd been gone longer than he'd meant to and didn't want to worry her.

She was just where he'd left her. That was the good news.

The bad news? She wasn't alone.

There was one thing this whole experience had taught Reggie and that was the taste of fear. She suspected that D.J.'s need to scout ahead was an excuse to let her sit for a while. She'd been too tired to argue the point; a couple of minutes of not having to move had sounded too good to pass up. After a long drink of water, she'd closed her eyes to give them a brief rest. Really, that's all she'd meant to do.

Evidently her exhaustion beat out her good intentions. She had no idea how long she'd actually slept, but she'd been jerked out of a deep sleep by someone kicking her foot.

She'd woken up furious and ready to rip into D.J. for his heavy-handed technique. Unfortunately, the man standing in front of her wasn't D.J. Heck, he wasn't even human. Her throat immediately closed up, preventing her from screaming for help. She just hoped that D.J. wasn't walking back into an ambush.

Her captor made no move to touch her once he was satisfied she was awake. Was he waiting for his buddies to catch up with him before the party started? God, she didn't want to think about it.

Then he actually smiled at her. "Reggie? D.J.?"

His accent was so heavy that it took her a second to recognize her own name. How did he know who she was?

"I'm Reggie," she said, pointing at herself since he seemed to be waiting for a response.

"D.J.?" he said again, making it sound like a question.

Did she out her friend or claim ignorance? It wouldn't exactly be a lie since she really didn't know where he was at the moment. He'd already been gone far longer than she'd expected him to be.

She settled for a shrug, holding her hands out palms up. She had no idea how well nonverbal communication translated from one world to the next. Under other circumstances, she would've found that idea fascinating, but right now, not so much.

But her taciturn companion evidently understood because he nodded and moved a short distance away. As soon as he did, she scrambled to her feet. When he started back toward her, she froze in place. She'd never outrun him, but she felt less like a prisoner standing up. Maybe it was stupid to feel that way, but there it was.

This Kalith was a definite puzzle. He was dressed in a manner similar to that of the others she'd seen, but there were differences, too. She'd guess he was younger, but that wasn't it. He stood ramrod straight, almost military in his stance. His clothing was uniformly dark except for an ornate insignia sewn to the front of his tunic.

He didn't seem inclined to talk, so she didn't try. Maybe he didn't speak English. He shifted slightly, his attention riveted on the other side of the clearing. What had he heard or seen that had him on full alert? *Please, God, don't let D.J. come charging into an ambush.* Maybe she could distract this guy.

She hesitated, but the Kalith's attention remained fully focused on that same spot. He held his weapon by his side, not exactly a threat but definitely ready to act if necessary. When he took a step forward, she bolted and ran in the opposite direction.

He hollered and charged after her. When she looked back, he'd sheathed his sword and was gaining ground on her quickly. That was all right. As long as he was concentrating on her, D.J. was safe. She put everything she had into getting away, but after the day she'd had, she was running on fumes. After just a few seconds, he was breathing down her neck.

Then in one fell swoop, he scooped her up in his arms. That did it. She totally lost all control, preparing to scream her lungs out, flail her arms, and kick as hard as she could. She tried to break free but nothing worked. The Kalith slapped his big hand over her mouth and just waited until she'd exhausted the last of her energy.

When she hung limp in his arms, he quietly carried her back to where she'd left her pack and gently lowered her to the ground. Once again he stepped back, holding up his hands as if asking her to stay put. Then he drew his sword again.

"D.J.," he said, pointing across the clearing with the tip of his blade.

She held her breath and prayed he was wrong.

• • •

Once again Cullen was going to leave it up to Cody to explain their findings. It felt almost as if the Paladin was showing off his star pupil. Cody could only hope that Devlin and the rest were even half as impressed as Cullen was by what Cody had dug up on those two guys in St. Louis.

They'd gathered in Devlin's office again. Cullen distributed hard copies of the information while Devlin spoke.

"Okay, everybody, listen up. Cullen tells me that Cody here has found the nails to seal the coffin on those two assholes in St. Louis. He's going to go over the highlights with us. The good news is, Sasha has already agreed to contact her father with the report."

Then he nodded in Cody's direction. "You're up."

Cody started at the beginning, careful to follow Cullen's advice not to drown them all in geek speak. He stuck to the facts, starting with Ray's e-mail to Reggie and going from there. By the time he got to the part where Todd had a flight booked to Miami the next afternoon, the room was unnaturally quiet.

Not bored quiet either. Deadly quiet was more like it. Ominous, even. If he'd had any doubts about the true nature of these men, they were pretty much laid to rest now.

They all had their eyes pinned on Cody, looking pretty damn fierce. It would've been scary if he'd been the real target of their anger. All of it was directed toward the two men who'd jeopardized an innocent woman's life for their own selfish reasons. That was bad enough, but the Paladins also stood to lose one of their own if D.J. didn't make it back from Kalithia with Reggie.

Cody concluded with the last few details and then turned it over to Devlin. The big man stood and looked around the room before nodding at Cody with a brief smile.

"Okay, guys, like I said, Sasha is going to contact her father immediately. She's asked that we hold off any direct confrontation until the Regents are notified. However, I've already called Jarvis and filled him in about what's going on. He's got men on the way to keep an eye on both targets until we get the official go-ahead. Either way, Lonzo and I are on a flight to St. Louis in three hours."

Then Devlin smiled again, but there was nothing friendly about it this time. "Jarvis has also promised that they'll take the bastards down if they try to bolt before the Regents decide to act. It's such a shame when communications break down."

The laughter in the room was edgy and dark, but Cody found himself joining in. His first concern was getting Reggie back safely, but they also needed to make sure she stayed safe once she was home. Besides, he wanted the bastards to pay for putting her through hell, not to mention everyone else who'd been drawn into this mess.

"Any questions?"

"I've got one." It was Trahern holding up his hand.

"Ask away."

Trahern briefly turned his icy eyes in Cody's direction before speaking.

"I was wondering when we're going to put my young friend here on the payroll. He's earned it. The rest of us have been sitting on our collective asses while he and Cullen have done all the work."

Now all eyes were on him. Cody expected Devlin to tell Trahern to butt out. Instead he was nodding.

"I've already spoken to Sasha about it. I was going to talk to Cody after the meeting. For now, let's just say we take care of our own."

Okay, a whole new cotton crop popped up in Cody's throat, spreading to his lungs and making it hard to breathe and impossible to talk. Payroll? Seriously?

Devlin tossed his empty cup in the trash. "Okay, everybody out of here. It's business as usual until you hear otherwise. Cody, stay where you are."

D.J. drew his sword and slowly started forward, fighting the urge to charge in and ask questions when the dust settled. Two things stayed his hand, the first being that the Other was making no threatening moves toward either of them at the moment. The second was that the bastard stood between him and Reggie.

"D.J.?"

Okay, how did that guy know his name? There was only one way that he could think of.

"Berk?"

The Other nodded. "Sent me."

D.J. still hesitated, but lowered his sword slightly. "What else did he tell you?"

"Barak. Hunter. Berk. Cave. Safety. Trust."

The Kalith repeated the words as if he'd memorized the speech without really understanding the complete meaning. Even so, it was the best news D.J. had heard in days.

He sheathed his sword and started forward, nodding his head as he went. "Trust. Come with you."

To keep the conversation going, he pointed at his chest and said, "I'm D.J. She's Reggie." Then he pointed at the other man. "You?"

The Kalith smiled and laid his hand on his own chest. "Javel."

D.J. finally locked eyes with Reggie. "I think this guy is a Blademate of Berk, that Sworn Guardian Devlin and Barak were going to contact."

He walked past Javel to offer Reggie a hand up off the ground. "Are you all right?"

"I am now. He scared the stuffing out of me. I'd fallen asleep, so I don't even know where he came from."

When she brushed her hair back from her pretty face, he saw dried tracks of tears. He immediately enfolded her in his arms, despite the risk of turning his back on Javel.

"God, Reggie, I'm sorry. I promise we'll get past all of this. Someday you'll look back and wonder if it even happened."

She snuggled closer. "Yeah, right. Like I could forget

staring up at twin suns or all these guys running around with swords."

Was he one of the guys she was talking about? Selfish as it was, he really hoped so. If she was going to haunt his dreams for years to come, it was only fair if he got equal time in hers.

Javel cleared his throat, a not-so-subtle hint that they had more important things to be thinking about at the moment.

"Guess that means we'd better get moving." He kissed her forehead before stepping back. "If this guy is on the level—and I think he is—things are definitely looking up for us."

"All right, if we must."

She turned her bright smile on the Kalith warrior and wiggled her foot. "I'm sorry I kicked you."

It wasn't clear how much English the guy understood, but he obviously knew what to do when a beautiful woman smiled at him. He tipped his head to the side and bowed slightly from the waist. His smile was a tad hotter than D.J. liked.

D.J. stepped forward, placing himself firmly between the Kalith and Reggie. The damn kid actually laughed. He might not speak D.J.'s language, but he definitely got the message.

Having made his point, D.J. held his hands palms up and out to the sides. "Where to next?"

Another message received. Javel pointed in the direction D.J. had been scouting out. That only made sense. Time to head 'em up and move 'em out.

He picked up his pack and Reggie did the same. When they were ready, he motioned for Javel to lead on. The guy knew the way better than he did, and D.J. wasn't crazy about letting someone he didn't know walk behind him carrying a sword.

Their small procession moved out at a comfortable pace. Evidently he wasn't the only one who realized how tired Reggie was. The suns hovered over the distant horizon, making it imperative they cover as much distance as possible before the pale light disappeared altogether.

Javel better call a halt in the next few minutes or D.J. was going to hamstring the guy. Reggie was doing her best, but it was getting dark to the point where he was holding her hand to guide her way.

Maybe the Kalith sensed D.J.'s growing irritation because he hung a sharp left turn and led them off the trail. About twenty yards later, they walked into a small clearing along the same stream they'd camped by the night before.

The sight brought back some fond memories, but somehow he doubted Reggie would be up for a repeat performance, not with Javel there. For that matter, neither would D.J. Making love to her wasn't ever going to be a spectator sport.

He stared out at the hills looming on the horizon. They were a whole lot closer now, which was a good thing. Really. But he couldn't help thinking about the fact that if they safely reached the barrier tomorrow, Reggie would be going back to her life and he'd go back to his.

Talk about total downers. There was no way the two of them could stay in touch, especially *close* touch, not with her job to think about. If she didn't track down D.J. for her boss, it would be seen as a failure. Eventually one of her coworkers would give it a shot. One way or another, the Knightwalker was going to have to disappear permanently.

Rather than obsess about things he couldn't change, he got busy and helped Javel gather wood for the fire. Once they had a nice blaze going, D.J. rooted through the pack to see what was left for dinner. He found three MREs.

At least they didn't take much effort to prepare. He handed one to Reggie and offered one to Javel, who sniffed it and wrinkled his nose.

Reggie laughed. "My opinion exactly."

D.J. faked an attempt to steal it back. "If you don't like my cooking . . ."

She whipped it out of his hands. "It's not like you've got any steaks tucked away in that pack. But since you've done all the cooking on this lovely vacation, I'll fix you dinner when we get back home."

Curious, he asked her, "Are you a good cook?"

She gave the MREs a pointed look. "If I can't do better than this stuff, shoot me now."

Javel's head swiveled back and forth, probably trying to follow their conversation. He didn't say anything, but there was a definite twinkle in his pale eyes right up until he took his first taste. The look on his face was absolutely priceless, but he stoically ate every bite.

After he was through, he got out his own pack and removed what looked like some kind of fruit. He offered one to Reggie and tossed a second one to D.J.

Reggie studied hers for a second. "Do you think we should?"

"I don't see why not, provided he eats his. The Kaliths I know thrive on our food, so it's probably a safe bet."

She nodded her thanks to Javel and bit into the fruit right after he started eating his. Her eyes flared wide, and she quickly took a second bite.

"This is delicious."

D.J. agreed. Javel smiled and nodded, clearly pleased with their reactions.

With dinner over, it was time to get some sleep. D.J. spread out his cloak for Reggie.

"I'm going to stand guard for a while."

Using words and hand gestures, he conveyed his intent to Javel. The Blademate nodded. He pointed toward the moon on the horizon and moved his hand in a sweeping arch to a point overhead. Then he pointed at himself. Guessing he was offering to split the watch with him, D.J. nodded.

Javel immediately stretched out on the ground some distance from where Reggie lay by the fire. Like most soldiers, he dropped off to sleep almost immediately. Reggie wasn't far behind.

Once they were both settled in, D.J. walked the perimeter a few times. After a bit, he sat down on a rock by the water where he could keep a close eye on their escort and still watch Reggie as she slept.

The strain of the past few days had done nothing to diminish her beauty or that incredible intensity that was so much a part of her personality. Considering all that had been thrown at her—kidnapping, murder, aliens— she was holding up amazingly well. Maybe there was a major meltdown hovering on the horizon, but so far she'd dazzled him with her strength and determination.

She stirred and murmured something in her sleep. Her eyebrows were drawn down low over her eyes as if she were concentrating. Her mouth was pursed and unhappy. Whatever was going on in her sleeping mind, it wasn't good.

He moved to sit closer and leaned down to brush her hair back from her face. Instantly, the worried lines on her forehead disappeared and she rubbed her face against his hand like a kitten needing a good scratch.

He froze, the position he was in uncomfortable and awkward. On the other hand, if she needed his touch, he'd pretzel it for the rest of the night.

Finally, he slid down onto the ground and sat cross-legged beside her, letting her hold his hand next to her face. The small connection soothed him as well.

Once they were home, he was going to miss this. He was used to being part of a team, but not a couple. One of many, not one half of a pair.

He couldn't let himself think like that. Sure, he had friends, people he mattered to—Cullen, Devlin, Trahern, Lonzo, Hunter. He even had friends who looked and talked exactly like that kid sleeping in the grass with his pale eyes and silvered dark hair. That had been a real kick in the ass—finding out that not everyone who lived on the other side of the barrier was a certified whack job.

Reggie shifted in her sleep again, this time turning away from him. She'd finally settled into deep, peaceful sleep. Evidently she no longer needed his touch to hold the bad dreams at bay. He drew his hand back to his side, missing that small connection. Rather than sit there and dwell on it, he walked the perimeter of their camp and a short distance beyond.

The hush of the Kalith night eased his restlessness. A light breeze rustled the tall grass with a soft murmur. Occasionally, a bird called out in the night, or a small animal scurried along the edge of the water.

Glancing up at the sky, he noticed the moons were now overhead. Time for the changing of the guard. He'd debated long and hard about whether to trust the young Blademate with watching over the camp while D.J. slept. Paladins had incredible stamina, but he'd been on full alert for days now. If he didn't get some serious shut-eye soon, it would start to impact his ability to fight.

Yeah, now that they were on their way to meet up with Berk and his men, the rest of the trip might go smoothly. But his years as a Paladin had taught him not to trust luck or even well-laid plans. Hoping he wasn't making a major mistake, he carefully approached Javel as he slept. Figuring a Blademate would have a hair-trigger response at being rousted out of a sound sleep by a total stranger—not to mention the traditional enemy of his people—D.J. stopped just short of sword range.

"Javel, rise and shine."

Pale eyes snapped open, full awareness quickly flooding into them. Javel automatically gripped his sword, but at least he didn't come up fighting. After a second, he sat up and stretched.

Still unsure of how much English the Blademate actually understood, D.J. kept it simple. "You okay?"

Javel nodded and stood up. After sheathing his sword, he gestured toward the ground and then toward D.J. Next he pointed at the moons overhead, again indicating the passage of time by pointing toward where they'd be in a few hours, and then on toward the hills in the distance.

D.J. nodded his understanding. Javel would stand guard until just before dawn. Then they needed to hit the road.

"Okay, we'll leave when you think we should."

The Kalith disappeared into the darkness, but D.J. could still sense his presence. Time to settle in for the remainder of the night. It was tempting to snuggle in next to Reggie, but he wasn't sure how she'd feel about it now that they had company. But, damn, just the memory of how it had felt to hold her close had him hard and hurting.

Common sense won out. If they were to come under attack, either from the Others prowling the area or even their buddy Javel, he needed to be able to move fast and furiously. He couldn't do that if his legs and arms, or other things, were tangled up with Reggie.

He made his bed in the spot Javel had vacated. Even so, he turned so that the last thing he saw as he drifted to sleep was Reggie's pretty face.

Chapter 21

*O*kay, so far, so good. Todd had made it out of the house without his wife doing more than her usual amount of bitching. Something about this unexpected business trip interfering with some plans she'd made. Probably another one of those godforsaken charity functions she was always dragging him to.

If he had any regrets about leaving her behind, that thought alone pretty much eliminated them. Never again would he have to stand there and listen to his wife and her clone friends prattle on and on about their latest cause.

He had far more important things to attend to, like retrieving his money and travel papers before hightailing it to the airport. To hurry things along, he helped load his own luggage into the back of the taxi before climbing into the backseat.

He wished this felt more like an adventure than running for his life. That thought had him spinning around to look out the rear window.

Stupid to think that someone might be following him, but it paid to be careful. Although what would he do if there *was* someone tailing him? It wasn't as if he was armed. Even if he did know how to use a gun, these days, carrying one into an airport was out of the question.

He took comfort from reviewing his plan, proud of how carefully he'd set everything in motion. He'd told his office assistant he'd be in a little late, but otherwise it was business as usual, including having her set up some meetings he had no intention of attending.

First up on his real agenda was to stop at the bank. He'd pay the cabbie to wait while he dashed in to retrieve his stash. Then it was off to the airport where he'd made two sets of reservations. He'd be flying from St. Louis to Miami under his real name. Once there, he'd dump all of his old identification and become Justin Camp before continuing on to his next destination.

How would it feel to shed his current life like an old skin he'd outgrown? Freeing? Scary? Not that it mattered. It wasn't as if he had any choice. Looking back, he should've told Ray that'd he'd handle the security breach himself. Trusting that idiot to be discreet had turned out to be a mistake of the clusterfuck variety.

He shoved away all thoughts of what-might-have-been as the taxi pulled into the bank parking lot and stopped.

"I need you to wait for me," Todd said, holding out a ten. "I shouldn't be gone long."

"Thank you, sir. I'll be right here when you come back out."

He opened the door. "There'll be another twenty in it for you if you get me to the airport in under thirty minutes."

The cabbie winked and grinned. "Don't worry about that, sir. You'll reach your destination in plenty of time."

On his way into the bank, Todd looked back. What was that all about? Right now the guy was on his cell, not paying any attention to Todd at all. For some reason, it reassured him that it was only nerves making him jump at shadows. It shouldn't take him more than fifteen minutes to clear out his safety deposit box and withdraw his fair share of the savings and checking accounts.

Then back to the cab and on his way to freedom.

Lonzo pocketed the ten as he watched Todd dart into the bank. Somehow he doubted he'd be getting that twenty the asshole had promised him for making sure he got to the airport on time.

"Yeah, Devlin, I've got him. Right now he's in the bank collecting all the nuts he's been squirreling away. Unless he's abandoning all of his luggage, he'll be back. Besides, Jarvis and his men are watching the other doors. They'll snag him if he tries to ditch me."

Lonzo laughed. "You should've seen the man watching to see if we were being tailed. Has he never heard of a GPS chip in a cell phone? The guys got here before Todd had time to walk in the door. What an idiot."

"Don't forget that idiot is responsible for putting D.J. and Reggie through hell."

"Trust me, I won't."

Devlin was still talking. "Promise me you won't lose him. When D.J. gets back, he's going to want to have a personal talk with Todd baby."

Then Devlin paused for a long second. "And if he doesn't get back, I'll be the one having that conversation with him. I hope the carpet in Jarvis's office doesn't show bloodstains."

Lonzo understood exactly how the man felt. "Under the circumstances, I'll spring for a new carpet myself."

A movement at the bank door caught his attention. "Oops, gotta go, boss. My fare's on the way back. He already gave me a ten-dollar tip and promised me a twenty if we hauled ass to the airport."

Devlin's chuckle was a grim rumble. "I'll spot you the twenty if he doesn't cough it up."

"Sounds good. Keep me posted."

Before Lonzo hung up, he had one more thing to say. "Dev, I really hate this shit. After this is over, Jarvis agrees it's time we clean house around here."

"Tell him I'll buy the brooms. Watch your back."

Lonzo slid his cell back in his shirt pocket and started the car. When Todd got in, Lonzo popped the top on a very special bottle of water and held it out to his passenger.

"It's a warm one today, sir. I noticed you were sweating quite a bit and thought you might like a cold drink."

If Todd refused it, Lonzo would go to Plan B, which involved a big, fat syringe full chemicals to knock the guy out for the duration of the trip. While shoving a needle in the bastard held some appeal, it increased the chance of some civilian seeing what was up and calling the police. They couldn't risk that.

But Todd accepted the bottle and immediately took a long swig. "Thanks, I appreciate it."

Knowing the drugs should kick in within a couple of minutes, Lonzo pulled out of the parking lot and dutifully headed for Todd's next stop. It was an airport, but a private one. Before the guy resurfaced, he'd be tucked into a special room located far underground in the caves of southern Missouri that housed the Paladin headquarters in the Midwest.

But just in case the drugs didn't do their job fast enough, Lonzo flipped a switch that locked both doors in the backseat. Short of chewing through glass and metal, there was no way Todd would escape the confines of the taxi anytime soon.

Lonzo checked the rearview mirror. Todd was already starting to blink, as if trying to bring his eyes back into focus. Satisfied that his passenger wasn't going to be a problem, Lonzo cranked up the radio and sang along.

Sometimes the good guys actually won.

By late morning, they'd already been following Javel for hours. From where they now stood, D.J. could see the rock Barak had described to him. It definitely sported the profile of an old man, complete with an oversize nose and what could be ears. Allowing for the steep terrain ahead, they should be able to reach it in under half an hour.

Damn, his backside was definitely dragging, but each step took them that much closer to home. He had to believe that. The alternative was unbearable. It was also hell to be this close to Reggie and not touch her. He craved any kind of skin-to-skin contact and would've been content simply holding her hand. If that wouldn't have slowed down his response time in an emergency, he might have given it a shot.

Reggie paused to look back at him. "D.J., how sure are you that we can trust him?"

Their Kalith escort had ranged out in front of them, momentarily out of sight as he scouted the trail ahead. It didn't translate to Javel being out of hearing though. While his understanding of English seemed to be spotty at best, it didn't pay to underestimate the man. Pretending to not understand their language was one heck of a way to spy on them.

D.J. kept his answer to a soft whisper. "He's definitely leading us in the right direction, and he had plenty of chances to attack while we slept. For the moment I'm willing to give him the benefit of the doubt."

Reggie nodded. "Any sign of those other guys? The ones who were following us?"

"Not so far this morning. I've been watching behind us and no dust clouds. Of course, they could've cut across country same as we did."

She held up two fingers and crossed them. He mirrored her actions. "Yeah, me, too."

The day had been uneventful so far, but that didn't mean much. When dealing with the crazies of Kalithia, there was no predicting when hell would break loose. It had been quiet since Javel found them the day before.

Maybe too quiet.

D.J. kept a wary eye on the trail ahead, watching for their Kalith escort to return, and never letting more than a minute or two go by without checking behind them. Reggie picked up on his growing tension and was doing her own fair share of scanning the surrounding terrain.

To break the strain, he struck up a conversation. "So what's the first thing you're going to do when we get back?"

She grinned at him and rubbed her hands together in glee. "Find the nearest coffee shop and get a gallon to go, complete with all the trimmings. Double shots, double cream, double sugar, double foam, double everything. Oh, and sprinkles. Definitely lots of sprinkles."

He understood why coffee would be at the top of the list. "Having a problem with caffeine withdrawal, are we? Yeah, I get that. A big greasy hamburger and fries sound good, too. What else is on your agenda?"

"I haven't really thought much past the coffee run."

Reggie's eyes slid to the side and there was a definite hint of pink in her cheeks that hadn't been there before. She was definitely hiding something. Did it involve him?

"Okay, lady, somehow I don't believe you. I think you've got something decadent planned. Something that involves ice cream and chocolate sauce."

He waggled his eyebrows. "Come on, Reggie, 'fess up."

Her blush deepened, meaning he'd hit a little too

close for comfort. Okay, so maybe he should update his own list. Rather than call her on it, though, he changed the subject.

"So, I'm curious. How long are you going to give me to hide my tracks before you point your boss in my direction? Maybe I'll borrow your Ruby avatar for a while. Think I'd make a pretty woman?"

Reggie whacked him on the arm.

"Darn it anyway, D.J., that's not funny! After all of this, how could you think I'd turn you in? Not to mention the fact that I've probably already lost my job over this mess."

He held up his hands in surrender. "Whoa, Reggie, I was just teasing. Seriously, if siccing your boss on me will ensure you keep your job, don't even hesitate. I can take care of myself."

She glared at him and then turned away, but not before he saw the tears welling up in her eyes. Okay, now he felt like a total jerk. But before he could apologize, Javel came running down the hillside, his sword drawn.

D.J. dropped his equipment bag on the ground, at the same time shoving Reggie behind him. He drew his own blade and pulled his gun out of his waistband. Javel slid to a halt just out of reach, his eyes wide, his breathing ragged.

He pointed back in the direction they'd come from with his sword. "Kalith!"

Then he pointed where they'd been heading. "Cave! Close!"

Right now D.J. would give his left arm for a Kalith/

English dictionary. Was the Blademate telling him they were about to be attacked by Kalith warriors? Or that the Kalith hunting party had taken control of the cave? How the hell was he supposed to figure it out? A wrong decision here could easily prove fatal for all of them.

He held his hands out and shrugged his shoulders, hoping to convey his confusion to the young warrior. "Berk?"

Javel immediately shook his head and pointed behind them again. "Berk, cave. Kalith come."

He held up five fingers and then two more. Okay, that was clear enough. Berk was waiting at the cave. The seven Kalith weren't his men. Time to find a defensible position. Hard to do when he had no idea how long they had to prepare.

Looking around, he ran through the options in his head. There was only one acceptable choice. D.J. would hold off the approaching Kalith while Javel got Reggie to the cave. Once there, Berk could send reinforcements.

"Reggie, you go with Javel. Now."

He infused as much authority into his voice as he could, hoping she wouldn't argue. Yeah, right, like that was going to happen.

"No, there are too many of them for you to fight alone. I'll hide up there," she said, pointing toward the trees on the hill. "That way Javel can help you."

"And if we both get killed, Reggie? What would you do then? Please just go with Javel. He can get you to Berk. The Guardian and his men will see you get home."

He grabbed her arm, meaning to shove her at Javel.

Instead, he kissed her hard and fast, hoping she'd understand what he was trying to tell her, what he had no words for. Then he did push her toward Javel.

He pegged the young Blademate with a hard stare. "Take Reggie to Berk. To the cave."

With a grave nod, Javel held his sword up in salute and started dragging Reggie up the trail. "To cave. To Berk."

She fought against his superior strength. "D.J., if we go, you'll die. Don't do this. It's suicide!"

"Damn it, Reggie, go! I'm harder to kill than you know. The longer you argue, the longer it will be before Berk can send reinforcements. Run!"

All the fight went out of her, and she let Javel tow her along. D.J. couldn't tear his eyes off her. Watching her leave felt as if his heart was being ripped out by the roots. Hell, maybe it had been. He suspected she'd taken over complete ownership of it from the first moment they'd met.

He just wished he'd told her.

Then he turned to face the oncoming enemy with a sword in one hand and his Glock in the other. Guns against blades might not be a fair fight, but he didn't give a flying fuck. He'd kill the bastards with his bare hands if that's what it took to give his woman time to reach safety.

As the enemy came around the bend, he screamed out in challenge and charged into battle, firing as he ran. His first shots laid two out flat and crippled one more. All three went down screaming. The rest immediately backed off to regroup. Four against one made for slightly better odds, but not by much.

God, how many of these bastards had he killed over the years? Dozens? Hundreds? It didn't matter. A few had returned the favor. Normally, he didn't worry about that much. Sure, it hurt like hell and never got less scary to feel the last breath leaving his body.

But with his fellow Paladins there, he always knew someone else would step up to take his place. Later, when the blood quit flowing, they'd carry him up to the labs where Laurel or one of the other Handlers would jump-start his return to the living.

Not going to happen now, not here. For the first time in recent memory, he was scared. Not for himself, but for Reggie. He'd kill every crazy Other in this whole fucking damn world if that's what it took to keep her safe.

Okay, the assholes were working themselves up to another charge. They were doing their damnedest to encircle D.J., but he danced backward to keep from being surrounded.

He lunged forward, his blade catching the one on the right deep in the abdomen. Before D.J. could jerk his sword free, though, he felt the slide of steel cutting through his upper thigh. For the moment, adrenaline overrode the pain. As long as he didn't bleed out, he'd continue to whittle down the number of Others still on their feet.

They babbled at him in Kalith, clearly taunting him. Just for grins, D.J. added his own litany of insults to the

chorus. Lunge and thrust. Cut and bleed. The truth of
his reality.

He hated knowing that once again Reggie had a
front-row seat to the travesty that was his life.

That new burst of fury took down another enemy,
leaving the scum writhing in the dirt, trying to hold in
his intestines with bloody fingers. D.J. finished the poor
SOB off and was repaid for his kindness with another
superficial wound from one of the remaining Others.

This time, when he lunged, his wounded leg gave
out, leaving him pitching forward into the dust. He managed to block the first swing of his opponent's sword.
The second, not so much. He fought off the waves of
darkness as long as he could, trying to hold on, to fight.
They finally proved too much and the battle was lost.

As the last wave of pain crested and flowed over him,
his desperate mind imagined Reggie hovering over him,
tears streaking down her face. If the image was real, he
hated knowing she had to see him like this. But of all
the times he'd died, seeing her sweet face was the best
good-bye ever.

Chapter 22

$\mathcal{T}$odd felt like hell. All things considered, it was an improvement over the last time he'd regained consciousness. That time he'd been pretty sure he was dying and had felt bad enough to hope he was. Now he was very much afraid he was going to *live*.

He pushed himself upright, moving slowly to ward off the waves of nausea that threatened to overwhelm him again. Once he was almost vertical, he squinted at his surroundings.

Where the heck was he? And how did he get there? Why was he barefoot and in surgical scrubs?

The room was empty except for the stainless-steel table he was sitting on. Heavy chains that ended in leather straps with buckles dangled from all four corners. He supposed he should be grateful that he hadn't been restrained. Of course, it probably meant his captors were sure he wouldn't be able to escape.

The last thing he remembered was . . . oh, yeah,

he'd taken a cab to the bank. He had vague memories of filling his briefcase with money. He'd paid the taxi driver to wait in the parking lot for him. That much he recalled. Beyond that, though, things became jumbled.

Slowly the fog in his head dissipated, and the memories became clearer. The driver had offered him a bottle of water. It had tasted cold, refreshing. They'd left the parking lot. After that, nothing.

And then it hit him—that rat-bastard cabbie must have drugged him. The question was, why? Robbery made sense, but there was no way the guy could have known in advance that Todd had been headed to the bank to pick up a wad of cash. Did he keep a bottle of drugged water on hand just in case?

Considering the only other explanation, he almost hoped that's what had happened. However, he wasn't in the habit of lying to himself. After studying his surroundings some more, he admitted the truth of the situation. There was only one place he could think of that would have walls made of natural limestone. Even the air had a damp, cool feel to it, not quite the same as normal air-conditioning.

Had Ray sold him out? Not that it mattered. However Todd had come to end up in this stark room, there wasn't a doubt in his mind that he was deep inside the Paladin headquarters. He rubbed his hands up and down his arms, trying to ward off the shakes.

Fear was such an ugly thing.

If he couldn't corral it, he'd soon be running in circles screaming. If he thought it would help, he'd stretch back out on the stainless-steel table and pray for oblivion to take over again. Maybe the next time he'd wake up to find that this had all been a nightmare.

Instead, he slowly lowered his feet to the floor, unsure his legs would support his weight. The only way he managed to stay upright was to hold on to the edge of the table with a white-knuckled grip.

"What next?" he asked.

He didn't really expect an answer, but got one anyway when across the room, the doorknob turned.

Todd had never met Devlin Bane in person, but there wasn't a doubt in his mind that was who'd just walked into the room. The guy was enormous. His shoulders barely cleared the door frame, and he had to duck to enter the room.

Okay, that was an exaggeration, but not much of one. A second man followed Bane into the room. This guy he'd seen before. It was the cabdriver—and the bastard had the balls to laugh when he realized he'd been made.

Todd refused to cower and glared at the two Paladins.

Bane crossed his arms over his chest and spread his feet, planting himself in the center of the room while his buddy circled around behind Todd. It was impossible to watch them both, so Todd didn't bother to try. There was no mistaking the top dog anyway.

Todd went on the attack. "Gentlemen, care to explain yourselves? Because from where I'm sitting, you're both in a world of trouble."

Bane actually looked amused. "Lonzo, he's disappeared off the face of the earth, and he thinks we're the ones in trouble."

Lonzo drifted closer to the table. Todd instinctively shifted toward the far end, which only made his tormentor laugh.

"The Regents have always allowed you Paladins too much slack, but you've crossed the line this time. When they find out what you've done, they'll be shoving needles full of poison in your arms before you have a chance to ask for mercy."

This time it was Devlin Bane who laughed. "What makes you think they don't already know? They sure take a dim view of being ripped off. We've traced that money you carried out of the bank this morning right back to their accounts."

No way. He'd covered his tracks too well. "That money is mine, free and clear. I was hiding it from my wife."

"Yeah, that much I believe. I have to tell you, Todd—" Then Bane stopped. "Wait, you don't mind if I call you Todd, do you? After all, we're going to be spending quite a bit of time together."

"Call me whatever you like."

Bane shrugged his shoulders. "Anyway, I was about to say that your wife wasn't so thrilled when the bank called to see if you were unhappy with their services. Seems she had no idea you'd withdrawn such a sizable chunk of change from your joint accounts."

Lonzo crowded closer. "I wouldn't be in a big hurry to return to the bosom of your family, Todd. I'm seeing a divorce lawyer in your future. Well, provided you even have a future."

Okay, this was not going well at all. Acid burned the back of Todd's throat, and he had to tuck his hands under his armpits to keep them from shaking. He hated—*hated*—showing any sign of weakness in front of these jackals.

"Don't threaten me, you bastard. I don't even know what you're talking about."

"Then let me fill in the blanks for you." Bane's eyes burned hot and hard. "You and your broken-nosed buddy Ray arranged for Reggie Morrison to be kidnapped and taken across the barrier into Kalithia."

"If so, that was all Ray's idea. I had nothing to do with it."

The Paladin leader gave no indication that he'd even heard a word Todd had said. "One of my men, D.J. Clayborne, crossed into Kalithia to retrieve her. Seems Miss Morrison is a personal friend of his. By extension, that makes her a personal friend of mine."

Lonzo joined in, his smile showing way too many teeth. "And mine. Oh, and Blake Trahern's, too. I know you've heard of him. The man's a legend in our world. A real hard-ass killer when he takes a dislike to someone. I'm sure you'll understand why you're currently at the top of his hit list. Last I heard, he was putting a nice dull edge on his favorite sword in your honor."

Devlin picked up where Lonzo left off. "You see, Todd, here's the thing. When you depend on each other in battle, you become closer than brothers. Attack one, you attack us all. We're not like the Regents, who handle their problems around a conference table."

The door opened again. Todd felt a momentary flicker of hope, only to have it die as quickly as it had been born. The man walking into the room was none other than Chaz Willis, one of the most powerful Regents in the organization.

"Devlin, good to see you again."

"Hi, Chaz. Welcome to the party. Lonzo and I were just explaining to Todd here that he really screwed up big this time. I assume Sasha brought you up to speed?"

"Yes. Right now she and Larem are monitoring the situation. As I understand it, they're with Hunter Fitzsimon waiting for word from Sworn Guardian Berk in Kalithia. They'll relay any new information directly to me."

It took Todd several seconds to make sense of it all. The Regent was known throughout the organization as a real mover and shaker. Recently, his daughter had taken charge of the Seattle region. There'd been rumors that she'd gotten involved with one of the freaks from Kalithia the Seattle Paladins had adopted as their own.

Todd had refused to believe it, figuring that at the first hint of such a thing happening, Sasha Willis would've been relieved of duty and dragged back home in shame. Obviously he'd been wrong about that.

Either way, he wished he'd taken the time to investigate the situation himself. It was obvious the Regents and Paladins were going to present a united front on this. He was so screwed. On second thought, maybe he still had a few cards to play.

"Okay, what's it going to cost me? I have more money that you haven't found yet. Say the word, and it's yours. Just return my new identity papers along with an airline ticket, and I'm gone."

All three of the men stared at him as if he'd just sprouted a second head. He sure wasn't feeling the love. "What? You can't tell me that the organization wouldn't like to get back more of the money Kincade skimmed off the top."

The Paladin leader looked at Chaz, who shrugged. "You tell him, Devlin. I'm just here so that I can report back to the Board of Regents exactly how this problem gets handled."

The chill in Bane's eyes made it feel as if the air conditioner was working double overtime. Certain parts of Todd's body shrank up, not from the cold, but from fear, pure and simple. This must be how the guilty felt when the judge was about to pronounce sentence, taking away their freedom and maybe their lives.

"Todd, you obviously are not understanding that you are in some seriously deep shit. Let me explain how this is going to play out. Right now, it's like you've had a stay of execution while we decide what to do with you. Personally, I figure the world would be a better place without you and your friend Ray in it. By the way, he's singing like a canary. I've never seen anything like it."

Todd had expected no less from the jerk. Ray would rat out his own mother to save his skin. Todd just wished he'd been the one given the chance to sing his way out of this mess. Instead, Ray had tossed him to these wolves.

"Just so you know, it won't save him. We've already made sure that the police found the body of the guy he killed in that warehouse back in Oregon. They've also found the gun, with Ray's prints on it. They'll be coming for him soon. Ironic, don't you think, that he might end up being the one with a needle shoved in his arm?"

Todd flinched. How much worse could this get?

Devlin kept right on talking, burying Todd's hopes deeper and deeper. "You, on the other hand, are going to sit right here in this room until all this plays out."

"What do you mean?" Not that he really wanted to know.

"The cave your buddy shoved Reggie into over in Kalithia was blown to hell and back before D.J. could find her and bring her home. We're operating under the assumption that they got away and are trying to find another route home. Our contacts in Kalithia are currently hunting for them to make sure they find a safe place to cross back to this side. With luck, D.J. and Reggie should be home soon."

Lonzo picked up from there. "If so, you'll live. You'll wish you were dead when D.J. gets done with you, but you'll live. But if they don't make it back—"

He stopped briefly, obviously having trouble getting past that thought. Todd wanted to stick his fingers in his ears before the Paladin regained his ability to talk again. Too late.

"If they don't make it back, then no amount of luck will save you. No, it will be just me and Devlin and you, alone in this room. Only two of us will walk back out that door. So, Todd, if you believe in God, I'd start praying for the health and well-being of D. J. Clayborne and Reggie Morrison. If they die, you die. It's that simple."

This couldn't be happening. Not to him. Todd tried to catch Chaz's eye.

"You're a Regent, not a murderer! You can't let them get away with killing me."

But for a moment, Chaz looked every bit the deadly warrior as the two Paladins. "Todd, they're not getting away with anything. They're operating under direct orders from the board. You endangered not just that young woman but one of our Paladins as well. Plus, you've put the whole organization at risk."

He turned his back to Todd. "Carry on, men. I'll be in touch as soon as I hear anything. Try to keep the bloodstains to a minimum."

Devlin nodded. "Yes, sir, we will."

This nightmare just got worse and worse. But the scariest part was the way Devlin Bane smiled the whole time Chaz was talking.

Chapter 23

$\mathcal{B}$y the time Reggie and Javel scrambled to the top of the hill, the clash of weapons was already echoing through the air. Each clang of steel against steel made her flinch. She was a coward for running away with Javel while D.J. was back there fighting for his life. For *her* life.

Even if she'd only be in his way, it still meant that she'd left one man to face a mob of killers. She turned back to watch, Javel at her side. He held his sword in a death grip as if he, too, wished he was down there in the midst of the fight.

Oh, God! Even from this distance she could tell D.J. was badly hurt. His black clothing hid the blood, but the maroon-stained mud at his feet told the real story. For the moment, it appeared that he was holding his own. Only a couple of his enemies were still standing, both of them wounded as well. Maybe, just maybe, he'd hold out until help arrived.

No sooner did that cross her mind than the Kaliths double-teamed him, their blades flashing bright in the sun. D.J. fell forward, still fighting even as he went down. She screamed, ready to kill anyone and everyone who got between her and her fallen lover.

Before she could run one step, a rock-hard arm clamped around her waist and a callused hand gripped her gun hand. She was left with her feet touching nothing but air.

She fought. God, how she fought. She was sick and tired of being manhandled. This time was the worst because her captor was keeping her from getting back down there to where D.J. lay crumpled and so horribly still. From out of nowhere even more Kalith appeared beside her. Javel lowered his sword.

Was he going to surrender rather than fight? Then, with a shout, he led the charge down the hillside. Everyone was moving except her and her captor.

"Let me go! I've got to get down there!"

A deep voice spoke right next to her ear. "Reggie Morrison, if you will stop fighting me, I will take you back to D.J. as soon as it is safe. Those are my men with Javel. I am Sworn Guardian Berk. I'm sure that D.J. mentioned my name."

His patient words wormed their way past the panic in her head, stealing away her need to fight. When she went slack in his arms, Berk eased her down to the ground long enough to remove the gun from her hand. Once she was disarmed, he gently lifted her in his arms and carried her back down to where the man she loved lay sprawled in the dirt like a broken toy. She could only pray he wasn't beyond repair.

Ten minutes later she knelt in the dust. She couldn't breathe. She couldn't talk. It hurt so bad. The pain just wouldn't stop coming.

The Kalith who'd introduced himself as Sworn Guardian Berk had felt for D.J.'s pulse. Then Berk immediately removed his cloak and used it to cover D.J.'s still form.

Even if the Sworn Guardian didn't speak English, the message was clear. D.J. was dead. And all because of her. There was so much she hadn't told him—how he made her feel, how much she loved him. She was a coward two times over. Once for not staying to fight by his side. Then again for not 'fessing up to how she felt about the man.

He'd died not knowing. Somehow she was going to have to live with that.

Berk stepped between her and D.J.'s body and offered her a hand up off the ground.

"There's nothing left for us to do here. My men will handle the dead. Your people will be waiting for you."

"They aren't my people."

But she supposed they were, at least more so than the men and women who now surrounded her.

"Can you walk or do you need me to carry you?"

"I can walk."

Or would die trying. She almost hoped she would.

Berk and Javel flanked her as they started the long trek up the hill. About halfway, she glanced back.

Four of Berk's men had spread out a blanket and were gently lifting D.J. onto it. They folded his hands over his chest and placed his bloodstained sword at his side.

What had she been thinking? She tugged on Berk's sleeve. "We can't leave him here. D.J. needs to be buried in our world, not here."

Berk flinched and looked horrified. "Why would you do that?"

She would've thought the answer to that question was obvious. "Because he belongs there. His friends will want to say good-bye."

Berk appeared puzzled. "You do know that he is a Paladin."

"Of course."

He stared at her for a few seconds and then looked back down at the slow procession of his men as they started up the path to where they stood. "It is my guess that he never fully explained what that means."

She wasn't in the mood to play guessing games. "What are you talking about?"

"I believe it is best to let D.J.'s friends explain what happens when a Paladin dies. Suffice it to say that, with luck, all will be well."

He glanced up at the suns overhead. "But now, time is running short, and we must get to the barrier if we are going to be there when Barak brings it down again. My own talent for working with the energy is less predictable. If we miss the opening, it could be another twelve hours before you see your homeworld again."

Before she could protest, he marched up the path, leaving her no choice but to follow.

Her eyes, still swollen from crying, had a hard time adjusting to the dark interior of the cave. Berk and another of his men pulled out blue gemstones about the size of golf balls and murmured over them. A spark flickered deep inside the stones, gradually growing in intensity until the stones cast a soft glow throughout the cavern.

Once again, she stood facing a shimmering panel of light that stretched across the back wall of the cave. This time she didn't see its beauty or feel any desire to reach out to touch it. All it was to her was a means to get back home. Maybe someday she'd make sense of all that had happened during the past few days. Right now, she was too tired, too shattered, to do more than stare at the shifting patterns.

Berk and his men hovered nearby, neither crowding her nor offering her platitudes that would do nothing to ease her pain. Berk had told her one last time as they'd entered the cave that all would be well. She'd snapped at him to shut the hell up.

The familiar sickly green streaks appeared in the barrier as the other colors faded in intensity. She could sense growing excitement in those standing near her. Perhaps they were as happy to see her leave as she was to be going.

With a quiet whoosh, the barrier disappeared altogether, revealing a bunch of men spread out over the width of a cavern that mirrored the one she stood in. All were armed with swords, but immediately sheathed them as soon as they got a clear look at Reggie and her companions.

One limped forward. "Berk, I see you found Miss Morrison, but where's D.J.?"

Then he spotted the burden that four of Berk's men still carried. "Oh, shit, no."

His eyes immediately sought hers. "Miss Morrison . . . Reggie, I'm so sorry. My name is Hunter Fitzsimon, and I'm a friend of D.J.'s. We all are."

A tall silver-eyed man brushed passed them, along with another man who was obviously a Kalith. She'd spent enough time around his brethren in the past few days to recognize him for what he was. They replaced Berk's men as pallbearers. Everyone stepped aside to allow them to pass. The silence in the two caves became oppressive.

Hunter then offered her his hand, leading her across the line in the cave floor that marked the border between Kalithia and Earth. He quietly spoke to Berk in a voice that sounded as if his vocal cords had been badly damaged at some point in the past.

"We'll be in touch. Thanks for . . . well, just thanks."

His words reminded Reggie of her own manners. She sought out Javel in the cluster of Kalith warriors and mustered up a small smile for him.

"Javel, thank you for your help."

Although he might not have understood her words, he clearly understood her meaning, offering her a shy smile in return. Next she spoke to Berk.

"I appreciate everything you've done, even if I haven't always acted like it. Thank you for bringing me—" She stopped, choking on the words. "For bringing *us* home again."

He bowed his head to her before turning his attention back to Hunter. "I don't think D.J. ever told his woman the truth of what it means to be a Paladin. I fear she is in for a shock if someone doesn't warn her about what is coming."

Hunter closed his eyes and slowly breathed in and out through his mouth. "I'll see to it. Tate can help with that. She's had experience in that area."

Reggie let their words flow around her, not really caring what they were talking about. She already knew that she could never tell anyone about what had happened. Most people wouldn't believe her in the first place, and it was no one's business what she and D.J. had shared.

Rather than linger to see what else Hunter and Berk had to talk about, she walked toward the circle of sunshine that marked the opening to her home planet. She breathed deeply, filling her lungs with the heavy, cool air of the Pacific Northwest. It tasted sweet to her senses. The first real step back to her life.

The one that would have a huge, gaping hole in it without the Knightwalker.

She stepped out of the cave to find herself perched

on a rocky ledge halfway up a cliff. Good thing she didn't have a problem with heights. Even if she did, sidestepping along a narrow ledge was small potatoes compared to everything she'd been through the past few days.

When she reached the main path, she looked at the beach below and the wooded hillside above. Up or down? Seeing that the tide was running high, she opted for up. Maybe she was supposed to wait for Hunter, but if she stopped moving, she wasn't sure she'd ever get started again. The thread of stubbornness that held back her rage and grief was frayed and stretched to the point of snapping. If she was going to go into a complete meltdown, she wasn't going to do it out here on this god-forsaken hillside.

As the trail wound upward, the trees gradually thinned out. As she reached the edge of the woods, a familiar figure came into view.

She screamed his name and took off running. "Cody!"

When she reached his waiting arms, he crushed her against his chest and she held on with all her strength.

She was finally home.

Reggie closed her eyes and counted off the firsts she'd experienced since that night D.J. had appeared at her door. She'd met her first Paladin and visited another world. Aliens had kidnapped her and then she'd been rescued by some more. She'd seen her first fight to the death, and then made love with a man outside, under the stars.

The list went on and on.

But as weird as all of that was, the strangest part was listening to Tate Justice explain how Hunter had died out in those very same woods that bordered her backyard. Not only that but he'd somehow pulled through despite being dead or maybe just mostly dead. An image from the movie *The Princess Bride* kept playing out in Reggie's head. Who knew, maybe Westley had been a Paladin. He sure had the sick sword skills to fit the part.

She must be losing her mind. Here she was, being whisked back to Seattle in a helicopter, and all she could think about was a movie. She wished Cody had been able to come with her. There hadn't been room for everyone, just her, Trahern, and D.J.

For the hundredth time, she had to pull her eyes away from the plastic body bag stretched out on the floor at her feet. Up until now Trahern hadn't said more than a handful of words to her, but then he took her hand in his much bigger one. Some part of her mind noticed that his calluses matched the ones on D.J.'s hands. For whatever reason, that comforted her.

"You'll be good for him."

She whipped around to look at Trahern directly, definitely seeing a lot less ice in his silver-gray eyes than had been there earlier. "What do you mean? We hardly knew each other."

That was a lie.

She studied her companion. He and the others obviously believed D.J. would come back from death. God, she hoped they were right, and not just because if they were delusional, she was surrounded by crazies. But either way, if Trahern was also thinking there'd be some kind of future for her and D.J., he was mistaken.

Wasn't he?

"Don't play coy, Reggie. We all know that you've had our boy there tied up in knots for a while now. Hell, I've known him for years, and I've never seen him act like that. He took pride in being able to outdance any other hacker out there."

She rolled her eyes. "Yeah, that's a basis for a long-term relationship—seeing which one of us can outhack the other."

Trahern shook his head. "That's not what I meant. It's that you *get* each other. In our little corner of the world, do you have any idea how rare that is?"

She noticed that he wore a wedding band. "You found someone."

For the first time, he really smiled. "Yeah, I did. I know Tate talked to you about what she went through with Hunter. Brenna saw me die, too, only she was also shot in the process. If it hadn't been for her pigheaded stubbornness, I wouldn't be here with you today."

He looked away, as if afraid of letting too much of what that had meant to him show. Then he leaned to the side to get a better view out of the window.

"We're almost there. Devlin's wife, Dr. Laurel Young, is waiting for us. She's our best Handler—that's what they call the docs who patch us up. If anyone can pull D.J. through for you, she can."

"Is she the one who brought you back?"

"Yeah, she was." He stared out the window, a small smile playing at the corner of his mouth. "I obviously was in no shape to know what was going on, but I have it on good authority that Laurel and my Brenna kicked some serious butt to make that happen. Grown men quivered in their boots and ran for cover."

He squeezed her hand one last time. "I have a feeling that you and Laurel will do the same for D.J."

The gesture meant more than he knew. "Maybe all that's true, but there's no guarantee he'll want to have anything to do with me after all this. None of this would've happened if I hadn't started poking my nose around in his business."

Once again Trahern smiled down at her, humor twinkling in his eyes. "You're not going to believe me, but you should. Poking that pretty little nose of yours in D.J.'s business is probably the best thing that ever happened to him."

It was obvious she wasn't going to convince the man he was wrong. When the helicopter landed, he was the only one smiling.

Chapter 24

*I*n and out. In and out. The sound of air rasping through the bellows in D.J.'s chest was the first sign he was on the long trip back to the living. Underneath the whisper of his lungs was the soft backbeat of his heart, slow at first but then picking up speed, running ragged for a while until it finally settled back into a rhythm.

Cold, bone-chilling cold. Gradually, his blood remembered the pathways throughout his body and brought warmth flooding back to his extremities. Not to mention pain. Lots of it. Dead men don't hurt. Men coming back to life do.

God, he hated this whole fucking process. It never got any easier; if anything, it got worse. They said it beat the alternative. Sometimes he wasn't so sure.

Hearing was always the last sense to disappear and the first to come back. The soft rumble of voices slowly translated themselves into individual words. Eventually, he'd remember who was talking and understand what was being said.

One word stood out: Reggie.

His whole body jerked and twisted to the tune of rattling chains. No amount of jerking would free him from his restraints, but he fought them anyway.

"D.J., settle down. You'll rip out your stitches."

Laurel's voice, calm as always. She wasn't the one he needed to hear. Not this time. He erupted in another burst of rebellion.

A pair of heavy hands came down on his upper arms, pinning him down. "Damn it, D.J., cut this shit out. You're bleeding all over the place."

Trahern. Wrong again. With his arms in lockdown, he kicked his feet and tried to force words out of his mouth. No, not words. Just one.

"Reggie!"

Success. He whispered her name again. "Reggie."

Having had his say, he settled back down and waited for answers. Evidently deciding D.J. was going to behave himself, Trahern removed his hands and stepped away. Someone took his place. Someone who smelled like flowers.

Reggie.

"D.J." She spoke in that hushed voice people used in churches and hospital rooms. "I'm right here."

His lungs' fledgling attempts to breathe deeply drew in just enough of her scent to tease his senses. Her soft hand cupped his cheek, her fingers trembling.

"This. Scared. You." Stringing words together was a bitch right now.

"Not at all," she whispered as she brushed his hair back off his forehead.

He could hear the fear in her voice. "Liar."

Reggie choked a bit. "Yeah, well, I'll get over it."

Laurel entered the conversation again. "D.J., you know the drill. Everything is looking good right now, but you need to sleep, and so does she."

It was early in the recovery process, but maybe he could pry his eyes open. A quick glimpse of Reggie. All he needed. Only one eye cooperated. It was enough. She was crying. Damn it. He hated that, hated himself for wanting Reggie to be there even knowing what it was costing her. The sooner she left, the sooner she'd forget.

"Go, Reggie," he croaked.

She nodded. "Okay, but I'll be back."

Not what he meant. "*No!* Go away. Home if you can."

God, he needed her to leave. Now. Because he didn't know if he'd ever find the guts to let her go again.

"But, D.J., I want to be here."

When her hand caressed his bare shoulder, he wanted to purr. Instead, he screamed, rattling his chains with every ounce of strength he could muster.

"It hurts, damn it. *Go!*"

Laurel interceded. "Blake, get her out of here before this idiot destroys all my hard work."

His Handler sounded frustrated or maybe it was disgust he heard in her voice. He heard the shuffle of feet and the deep rumble of Trahern's voice. When D.J. could no longer hear them, he gave up, surrendering to the bleakness that was his life.

Laurel came closer, her cool hands checking his vitals with her usual efficiency. "D. J. Clayborne, I never thought you'd be such a coward."

So it had been disgust. That was okay. He disgusted himself.

"Sorry."

"It's not me you should apologize to. The question is whether you'll get the chance to apologize to Reggie. After that display, it would serve you right if she actually did what you told her to. Luckily, I'm betting she's got more gumption than that."

Laurel gave his hand a quick squeeze. "By the way, if you need lessons in groveling, I'll have Devlin give you a few pointers."

Rather than respond, he slept.

Reggie peeked into Laurel's lab through the small pane of glass in the door. D.J. was sitting up, looking a heck of a lot better than he had three days ago. She'd spent the time since he'd kicked her out resting up and trying to piece her life back together.

She'd sent an e-mail to Mr. DeLuca explaining that although she was feeling better, she'd been called out of town on an emergency. After apologizing for being out of touch for so long, she'd offered her resignation if he wanted it. She hoped he did.

As a final gesture of goodwill, she told him that she'd had it on good authority that the Knightwalker had died. Maybe he wouldn't believe her, but she was confident he wouldn't find any further trace of the iconic hacker.

According to Cody, they'd already managed to track down the bastards who had started all of this. So if she wanted to go home, she could. Cody was planning on heading back to Portland later that afternoon. He'd made special arrangements to make up the finals he'd missed, but then he was going to move up here to work for the Regents while he finished school at their expense. Turns out he shared the same DNA as the Paladins.

Who would've seen that one coming?

His future was set. He'd found a place where he belonged. She was truly glad for her friend, if more than a bit jealous. Her own future was definitely up in the air, but she had some thoughts on the subject. It would all depend on how the next few days played out.

"Are you ready?"

She glanced up at Trahern. "If you're sure my plan will work."

The Paladin stared through the window, his expression a bit haunted. "God, I hate this place. It helps knowing Brenna is always waiting for me. But I've got to tell you, Reggie, if you're not up for the long haul, for both your sakes, go back to Portland."

She'd been up most of the night debating that exact subject. After pacing the floor and making lists of pros and cons, she'd come to the only decision she could live with.

"All of this is killing him. D.J.'s computers might let him connect with the rest of the world, but they're still cold comfort. He needs me."

She stepped back from the door. "And I need him."

Trahern looked down at her. "D.J. might be stubborn, but he's not stupid. Like I said, you'll be good for him. Tell him that. Better yet, show him."

She grinned. "Don't worry. I will."

"We'd better get moving. Laurel plans to discharge him in half an hour so he can catch his flight to Missouri. I tried to talk him out of going, but you know D.J."

"Yeah, I do."

Trahern held the door for her as they walked out of the building. "Devlin promised to have him back in a couple of days. I'll let you know when I have specifics."

"Good. I'll be back from Portland in plenty of time."

"This is a good thing you're doing, Reggie."

She hoped so. She really did.

Todd swore this godforsaken cell got smaller every day. Other than when his captors brought him food three times a day, he'd been alone the whole time.

The bastards had yet to tell him if that Paladin and Reggie Morrison had made it back from Kalithia in one piece. Since he was still breathing, he had to guess they had. Bully for them. They were free. He wasn't.

Eventually they were going to have to let him go if they wanted the money back that he'd hidden away. Kincade wasn't going to lead them to it if he hadn't by now, which made him wonder where that guy was and what their long-term plans were for him.

He could hear footsteps approaching out in the hallway. That wasn't unusual, but he couldn't see who it was because this nine-by-nine room had no windows. He paused to listen. Whoever was out there had stopped right outside his door.

"Who's there?" he demanded.

No answer.

It wasn't mealtime, so whoever it was had other reasons for being there. His stomach lurched, a common occurrence since fear had become his constant companion.

He backed away from the door until he was flat up against the opposing wall, wedged between his cot and the bare toilet. Finally, he could hear a key being fitted into the lock and the knob turned.

When the door opened, it revealed a man who was a total stranger to him. If he had to guess, the guy was a Paladin because he had that same obnoxious arrogance that was second nature to both Jarvis and Devlin.

He also had a smile that made Todd's balls shrink up tight. Who was he? Then he knew.

"D. J. Clayborne, I presume."

The smile widened. "Right on the first guess, Todd."

D.J. sauntered into the small room as if he owned the fucking place. He studied Todd's stark surroundings with a sneer. "Quite a demotion from your usual lifestyle, don't you think?"

"Cut to the chase, Clayborne. What do you want?"

"I want you to rot in hell, but then you'd give the place a bad name. Personally, I think it would be more fitting to shove you across the barrier like you did Reggie

Morrison. I'm sure some of your late, but unlamented, associates have family or friends who'd like to talk to you."

Dear God, no! They'd kill him. Todd's voice cracked when he tried to set the record straight. "She made it back alive."

"She did. I didn't." D.J. smiled again. "I've got to tell you, Toddy, you have no idea how much I hate being killed. It tends to piss me off."

Then he stepped closer, his hands flexing. "Sorry to have kept you waiting, but at least I'm here now."

Then using those lightning-fast Paladin reflexes, D.J. had Todd in a chokehold. "So here's the deal, you scum-sucking bastard. When Jarvis and Chaz Willis ask you a question, you will answer. It's that simple. If I hear that you've been uncooperative, I'll be back, and then we'll make that little trip to Kalithia. Of course, yours will be one way."

Todd couldn't breathe enough to speak, but it was due to absolute terror rather than D.J.'s powerful grip. He managed to nod, feeling like a bobble-headed doll as he tried to convince this cold-eyed killer that he would be telling the truth.

D.J. let go, shoving Todd backward hard enough to bounce him off the wall. "Fine, but just so we understand each other, I'll spell it out one more time. You tell them what they want to know or you die. Are we clear?"

"Yes," Todd whispered, rubbing his throat to ease the pain.

"I knew you'd be smart about it."

As D.J. backed up a couple of steps, Todd breathed a sigh of relief. He'd been terrified of this moment for days, but it looked like he was going to escape with a bruised neck. He'd always known that he'd have to give them all the information he had if he wanted to walk out of here in one piece.

"So we're good."

"Well, no," D.J. said, shaking his head. "There's one more thing."

Before Todd could ask what it was, D.J. cut loose with a punch that shoved Todd's belt buckle straight through to his spine. Then he followed it up with one more to Todd's nose. Todd hit the wall and slumped to the ground with blood dripping off his chin.

D.J. stood over him. "The first one's from me. The second's from Reggie."

Then he grabbed the threadbare towel off the sink and tossed it to Todd. "If they ever let you out of here and you want to live, stay away from me and stay away from her."

Once again Todd nodded. Evidently satisfied that he'd made his point, D.J. walked out and locked the door behind him.

Chapter 25

"*T*hanks, man. I appreciate the ride."

Lonzo pulled over in front of D.J.'s place. "Glad to do it."

Before D.J. got out he had one question he needed to ask his friend. "Lonzo, I did the right thing, didn't I? Sending her away, I mean."

"Personally, I think it was damn noble of you. Stupid as hell, but noble."

Then Lonzo punched him on the arm. "However, if there was ever such a thing as a do-over, I suggest you reconsider your decision. We all like Reggie. A lot. In fact, if you didn't already have dibs . . . but you clearly do."

Not exactly the answer D.J. had been hoping for. Then he noticed Lonzo had left the engine running. "Aren't you coming in?"

"No can do. Wish I could stay to tuck you in, but Trahern needs me back at headquarters. You gonna be okay on your own?"

"Yeah, I'll be fine."

"Don't forget that Laurel ordered you to take the next week off. She said if you show up, she'll get Sasha to dock your pay double for every hour you're there."

"I remember."

Although how was he supposed to spend a full week with nothing to do and no one to do it with? Physically, he was back to normal. That didn't mean he was ready to be alone. Yeah, he'd told Reggie to go home to Portland, but it still pissed him off that she'd actually gone. He wasn't being reasonable, but right now he didn't give a flying fuck about reasonable.

"Call if you need anything."

He climbed out of the cab of Lonzo's truck, moving more slowly than he really needed to. "I said I'll be fine."

Eventually. Maybe.

As he approached his front door, he could hear music playing. Strange. Usually his neighbors were gone during the day. Even when they were home, their taste in music ran toward the classical end of the spectrum. He was pretty sure what he was hearing was straight out of Nashville.

Huh, it was coming from his place. Had he left the radio on? He didn't think so. He turned the key in the lock and shoved the door open. For sure he hadn't left the lights on. What the hell was going on?

Two steps inside the door, he stopped. What was that smell? Roses? He'd noticed that same exact scent just recently. Reggie.

A new surge of energy poured through his veins. He wasn't sure if it was anger or hope. After he'd mustered up the gumption to order Reggie to leave him alone, she had done exactly that. He hadn't seen her again and assumed she'd gone back to Portland. What if she hadn't? His equipment bag hit the ground with a thud. He lifted one foot and moved it forward, then the next, managing to keep going until he reached his living room.

It was empty. Had she come and gone? He tried the kitchen next, hoping his heart wouldn't burst in his chest before he found her. There was something that smelled of oregano and tomato sauce in the oven, but still no sign of Reggie.

That left his office . . . and the bedroom. Okay, that thought sent him bolting down the hall. His bed was made with the blankets turned back. It looked neat, tidy even. Welcoming and with a predictable effect on the fit of his jeans. He backed out of the room and headed for the only place that was left.

The door was closed but he could hear the rapid click of a keyboard in the hands of a master. He should've guessed Reggie would be playing with his equipment. Okay, that wasn't the smartest analogy he could've come up with.

Why was she here? Only one way to find out.

She'd heard him come in. It was all she could do not to go charging out to meet him, throwing herself into D.J.'s arms. But if she was going to tread on the minefield of getting past his defenses, she needed to move cautiously and let him come to her.

Just as the door opened, she finished the e-mail she'd been composing and hit the Send button before looking in his direction. When she finally did, she couldn't say a word. All the earlier images kept getting in the way: D.J. fighting for his life before going down under the combined assault of the last two Others. Berk's men wrapping D.J.'s dead body in a blanket. Flying back to Seattle with his body bag at her feet. The horrific process of life returning to where there had been only death a few seconds before.

It was hard to believe he was really standing there, so handsome, so alive. He didn't look particularly happy to see her, but she'd come too far to run away now.

"Hope you don't mind that I let myself in."

He finally stepped into the room. She jumped to her feet. He towered over her enough when she was standing. He crossed his arms over his chest and glared down at her.

"I told you to go home."

She offered him a smile, but it wasn't exactly a happy one. "I did. I just didn't stay there."

"Why are you here?"

"Where else should I be?"

"Damn it, Reggie, I'm in no mood for games. Why are you here?"

Time to throw down the gauntlet. "Because I felt like a coward standing on that hillside with Javel and Berk while you were down there fighting."

He started pacing, snagging one of his tension balls off the desk and working it hard. "I'm a trained warrior,

Reggie. You aren't. If I'd let you get killed, you would've stayed that way."

She picked up one of the other toys and tossed it from one hand to the other. "That's not why I felt like a coward. And since you brought it up, why didn't you tell me about your Paladin abilities?"

He did an about-face to look away from her. "I didn't want you to know the truth of what I was. Even if we didn't have a future together, I didn't want you to think you'd slept with some kind of freakish monster."

He spoke in a perfect monotone, but that didn't disguise the pain in each word he said. If she could get her hands on whoever had labeled him a monster in the past, she'd kick their collective asses off the Space Needle.

"You're not a freak or a monster."

His laugh was ugly. "Try convincing my mother of that."

"Tell me about her."

At first, she didn't think he was going to, but then he started speaking, slowly, but then the words picked up speed as he continued. "My father died when I was still a baby. Evidently he never told her what he really did for a living or what he was. Anyway, she turned to religion in a big way. Most of my memories of my early childhood were centered around the church, and that was okay, at least at first."

He wandered over to stare out the window. "But when she noticed that I healed almost overnight, she started freaking out. That was bad enough, but then

I fell off the garage pretending to be a superhero and broke both legs and an arm. As you can probably guess, the hospital staff didn't quite know what to make of a kid who was busted up one day and bouncing on the bed the next."

"Did the church think it was a miracle?"

Reggie would have, but it was clear that wasn't how it had played out. It hurt to see D.J. looking so alone. She eased closer, slipping her hands around his waist and laying her face against his back.

He sighed and finally answered. "No, they thought I was possessed. When the prayers and the beatings didn't work, my mother couldn't live with the shame . . . or with me. At least she abandoned me outside a hospital. Guess I should be grateful for that much."

Reggie wanted to punch somebody. She kept her touch gentle, but let her fury boil over in her words. "Damn it, D.J., she doesn't deserve your gratitude for anything. How could she do that to her own son?"

He shrugged. "As near as I can tell, she was a kid herself and running scared. I did okay without her, especially when one of the local Paladins tracked me down after I fell playing a game of pickup basketball in college and broke my leg again. With the dawn of the computer age, the Regents started scanning hospital reports for stories like mine."

"You found somewhere to belong. With the Paladins."

He finally turned back around. "I owe them everything. When I showed a talent for computers, they paid off my student loans and bought me the best equipment on the market. We're family—or were. Guess I'll find out for sure when I go back to work next week. I, uh, broke a few rules."

God, because of her, he'd lied to his friends. Not only that, she'd bested him at the one thing he'd excelled in. With the job his mother did on him, he probably thought that his sword arm and ability to outhack the vast majority of the computer geniuses in the world were his sole talents.

How could she fix this?

"This is my fault, D.J. Surely Devlin will see that when I talk to him."

D.J. held her out at arm's length. "No way are you dealing with him. You're going home to pick up the pieces of your life."

He was still trying to protect her, the sweet fool. Time to set the record straight. "Nope, sorry, that's not happening. I'm here and I'm staying."

Anger flashed hot in his dark eyes. "Damn it, Reggie, no. You've seen my life. I spend most of my time wading in blood and watching my friends die over and over again. Sometimes they don't make it back at all. Someday I won't. I won't ask you to share that life with me."

Okay, time to play hardball. "I told you I felt like a coward, but you're wrong about why. I thought I'd missed the chance to tell you how I felt about you. You might not want me, but I'm not walking out that door without telling you."

She had his attention now. "I love you, D. J. Clayborne. I love everything about you. You and those friends of yours suffer in silence to keep people like me safe. That's such a powerful gift, and we don't even get to thank you for it. You keep your lives secret so the rest of us don't have to deal with the ugliness that's part of every day you pick up your sword."

D.J. stared at her in shock, shaking his head as if he was having trouble deciphering her words. Finally, he stumbled across to his computer chair and dropped into it. She followed him, climbing up in his lap.

"What I don't understand is how you can be so brave when it comes to facing off with those Kalith crazies, but scared when it comes to trusting me. In case you haven't noticed, I'm not your mother."

That earned her a small smile. "Believe me, I noticed."

She tossed the toy aside to cradle his face in both hands. "Then don't punish me for her crimes. I'm not going to run away, and I'm not going to leave, not unless you force the issue. We both know that it would be stupid to walk away from what we've shared, and you're not a stupid man. Or are you?"

Her heart lodged firmly in her throat while she waited for him to answer. It took forever—at least ten seconds.

He swallowed hard and whispered, "No, I'm not stupid."

Her heart stuttered when he turned his face to nuzzle the palm of her hand. "I didn't think so, which leads me to the next step."

"Which is?"

"Well, you don't want to ask me to share your life. I get that. So that leaves me with only one thing I can do."

"Which is?" he repeated.

"I can ask you to share my life instead. There are downsides. I spend hours on the computer when I have a puzzle to solve. I collect all kinds of toys to play with while I'm hot on the trail of some handsome, world-class hacker. Also, I've been told I'm a bit stubborn, and I have a temper. Think you can live with that?"

His smile spread slowly, but lit up his whole face. "Yeah, I think I can live with that. Besides, Lonzo told me that if I ever got a chance at a do-over, I should make a smarter decision."

"I like your friends."

"Good, because you'll be seeing a lot of them."

"Not right now though. I want some serious alone time with you—no Paladins, no Kaliths, no friends. At least not for a day or two."

"Not a problem. Laurel and Sasha ganged up on me and ordered me to take a week off. And suddenly, I have a few ideas about how to fill that time."

He muscled them both up out of the chair and carried her down the hall toward his bedroom. He tossed her into the middle of his king-size bed and followed her down.

There was a lot of hunger in his smile. "What do you say we start here and maybe end up in a Las Vegas wedding chapel? How does being Mrs. Darnell Jacob Clayborne sound?"

She considered the matter. "I like Mrs. D.J. better, but I'll take you any way I can."

His dark eyes turned serious. "Call me whatever you want as long as you love me."

She tugged him down for a long, hot kiss. When she pulled back, she cupped his handsome face and smiled.

"Then I'm just going to call you mine."

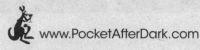

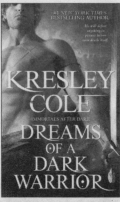